The Lost Alpha

KIMBER STONE

Copyright © [2024] by [Kimber Stone]

All rights reserved.

No portion of this book may be reproduced in any form without written permission from the publisher or author, except as permitted by U.S. copyright law.

Dedication

This book would not have been published if it weren't for the quick thinking and hard work of Leah, Jenny and Aurora! I dedicate this to you Ladies. Marc came in clutch at the end, so the dedication belongs to you as well.

I also dedicate this book to Avalina and Steph for all their help and guidance along the way!

My loving Husband and daughter also deserve a dedication for their patience while I wrote this story.

My final dedication goes to all those who feel lost in this world, may you find the light that will guide you to where you belong.

CHAPTER ONE

Chapter 1

Olivia

The trees swayed back and forth in the cold wind, as I stared out my bedroom window at the gloomy, grey sky. The sky was mirroring my current mood. I had no reason to be moody, but I felt on edge, like something was coming. For the life of me, I couldn't figure out what that was. Even Evie, my wolf, was pacing in my head to the point I was starting to get a headache.

"Evie, what's going on? I've never felt like this before. Could we be sick?" This scenario was highly unlikely since, as a werewolf, we didn't get sick. Our healing abilities kept us in good health.

"I honestly don't know, Olivia. Something big is about to happen, but I'm not sure when or what." This did nothing to calm my nerves, so I decided to link my best friend, Amber, to meet up. She's always great at taking my mind off things.

Amber and I were both ranked wolves of the Onyx Crescent Pack. She was the beta's daughter, and, lucky me, I was the alpha's only child, which made me the next in line to take over the pack, something I'd never been happy about if I was being honest. It's not that I didn't think I'd be a great leader. I knew I'd be much better than my father, Alpha Francis. I just felt like the position wasn't meant for me somehow. Don't ask me why. I just felt it in my bones.

Since we were toddlers, Amber and I had been inseparable, and she was going to be my beta once Dad decided to hand over the pack. Onyx Crescent was a smaller pack of about a hundred and fifty.

Typically, I should have taken over the pack when I turned twenty-one, but Dad had control issues. He insisted he was perfectly capable of running the pack still and would give it to me when I was ready. Here we were five years later, and I was still no closer to being sworn in as alpha - not that I minded, I had no desire to be in charge of this goddess-awful pack. My father would never let me run it the way I would want and his way of running it was tyrannical, I wasn't like him at all. Dad wouldn't come out and say it, but I also knew he didn't like the thought of a woman taking over his pack; he was holding out for me to find my mate.

As I came down the main stairs of the pack house, I saw Amber waiting for me by the giant bay windows near the front door. "Hey, Cupcake!" I yelled across the room at Amber as she turned around, laughing at the crazy nickname I called her by. She's little, like a cupcake, and as a kid, she always loved to eat as many cupcakes as she could at parties, so the name kind of stuck to her.

"So, what's going on that you needed to meet up so desperately?" she asked.

"I don't know. Evie and I are on edge, and we need to get out of here, and find something to occupy our minds."

"Shall we go for a run then?" she asked.

Evie started prancing in my mind at that suggestion. She wanted to stretch her legs.

"Alright, Evie is down. Let's go!"

Amber

When Olivia linked me, I was in the middle of arguing with my father. He wanted me to travel around the other packs in our territory to find my mate. I was in no rush and wasn't desperate enough to travel around looking for my soulmate. When it was meant to be, we would find each other.

I was grateful for the distraction and told my father that Olivia needed me. He couldn't argue with that, and as fast as my little legs could take me, I ran for the front stairs. I only had to wait a few minutes before I heard a loud "Cupcake" coming from Olivia. That crazy nickname she gave me when we were six and still, to this day, wouldn't go away.

I just laughed at this point and asked her what was up. She seemed on edge, which was not normal for Olivia. She was usually calm, cool, and collected. I suggested a run which her wolf was happy about, and so was my wolf, Lana.

As we stepped outside, a huge gust of wind blew and almost knocked me to my knees.

"Ugh, maybe a run wasn't such a great idea, with this weather."

"Oh come on, it's too late to change your mind. You've gotten Evie's hopes up," Olivia cackled at me. "A little wind never hurt anyone."

Easy for her to say. She was a statue standing tall at five-six with muscles for days, and there I was a measly five foot; that got pushed around by the wind. I always joked it was a good thing I had gotten the brains for the beta position since I was lacking in the brawn department, in human form anyway.

In my wolf form, I was unstoppable, Lana was mighty and fierce. No one could beat me at training in wolf form. I was too quick and slipped away from everyone, and they didn't see me coming; I was a little ninja wolf.

We made our way to the trees and stripped out of our clothes. Within seconds, I heard the familiar sound of cracking bones, and there was Evie standing tall in all her glory! She was large as alphas were, with a beautiful light brown coat flowing in the wind and bright green eyes. She was a sight to be seen. I didn't waste any more time; I let Lana take over and shift. She shook her dark brown chocolate fur and blinked her big blue eyes at Evie.

"Shall we go towards the waterfall?" I linked Olivia and received no answer. Evie just started to run, and I chased after her.

We ran for a solid fifteen minutes when Evie stopped abruptly. Of course, my tiny but mighty wolf was running extra fast to keep up with Evie, and I didn't have time to stop, so I crashed into her, and we both went rolling like a giant snowball.

"What the hell, Olivia," I hissed through our mind-link.

"Don't move," she said. *"Do you smell that? I also hear something coming from over the hill."*

I sniffed the air and caught the scent of rogues, but not the usual rotting smell. There was something off about these rogues. "We should link the warriors."

And, of course, my fearless best friend answered with; "Why waste time? We're here. Let's check it out." I really didn't like the sound of that, but who was I to say no to my future alpha? So, we crept over the hill and came face to face with three rogues in human form; we were outnumbered. This was not good.

Chapter Two

Chapter 2

Olivia

The rogues were sitting quietly by the edge of the stream; they looked surprised to see us. A look of worry passed through their eyes as they looked between each other. One scrawny rogue who couldn't have been any older than eighteen put his hands up in surrender and spoke. "We mean you no harm. We were hunting and needed a rest."

Evie blinked at him, and Lana growled lowly next to me, not convinced that they were harmless. I linked Amber to go get us clothes that were stashed in the bushes so we could shift and speak with them. Before Amber moved, I expanded my alpha aura to root everyone in place so they couldn't attack me while I was alone.

Little did I know there was a fourth rogue farther away hiding in the bushes who wasn't affected by my aura in the least. As soon as Amber was in the bushes, he rushed out towards me. I shifted back to my human form instantly, not caring about my nakedness. The young rogue who spoke to us blushed and averted his eyes out of respect, which I found interesting.

As the fourth rogue got closer, I alpha commanded him to stop, but he just kept coming, which shocked me. It was as if I didn't order him to stop. As he lunged at me, I sidestepped and grabbed him by the throat, throwing him to the ground. I kneeled on his neck and chest, pinning him to the ground instantly. It was my signature move that no one seemed to expect.

In the time it took me to subdue him, Amber was back by my side, pissed as all hell. "Where did he come from? And why didn't your alpha command work on him?"

I shrugged my shoulders and shot back,

"I have no idea why it didn't work, but I'd love to figure it out." As I said that, the rogue started to struggle below me. I pushed my knee harder into his neck as a warning.

"If you want me to get off of you, stop struggling and answer me. Who are you, and why are you in our pack territory?"

The rogue glared at me but chose wisely to answer.

"My name is Daniel, and I'm part of the Blood Viper Pack. We were hunting and didn't realize we had crossed into another pack's territory."

I wanted to believe what he said, but rogues don't have packs; they were lone wolves or, at most, traveled a few at a time from place to place.

"Rogues don't have packs, Daniel. Why are you lying to me? I don't take kindly to liars."

He shook his head at me.

"Not all rogues are evil or lone travelers. We are a pack of forgotten, lame, abandoned wolves that choose to be a family and protect each other, which is the only reason I attacked you. I thought you were going to harm my friends. We meant no harm. We only wanted to find food to bring back to our pack."

As I listened to Daniel speak, Evie chimed in.

"*I believe him, Olivia. I have a weird sense of familiarity with him, and what he says is true.*"

Her words shocked me, but I had to agree with Evie that this man felt familiar. I was not sure how, though.

"I'm going to get off you and let you up, Daniel. I won't hurt you, but if you try anything, I won't hesitate to put you down again." Daniel nodded in understanding, and I let him go. He got up slowly so as not to make me uneasy. I grabbed a long shirt from Amber and covered myself before continuing the conversation.

Daniel

This hunting trip was not turning out how I thought it would. Seeing the woman with the alpha aura holding my friends captive, set me off. Before properly thinking it through, I lunged at her and ended up on my back with her kneeling on my chest. Not my finest moment.

Xander, my wolf, was snickering at me and shaking his head, trying not to laugh. "W*ow, it didn't take her long to take you out, buddy,*" he said.

"*Shut up, Xander. Aren't you supposed to be helping me here?*" I responded.

"*Not really. She's not a threat!*"

"*What do you mean she's not a threat? She had her alpha aura holding the guys down.*" Xander just sighed at my statement. "*What?*"

"Clearly, she's just trying to protect herself. She doesn't know who we are, and the two she-wolves are outnumbered. Although, seeing how she fights, I think you guys are the ones in trouble! Hahaha."

I blocked Xander out at this point and answered the she-wolf's questions that she had asked me. She called me a liar but then chose to release me, which I found weird. A sense of calm came over me through her, so I didn't ask any questions and just got up slowly.

Once I was up, the woman had finally covered up; not that I was shy about naked bodies, I just didn't think my mate, Annabelle, would appreciate me being so close to another naked female, explaining her smell on me was going to be fun.

"Who are you, if I may ask?" I said.

A puzzled look crossed the woman's face before she answered.

"I thought I was the one asking the questions here? My name is Olivia Stevens, the future Alpha of Onyx Crescent, and this is my future Beta, Amber Small."

Great, not what I wanted to hear. We didn't want any trouble, and I told her as much.

"Listen, Daniel, I'm not going to lie. You're lucky it was us that found you and not my father or our warriors. Please head back over the border before any trouble comes of this. I believe you are peaceful, but my father isn't a rational man. He will smell rogue and not give you a second to explain before killing you all."

She didn't have to tell me twice. I thanked her for being gracious enough to listen to me, then the guys and I took our leave with a quick wave and promised to never cross their border again.

Olivia

Once Daniel and his friends left, I turned to Amber, who was staring at me with a look I couldn't quite make out.

"How could you just let them go like that, Liv? Do you honestly believe they will never come back over the border?" she all but shouted at me.

"They were harmless, Amber. Evie believed Daniel, and so did I. Please trust me. For his sake, I hope he is a man of his word and stays out of our territory." She let out a deep breath.

"You know I trust your judgment. I'm just worried about what your dad is going to say to all this." The slightly terrified look that passed over her face set me on edge.

"Well...we just won't say anything to him about it, that's all."

"What won't you tell me about?" a sharp voice said from behind me.

I whipped around to see my father with his beta and two warriors looking less than impressed with me. I started to sweat, not sure what to say.

Chapter Three

Chapter 3

Olivia

The longer I stood there without saying anything, the worse I knew it would be, so I chose to suck it up and tell him the truth. If nothing else, I was an honest person.

"Amber and I were out for a run, and we came across some young wolves from another pack resting by the stream. They didn't know they had crossed into our territory, so I sent them on their way." I held my breath slightly after finishing my explanation, hoping my dad wouldn't want further details.

My hopes were dashed when he narrowed his eyes at me and asked,

"Is that it? Because I know there is more; otherwise, you wouldn't have told Amber you weren't going to tell me."

I gulped and responded.

"I didn't want to bother you with a harmless encounter. That's why I wasn't going to tell you." I bit the inside of my cheek, willing the Goddess to let this end now. Amber gave me a slight side eye with the same prayer in them, which, of course, my dad caught. I knew we were screwed the moment his face started to turn red and the vein on his neck began to bulge. He was seething, and I was about to get an ear full.

"Do you think I'm stupid?" he spat at me. "I know you are keeping something from me. I can smell rogue in the vicinity and another alpha's aura; who was he, Olivia?"

Another Alpha? What was he talking about? I didn't feel any other alpha aura.

"Evie, did you sense another alpha around?"

"Honestly, Olivia, I'm not sure. Daniel had a strange aura that I couldn't quite decipher." I tried to absorb what Evie told me, but my dad demanded my attention once again.

"Olivia, I'm waiting for the truth, and you know I don't take kindly to being lied to." By this point, he was practically foaming at the mouth, so I gritted my teeth and just let it all out.

"They weren't technically rogues. They are part of a pack. One of the boys was able to ignore my alpha command and aura, which I've never seen before, but he didn't say he was an alpha, and his friends didn't call him that either." My words just tumbled out, and it took a moment for my dad to digest everything I had just said.

"Are you truly that stupid, Olivia?" My dad was eerily calm, which made me extremely nervous. I didn't have to wait long for the volcano to erupt. "Of course", he wouldn't tell you he was the Alpha. That is the dumbest thing I've ever heard. How could you just let them leave? They crossed illegally into our territory, and now they are who knows where doing whatever they please on our land! This is Exactly why I am still Alpha, and you will be lucky if I ever allow you to be Luna one day."

I was used to my dad's tirades. This wasn't the first and certainly wouldn't be the last, but his last words were a huge slap in the face. It was like I was ten all over again when he told me in no uncertain terms that I wasn't good enough to be alpha and had better pray to the Moon Goddess I find my mate, and he was worthy enough to be the Alpha of Onyx Crescent.

"Go back to the pack house, the both of you. I will finish dealing with you later, Olivia. Right now, I need to make sure those filthy rogues have left, no thanks to you."

I didn't bother arguing with him. I bowed my head and shifted back into Evie for the run back. Amber followed close behind as both our dads glared at us.

Alpha Francis

I was in my office on a conference call with the Alpha from an allied pack discussing border security, when I suddenly felt a familiar yet foreign presence had crossed the border. I couldn't end the meeting just yet, so I chose to let it go. If something was truly wrong, my warriors or beta would link me.

An hour or so later, my meeting was done, so I linked my Beta and two top warriors to meet me outside the front of the pack house. When they were all gathered, I let them know that someone had crossed our border and we needed to go find out who it was. We shifted quickly, running towards the furthest border to the east. We slowed as we came into a clearing near a stream.

Ahead of us, I saw my daughter, Olivia, and my Beta's daughter, Amber. They were whispering about not telling me something. To me, this conversation was unacceptable, and I immediately made our presence known. Olivia was nervous and gave me some half-assed story about some lost wolves needing a break. I didn't believe her; I knew she was holding something back from me.

Eventually, I got the truth out of her, and I couldn't believe how stupid and naïve she could be. This was why she hadn't been made alpha yet; clearly, she lacked the critical thinking skills she needed for the job. Now, I had to go hunt down those rogues and make sure they never crossed our border again.

I sent her and Amber back to the pack house, vowing to finish our discussion later. Once the girls were out of sight, I turned to Shane, my beta, and let out an exasperated sigh.

"Shane, you come with me. We'll keep going east, and you two will go along the western part of the border." I nodded to my two head warriors, and they ran off as instructed; Shane and I shifted and continued towards the eastern border.

"I can't believe Olivia did this to us," I growled to my wolf, Sheldon.

"Maybe she was right, and they weren't rogues and were harmless?"

I honestly couldn't believe what I was hearing from my wolf.

"Are you as dense as she is, Sheldon? How could you believe she is right?"

"She's our pup, Francis. I love her and will always believe her; you should try it once in a while! She's all we have now since you—" I cut him off and blocked him out before he had a chance to finish that sentence. I did not need this condescending fleabag to lecture me. The rogues' smell was stronger as we got closer to the eastern border. However, it started to dissipate as it went past the line, signalling they had left.

"Alpha, they seem to have left just like Olivia said they did," Shane linked me.

"Don't act like my foolhardy daughter. We can never be too careful. It could be a trap!" I proceeded to stalk along the border to confirm with my own eyes they weren't hiding anywhere.

As I was about to admit that they were gone, Shane linked me again.

"Alpha, there is one smell here that smells so familiar. I know it can't be, but it smells like..."

"If you want to keep breathing, I suggest you don't finish that sentence, Shane. You know as well as I, that's impossible."

"You're right, Alpha. I'm sorry, my mistake." The look in his eyes said he was anything but sorry and skeptical, which really bothered me and put me on edge.

It couldn't be, could it? I had that problem taken care of years ago, and even if by some miracle...No! No, it was not a possibility, and that was that.

I signalled Shane to follow me. As we ran, I linked the warriors who found nothing on the western border. I told them to stay alert but head back to the pack house. We would meet in my office to discuss a better patrol schedule.

Chapter Four

Chapter 4

Olivia

As soon as I reached the steps of the pack house, I shifted and ran inside' nakedness be damned. All I wanted was to be alone to cool off. Amber linked me.

"Liv, I'm sorry that just happened. Do you want me to come with you to your room?"

I thought about it for a second. Honestly, I just needed to be alone.

"I need some space right now, Cupcake. I'll come see you once I've cooled down." I heard her chuckle and cut the link as I made it to my room and slammed the door behind me.

I was so angry at this point I was shaking, so I threw myself on my bed and screamed as loud as I could into my pillows. I was still breathing raggedly when a light knock came at my door.

"Please go away. I'm busy at the moment," I shouted.

"Too busy to talk with your mom?" My mom's quiet voice reached me. I couldn't bear the thought of hurting my mom, so I threw on a robe I had on the edge of my bed and went to open the door. My mom, the ever-elegant Luna that she was, gracefully came into my room and wrapped me in a big hug. The tension in my body instantly left as I melted into the hug.

"So, are you going to tell me why you ran through the pack house naked, as if your ass was on fire?"

I couldn't help but laugh at her depiction of me and sighed before I answered.

"I met some lost wolves while I was out for a run with Amber. They were harmless, but then Dad showed up and made a big deal out of it. It ended with him going to hunt them down and me being 'a huge idiot.'" I made air quotes for emphasis.

"Your dad loves you, Olivia. He only wants the best for you and the pack, you know that." Of course, she would take his side on this. No matter the situation, it never changed.

My dad would be a nasty son of a bitch, and my mother would smooth it over with the 'oh, he loves you' rhetoric.

To say I was slightly fed up with this constant loop would be an understatement, but in order to keep the peace and end this conversation, I just agreed with her. Feeling like she had fixed everything, my mom took her leave and told me to meet her for tea later if I felt like it. I gave her one last hug and closed the door behind her.

I sighed in relief that I could be alone now. As I approached the window, I saw my Dad and Shane come out of the woods. I figured now was a good time to get my punishment out of the way, so I threw on some leggings and a tank top and rushed out of my room towards my dad's office.

As I rounded the corner, I stopped abruptly, hearing Shane whispering to my father.

"Alpha, I know you think it's impossible, but I really feel Corey was there today! It smelled too much like him for it not to be."

I couldn't see my dad, but I felt the anger flowing off of him in waves.

"What did I say at the border, Shane? Keep bringing up Corey, and I will have to find a new Beta! It's impossible Corey was here. He would have never made it past twenty-five, and I say this loosely if by some miracle he did survive, that means you failed! You confirmed he was taken care of, did you not?" Dad seethed.

All I heard after that was Shane stammering as my dad shut his office door. I stood there frozen for what felt like an eternity, trying to make sense of what I had just heard. My brain was spinning a mile a minute.

"Evie? What was all that? Do you remember hearing about a Corey?"

"Liv, like you, I have no idea what to make of that conversation, but it's very suspicious."

"Yes, it was. I need to speak to Amber about this." I turned on my heels and ran for the stairs that would take me to Amber's room. I skidded to a stop and started pounding on her door. The door flew open half a second later.

"Jesus, Liv, what the hell is going on? You're pounding on my door like a crazy person." I shoved past her and closed the door, pressing my back against it. "Liv, you're scaring me. What's going on? Are we under attack? Is your dad shipping you off to another country?" I just furrowed my eyebrows at her.

"No, no, nothing like that!" I lowered my voice before letting her in on what I heard. "I was going to my dad's office to get my punishment out of the way and heard him yelling at your father."

She looked confused.

"Yelling at my father, what for?"

"I'm getting to that! So, as I was saying, he was yelling at your dad about someone named Corey!"

Amber looked at me with a blank stare.

"We don't have anyone in this pack named Corey!?"

"I know, that's what I found weird, but it gets better! It seems your father was supposed to have him taken care of."

"My father killed some random man named Corey?" She looked hurt that I was implying her father was a murderer.

"Amber, if he did kill him, it seems it was a long time ago, and at my dad's request...you know your father can't refuse anything my dad says without consequences." She nodded at this, knowing full well her father was a puppet whose strings were pulled by my dad.

We both stood there in silence for a moment, lost in our own thoughts, until Amber snapped her head up and looked at me with a question in her eyes.

"What brought about this argument you heard?"

"Right, I completely forgot that part. Sorry." I looked at her sheepishly. "Your father said he smelled this Corey person at the border when they were hunting down those wolves." If I thought Amber looked confused before the creases in her forehead deepened.

"There were only four wolves there, Liv. I know we didn't get the other three's names, but they were younger than us. You said that this Corey was taken care of a long time ago, so that takes them out of the running, and the other wolf was Daniel."

"I know, Amber, something is not adding up. We need to do some recon work and see what we can come up with. I'm going to ask my mom, Luna knows everyone in the pack! How about you ask around the Omegas? They are always more open with you. I find they are too proper with me, as I'm the future Alpha." Amber agreed, and we both went our separate ways to gather as much information about Corey as possible. We promised to meet back in my room in an hour.

I had the perfect excuse to speak with my mom since she had asked me to join her for tea earlier. I linked her as I headed down to the kitchen and asked her to meet me on the back porch of the pack house. Ten minutes later, I was sitting across from my mom with two cups of tea and some cookies between us.

"I'm glad to see you're feeling better, Olivia."

I nodded with a smile.

"Yes, much better, thank you. Mom, you know all the wolves past and present in our pack, right?"

"Of course I do, Olivia. It's my job to know every wolf." That was exactly what I wanted to hear from her. "Why do you ask?" She eyed me curiously.

"Well, you see, I heard some people talking about a man named Corey. I've never heard of anyone in this pack by that name, and I was wondering who he was." I was going to say more, but the look on my mom's face stopped me instantly. She had completely blanched; her mouth hung open, eyes wide with a look I couldn't read. She started to tremble in her seat. "Mom, what's wrong?" I was so worried she was about to faint on me.

"Nothing's wrong, sweetheart," she squeaked out. At this point, she had started to sweat and was dabbing at her brow with a small napkin. I knew there was something not right, but she refused to tell me anything.

I asked Evie what she thought about all this.

"Liv, this is so weird. I've never seen your mom not composed; something is absolutely going on here." I was glad to know I wasn't alone in thinking this reaction was off.

Before I could say anything more, my mom stood up and, with a tight smile, let me know that she didn't feel so good and was going to rest for a little while. I didn't want to add to her distress anymore, so I let her go and wished her a speedy recovery.

I had to speak to Amber right away. I started speedily walking towards my room and got to the door at the same time as Amber.

"Do I have a story for you," we both blurted out at the same time. We had a little giggle at ourselves and rushed into my room.

"You go first," I said to Amber.

She nodded and let me know that she had spoken to seven different Omegas.

"Three didn't have a clue who Corey was, but four of them acted so weird when I mentioned the name Corey. They started to sweat and claimed they knew nothing! I swear they knew something. I couldn't get anything more out of them as they walked away."

"I had a very similar experience with my mom, Amber. She went white as a ghost and started to sweat too, like the Omegas! She was distraught and excused herself to go lie down, faking sickness. We have to find out what is going on!" Amber couldn't believe what I just told her about my mother.

"Who was this guy to have everyone reacting like this?" she asked me, and I just shrugged my shoulders.

"I don't know, Cupcake, but I plan on finding out. We just need more information. Sadly, I don't think we're going to find the answers here. Any ideas?"

Amber thinks for a few moments and then snaps her fingers.

"I've got it, Liv! The Jade Moon Pack is a record-keeping pack. They have records dating back hundreds of years. Every birth, mated pair, death, you name it, they have it recorded in their archives."

My best friend was brilliant! I couldn't believe I didn't think of that. "Amber, I could kiss you. I'm so happy."

"Please don't. I'm saving myself for my mate." She tried to say that with a straight face but ended up laughing hysterically. Amber sobered up quickly with a worried look on her face.

"How are we going to get into their records room? They don't let just anyone out of the blue into their pack."

I know I should be worried, but a devilish grin slides across my face.

"Well, my brilliant best friend, you said the answer yourself before."

"I did?" She looks so confused. I felt bad for her.

"Yes, Amber. Your mate! Your father has been pushing for you to travel and find your mate, has he not? This is the perfect excuse to get out of our pack and into other neighboring packs. As your best friend, it only makes sense that I'm traveling with you, plus my sweet daddy dearest will be ecstatic to have me traveling in the hopes that I stumble upon the next alpha, I mean my mate." I couldn't help but roll my eyes and gag while I laughed. Amber laughed right along with me and agreed this was the perfect plan.

She left me not long after to go tell her father he was right, and she wanted to start looking for her mate. I felt a wave of excitement pass over me. We were going to uncover the truth about this Corey one way or another.

Chapter Five

Chapter 5

Daniel

Once we crossed the border back into neutral ground, I let out a frustrated growl.

"What the hell was that!" I screamed.

Our hunt did not turn out the way it was meant to go. Not only did we leave empty-handed, but we were almost captured by that female alpha and her beta.

"I thought the Beta was cute and feisty," Xander panted at me.

"Xander, we have our mate. Quit panting over some random she-wolf."

"Hey, you chose Annabelle, not me. I wanted to wait for our mate! I gave in and allowed you to take a chosen mate because I couldn't stand your whining about how much you loved her."

I was going to respond, but I didn't have the strength to argue with Xander right now. I pushed him to the back of my mind as I kept walking. I couldn't shake the feeling of familiarity I had with Olivia or how odd that whole situation was. I was so lost in thought that I didn't notice when Jacob came up beside me, and he startled me badly.

"Jacob, what the hell, man? Don't sneak up on people like that!"

"I've been calling your name for two minutes straight, Daniel. Are you okay?"

"I'm sorry. I must have been more lost in thought than I realized. What's up?"

"I was just wondering if the alpha will be mad at us for not bringing anything back? It's the first time we've failed, and I'm kind of scared." Jacob looked down at the ground with a worried expression on his face. He'd always been nervous, even as a kid.

I wish I was able to give him an answer that would take away his fear; I've always been an upfront person. I answered him the best I could. "Honestly, Jacob, I don't know. Alpha Arnold could be really mad or totally okay with our failure. Either way, don't worry. I'll take the brunt of his wrath since I'm the one who failed."

"Daniel, you've been protecting me since forever. I can't let you do that; we failed as a team." He tried to give me a reassuring look, but I knew better. I failed at scenting the impending danger.

"You failed at taking down Alpha Olivia, too. She handed you your ass!" Xander snickered from the back of my mind. He blocked me out this time before I could clap back.

Talk about kicking a man when he's already down, and so much for the other half of me. Xander could be such an ass sometimes.

"Listen, Jacob, once we get back, just let me do all the talking, and it'll be fine." I gave him a friendly clap on the back. He didn't look convinced, yet he smiled and tried to believe me. This was why he was my best friend.

We still had a forty-five-minute walk back to the pack. I fell back to a steady pace and lost myself in thought once again.

The earliest memory I had was when I was three years old. I never had parents. As far as I'd been told, I was found in the forest alone. I was living with Alpha Arnold and his chosen mate, Julie, who was the one who found me; his true mate was killed in a rogue attack on his old pack. Alpha Arnold wasn't a true alpha. He was a beta in his past life. He took care of everyone so well that he was voted as alpha of our small mixed pack.

When I was three, Jacob arrived in our pack with his older sister, Sarah. They had no parents either. He was always scared. I decided then and there that he was going to be my best friend. I would always protect him. He naturally gravitated to me for comfort and protection, so we fell into a steady rhythm throughout our childhood; no one dared to pick on Jacob because they knew they'd have me to deal with.

When we were eighteen, we learned that Jacob's father had left his mother. She ended up taking her own life due to depression from losing her mate and the hardships of raising two children alone.

Jacob didn't take the news well and started blaming himself for his mother taking her life. He would cry that if only he'd been less afraid as a kid, it wouldn't have burdened his mother as much. It took me close to a year to get him to stop blaming himself. It was quite the task. He was still so hard on himself and worried everyone would be mad at him when situations like today came up.

I was brought out of my thoughts by a high-pitched, excited squeal. I had just enough time to register that the body flying into my arms was Annabelle. She hugged me tight and gave me a hard, short kiss. "I missed you so much, my love," she whispered into my ear after she let my lips go.

"I've only been gone a few hours, Belle." I chuckled at her.

"I don't care if you're gone one hour or one minute! I will always miss you," she said shyly.

This made me smile, and my heart swell. "Want to know a secret?" I whispered back to her. She nodded back emphatically. "I missed you like crazy too!"

The smile she gave me could have blinded the sun. I enveloped her in my arms. She nuzzled my neck but stiffened instantly. Annabelle pushed me back with force, her eyes getting angry and dark; her wolf Erin starting to surface.

"WHO IS SHE?" Annabelle growled at me. I didn't bother to feign ignorance since I knew this was going to happen. I had hoped I could have told her what went down before she smelled Olivia on me, but I guess today wasn't my lucky day.

"No kidding, lover boy. Good luck!" Xander just had to pop in and add his two cents before he retreated with his tail between his legs, knowing what was coming for us.

I almost smiled and let out a laugh, but I knew Annabelle would think it was directed at her. I chose not to add fuel to the fire.

"Belle, it's not what you thi—" she cut me off before I even had a chance to finish.

"Oh, really? What am I supposed to think, Daniel? You smell like another female around your marking spot, a powerful female at that."

"Belle, I could never do that to you! I love you to the ends of this earth and back. Our hunting trip went sideways, and we ended up in that female's territory."

Annabelle just stared at me with icy eyes. "That still doesn't explain why her scent is around your neck, Daniel."

I let out a long sigh. "Belle, I tried to attack her, thinking she was going to harm Jacob and the others. She was strong and pinned me to the ground by my neck; that's why her scent is there."

She just blinked at me and shook her head. "Come on, Daniel, do you think I'm stupid? You were pinned by a female? You are one of our strongest wolves."

"She was an alpha Belle, an Alpha! She was strong and very well-trained. If you don't believe me, have Erin reach out to Xander; our wolves can't lie to each other."

I felt Xander's presence lighten slightly, knowing he was connecting with Erin. Annabelle stood stone-cold and squared her shoulders at me. After what seemed like an eternity, the corners of Annabelle's eyes started to crinkle, and a low, rolling laugh started.

"Oh, Daniel, she really dumped you on your ass that bad?" My cheeks heated up in embarrassment.

"Yes, she really did, Belle."

Xander popped into my mind, wearing the longest grin I'd ever seen on a wolf. *"You're welcome, lover boy. She was about to rip your head off."*

"Thank you, Xander. I owe you one!"

Annabelle finally relaxed and came back over to me. "So how are you going to make this up to me?" she cooed.

"Oh, I've got an idea or two," I said with a little laugh. Before she could say anything else, I scooped her up, threw her over my shoulder, and began to run towards our house as she screamed at me to put her down, all while laughing uncontrollably.

Chapter Six

Chapter 6

Daniel

We made it back to our house within minutes. I pushed open the door and headed straight for our bedroom. "Hang on there, lover boy," Annabelle giggled; you need a shower first! "There is no way anything is happening with that other woman's scent all over you."

"Okay, fine, I can do what I wanted while we're in the shower." I winked at her. Pivoting, I headed to the bathroom and put Annabelle down on the counter.

Before she could say anything, I crashed my lips down on hers and gave her a long, passionate kiss. Annabelle let out a seductive moan that instantly woke my manhood. I deepened the kiss as the smell of her arousal started to fill the bathroom.

I broke the kiss long enough to pull her shirt off, throwing it onto the floor; Annabelle's small, perky nipples instantly hardened through her lace bra as the cool air hit them. I bent down and slowly sucked her right nipple through the lace; she shuddered at the touch of my hot mouth.

I looked up and smirked at her, "You like that, do you, Belle?" She looked at me with hooded eyes and nodded her head with a lazy smile on her face.

I slid my palm over her left breast, eliciting a soft moan from her, which drove me crazy; there was nothing better than the sounds this woman made when I ravaged her. Annabelle reached for my shirt and pulled it over my head.

She trailed her eyes all the way down my chest, landing on the bulge in my pants. "See something you like, my love?" Her eyes darkened as she grabbed my pants in response and undid my belt lightning-fast. Before I had a chance to say anything more, she had my pants down to my ankles, and my cock sprung up to attention. "That's all for you, Belle. He's yours, and only yours."

Annabelle smiled and licked her lips. "Ooohh, the things I could do with him," she cooed.

I was done waiting. I shredded her bra, pulled off her pants in one swift motion, and picked her up. She wrapped her legs around my waist. Pinning my cock between our stomachs. I opened the shower door and walked into the enclosed space, pushing Annabelle against the cool shower wall; she let out a shocked squeal at the chill of the tiles.

I turned on the water. As the water heated up, it cascaded over us. I dropped my lips to Annabelle's and kissed her with all my love poured into it. The steam enveloped us, and the smell of both our arousal was making us both feral by this point.

"Daniel, I need you inside me," she pleaded with me. I couldn't disappoint the love of my life, so I pulled back enough to line my cock up with her entrance and slowly pushed myself inside my mate. Annabelle arched her back, letting out a loud, "YESSSSSSSSSSS."

That brought Xander forward. He pushed balls deep into Annabelle, which made her writhe against me while her walls contracted around my cock in the most delicious way. I could never get enough of this woman. I fell into a steady rhythm, pumping into her, making her beautiful breasts bounce.

I began kneading her right breast and lowered my head to suck on her left nipple. I felt her walls tighten around my cock; I knew she was building up and would soon explode over the edge. Annabelle was panting and moaning. I shifted our position slightly so that I was hitting her G spot. "Oh my god, Daniel, YES, just like that, please don't stop." She had dug her nails into my shoulders, so I knew she was starting to unravel. I picked up my pace and swirled my tongue around her right nipple.

I could feel she was right there. I whispered to her, "Let go, Belle," and bit down gently but firmly on her nipple; this was the action that threw her over the edge into the abyss. Annabelle's head lulled back as her pussy clenched my cock like a vise. I slowed down to help her ride out her orgasm as she shuddered in my arms.

She finally came down from her high, and I slipped myself out of her and gently sat her on the bench in our shower; she looked up at me with a happy, satisfied grin. "You didn't finish?" she asked, sounding a bit worried.

"This was all about you, love. I needed to make up for having another woman's scent on me, remember?! Don't worry. That was just a warm-up. There is plenty of time for my release later." I winked at her as she stood up and put her forehead against mine.

"Thank you, Daniel, for being the sweetest and most caring partner a girl could ask for." Annabelle pecked me on the lips and reached for the soap. She started to lather me up, paying extra attention to my marking spot, to make sure Olivia's scent was good and gone.

Annabelle rubbed the soap down my abs and down my treasure trail towards my cock. My cock twitched as she gently passed her hand over it. I growled lightly, which turned into a moan as Annabelle gripped my shaft, slowly tugging it up and down. My cock was getting harder by the second as she rinsed the soap off. Annabelle looked up at me with a mischievous grin, licked her lips, and slowly knelt down in front of me.

"What are you doing, you little minx?" I chuckled and let out a moan as she kissed the tip of my cock.

"I'm just repaying the favour and having a little taste. Is that okay?" she looked up at me through her eyelashes, innocently; it took all my restraint not to push into her mouth.

"Absolutely love, do whatever you want. Like I said, he's all yours." Annabelle didn't need any more of an invitation and slowly started to lick me from root to tip with her warm, soft tongue. I rewarded her with a low growl-moan combo, which spurred her on to take my cock into her mouth and swirl her tongue around the tip, while sucking just the way she knew I liked it.

I wrapped my hand into her hair as a guide, while she picked up the pace of her sucking; bobbing up and down, taking my length as if it were nothing; it was an impressive sight to see. I felt myself getting close to the edge, but this wasn't about me yet; I stopped her midway down my shaft. "Hey, I wasn't done yet! You were getting close. I could feel it." She looked quite annoyed with me.

"Not yet, Belle, I'm not ready to finish yet! You've got a few more orgasms to have first." I helped her off her knees and turned off the water.

Stepping out, I grabbed two big fluffy towels, wrapping Annabelle and myself in one. I picked her up bridal style and strode into our bedroom. I tossed her unceremoniously onto our bed as she shrieked.

I took this time to crawl up on the bed like a predator stalking my prey, kissing my way up Annabelle's legs until I reached the apex between her thighs. "My turn for a taste!" I gently pushed her legs apart and bent my head down, licking her pussy from bottom to top. "Hmmm, delicious," I mumbled. As I got to her clit, I gently sucked it into my mouth, causing Annabelle to arch off the bed.

Annabelle

The moment Daniel sucked my clit into his mouth, I lost it, arching my back off the bed. The things this man did to me were insane. We may not have been goddess-given mates, but our chemistry had always been through the roof.

As Daniel continued to suck on my clit he gently, yet firmly, inserted two fingers into my pussy, pumping in and out at a leisurely pace. I could feel the pressure building in my stomach. "Faster, please," I panted. I was rewarded with a quicker rhythm that made my insides hum in pleasure. "I'm so close, Daniel, please don't stop."

He curled his middle finger just right and hit my G spot. I was so close I was seeing spots in my vision; before I could fall over the edge, though, Daniel suddenly stopped and looked up at me with a wicked smirk. "Oh, my sweet Belle, I can't let you fall just yet! There is more fun to be had."

I couldn't believe he just did that; he didn't give me much time to process as he flipped me over, pulled me onto my knees, and slid into my pussy. "Oh shit! Daniel, you are so hard," I couldn't believe he was still this worked up after all the exercise we had been doing.

"You turn me into an animal, Belle. What can I say!?" he laughed as he thrust into me deeply, making me forget my own name. It didn't take long before he had me on the edge of orgasm again.

This time, Daniel didn't stop. He slammed into me over and over again until stars burst behind my eyes, and I came harder than I had in a long time. My head was swimming, and my pussy clenched for dear life. I rode out my orgasm and as I came down, I made a split-second decision, flipping us both over so that I straddled Daniel, and rode him.

He looked surprised at the move I just pulled, but his shocked expression soon turned into sheer pleasure as I sunk down onto his cock. When I reached the bottom, I twisted my hips and squeezed my walls. This earned me a very loud moan, which spurred me on to go faster and harder. I could feel another orgasm coming, but I wanted us to finish together.

Just as I was thinking I was going to come undone alone, I felt Daniel's cock twitch and tighten inside me. One last tight squeeze and we both fell over the cliff together. Daniel grabbed my hips and held onto them for dear life as he emptied himself inside me.

I was so exhausted from all the stimulation I slumped onto his chest and let out a happy sigh. We stayed like that for a few minutes. Daniel kissed my forehead and went to get up. "Where are you going?" I asked.

"I'm going to get a towel to clean you up." He tapped my ass and hopped off the bed. I giggled and snuggled into my pillow. A moment later, I felt a warm cloth wiping my sore, yet happy, pussy. Daniel was gentle as he cleaned and dried me.

"Thank you, my love, you are most definitely forgiven for earlier." I reached out and cupped his cheek with a huge smile on my face.

"Well, I must say, if this is my punishment for making you angry, I may have to get in trouble again, soon!" He gave me a cheesy shit-eating grin, which I gladly wiped off his face by hitting him with his pillow.

"You did not just smack me with my own pillow, did you?" He tried to look offended, but the laughter was hardly contained in his eyes. Daniel was about to start tickling me when he froze, eyes going distant as if he was linking with someone.

"What's wrong, love?" He sighed and got off the bed. "Alpha Arnold wants to see me and discuss what happened today on our hunting trip." He rubbed his palm down his face, suddenly looking tired.

"Well, I'll go with you to their house. I have to pick up Gabriella from Julie. She fell asleep, so I left her to nap, when I went to meet up with you in the forest. As much fun as we just had, Mother Duty calls, and honestly, I missed my baby!"

We got dressed quickly and made our way over to Alpha Arnold's, holding hands like two love-sick teenagers; I was smiling, but I could tell Daniel was nervous. "It will be okay, Daniel. I promise you did nothing wrong." I brought our joined hands up to my lips and kissed the back of his hand.

Daniel looked down at me with a sweet look on his face, a cross between love, skepticism, and the desire to believe me. "Thank you, Belle. It will be okay because you're here with me." He smiled as we walked up the steps to the Alpha's house. Letting out a deep sigh, Daniel knocked on the door, ready to face any criticism or punishment the Alpha might hand out; all I could do was squeeze his hand in support.

Chapter Seven

Chapter 7

Daniel

I knocked on Alpha Arnold's door and waited anxiously. After a few moments, there was no answer.

"Maybe we should just go in? He did ask you to come." Annabelle shrugged her shoulders.

"You're not wrong, my love, but I just feel weird walking into his house," I sighed. We waited a few more minutes. I even knocked again; standing outside his house forever didn't seem like a much better option. I decided to suck it up and just walk in. No one really locked their doors around here, so there weren't any issues with Annabelle and me walking in.

Once inside, it was quiet. I was beginning to wonder if they were even home. Maybe I had misunderstood the mind-link? Before I could wonder anymore, we heard voices coming from the library. "Arnold, are you going to tell him finally?" That came from Julie.

"I don't think it's the right time yet, Jules! I want to find out what happened today first; then, I will decide if we should tell him or not."

Annabelle raised her eyebrows at me in silent question once we heard Alpha Arnold say what he did. All I could do was shrug. I was as clueless as she was.

I think they smelled us because they fell quiet suddenly, and Alpha Arnold called out, "Daniel, is that you?" As he walked out into the hallway to see for himself.

"Yes, Alpha, it is Annabelle and I. No one answered the door, so we just came in; we're sorry for intruding." Both Annabelle and I bared our necks to Alpha Arnold as a sign of respect.

"Don't be silly. You're not intruding; I called you over, remember?" He smiled and patted me on the back, which was slightly off-putting. Alpha Arnold was not cruel by any means, but he also wasn't the warmest individual. So, to have him be so cheery and accommodating kind of sent me for a loop.

Julie joined us at this point, carrying my sweet little angel, Gabriella. I smiled at her, and she let out the happiest little baby squeal; it melted my heart instantly. I bent down to kiss her forehead, before Julie handed her to Annabelle. "Thank you, Julie, for watching our little angel." I smiled at her.

"It was my pleasure! Gabriella is the sweetest little pup. I'll watch her anytime you want," she said as she tickled Gabriella's little tummy, causing her to burst into a fit of laughter.

"Ok, my little giggle bug, your daddy needs to have a meeting with the Alpha!" Annabelle said to Gabriella.

"I'll see you at home later, Belle." I gave her a quick kiss on the top of her head. She smiled at me and walked towards the front door.

"Shall we go to my office?" Alpha Arnold gestured towards his office down the hall. I nodded and followed him into the room. It wasn't a very big office, but it had comfortable chairs and large windows that gave the space tons of natural light and a great view of the forest.

I was slightly nervous about speaking with the Alpha, but once I looked out the windows, I relaxed a bit. "So, Daniel, care to let me in on what happened today?" Alpha Arnold didn't waste any time, he quirked his eyebrow at me.

I gave a little sigh and went into the whole sordid tale from the beginning. Arnold nodded his head throughout the entire story without saying a word. I swore I saw a hint of amusement pass through his eyes as I told him the part about Olivia dumping me on my ass; he managed to keep his face neutral the entire time.

I came to the end of my story and finished. "I'm really sorry, Alpha Arnold. I didn't mean to fail our expedition. Please take out any punishment on me! The others were listening to my directions, which led us into the other pack's territory, and it's my fault I attacked their future Alpha, Olivia."

I hardly breathed before continuing, "I have to say, it was a weird experience. Olivia seemed to trust me without any reservations, and she said she felt a familiarity with me; I felt like I knew her from somewhere, too. We both know that's impossible, but it was such an odd feeling."

A look of surprise and concern passed over Arnold's face, before he cleared his throat to speak.

Alpha Arnold

When Daniel told me he felt like he knew Olivia and the feeling was mutual, I got a tad nervous. I wasn't ready to speak to Daniel about things from his past yet. Sure, it probably would have been the ideal time, but there were still too many variables. I needed things to be lined up better before talking with him.

I cleared my throat before I spoke, hoping he hadn't sensed any of my nervous energy. "Daniel, first off, it wasn't your fault you ended up in their territory; that part of the land is actually not theirs to begin with." Daniel looked at me with a puzzled look on his face. "Let me explain, Alpha Francis of Onyx Crescent has always been greedy. For years he has been expanding his borders, and since we are the only two packs that are this close to one another, he gets away with it."

Daniel looked like he was about to say something, but I cut him off before he had a chance. "I know what you're thinking, and yes, I have contested it in the past, but Alpha Francis has poisoned the other packs in the area against us; he makes them believe we are rogues. The other packs refuse to acknowledge us as a pack because we are such a mixed group of wolves."

"That makes sense, Alpha. When Olivia had me pinned, she called me a rogue and wouldn't believe that we weren't rogues." Daniel looked thoughtful as he said this.

I gave him a reassuring smile. "See? You have nothing to worry about. I'm not mad at you or the others. If anything, I'm mad at Alpha Francis and his greedy pack." A look of relief crossed Daniel's face, and I could see him visibly relax.

That didn't last long, though, as he furrowed his brow and asked, "What about Olivia? I still can't shake the feeling that I have met her before."

Damn it, I thought I had dodged that bullet; I took a moment to look thoughtful before I spoke. I hoped that my answer would get him to let it go. "Maybe you knew each other in a past life, Daniel. You know that we reincarnate, and the goddess works in mysterious ways. I wouldn't be too worried about it. It's not likely you will see her again, so you can move on with your life."

I was satisfied with my answer. Daniel, on the other hand, looked like he was wrestling with himself, wanting to say something more, but ultimately, he chose to nod his head and agree with me. I didn't want him asking any more questions, so I stood up and gestured him towards the door. "That was a nice chat, Daniel. I don't want to keep you from spending time with Annabelle and Gabriella; you go home now!" Seeming slightly unsure of himself, Daniel got up, thanked me for not getting angry about everything and went on his way home.

"So, did you tell him, Arnold?" Julie came up behind me and poked me in the back.

"No, Jules I did not. He isn't ready to know about his past yet. If we want our plan to work, we have to wait a little longer." I cupped her cheek lovingly, and she leaned into my touch with a sigh.

"I sure hope you know what you're doing, Arnold. I love Daniel, and he deserves a lot better than he's been given his entire life."

I looked down at Julie sadly, and sighed, "I care a lot about him too, Jules, and I'm doing all this to see him thrive and have an even better life, one he could have never imagined for himself."

Julie went up on her tiptoes and gave me a sweet kiss on the lips. "Do you think he heard us talking about it when he came into the house earlier?"

I contemplated it for a moment. "I honestly don't think so, Jules. He would have said something about it."

She looked satisfied with my answer. "Come now, my Alpha, it's time for dinner." I wrapped my arm around her shoulders, and we walked into the kitchen to eat together.

Daniel

I left Alpha Arnold's house in a daze. He wasn't mad at me for almost getting myself and the other boys captured. However, that conversation left me more confused than ever. I know the feelings I had towards Olivia, and the answer Alpha Arnold gave was so strange! Acquaintance from another life? The goddess works in mysterious ways?

I asked Xander what he thought about all this. *"You know me, Daniel, I'm rarely lost for words."* I had a good chuckle at that. *"Are you done trying to be the funny guy?"* He half snarled at me.

"Geez, someone's cranky!"

Xander ignored my remark and continued, *"You asked for my opinion. Do you want it or not?"*

"Yes, yes, go ahead," I relented.

"As I was saying, I'm slightly lost for words at the moment." He paused, expecting me to laugh again or hit him with a witty comment. I refrained and urged him to continue. *"I can't for the life of me understand that man's answer. He was dodging that conversation like a professional athlete. What also bothered me was the look of concern at the topic, and his sudden nervous energy for no reason."*

"I agree, Xander. Plus don't forget that conversation Annabelle and I walked into. What does he have to tell me? Why is he waiting? Things *just aren't adding up."* Xander agreed that we needed to do some investigating on our own, since Alpha Arnold wasn't going to help me.

I walked into our house, and Annabelle ran right over to me and gave me a big hug. "How did it go, my love?"

I looked down at her with a tired smile. "It went better than I expected, Belle!" I told her about the entire meeting and about what Alpha Arnold had said about Olivia.

"So, he didn't tell you anything then?" She looked a bit shocked. "I guess you didn't give him the answers he was looking for?!"

I shrugged my shoulders at her. "Something doesn't add up, Xander and I feel like Arnold is hiding something from me."

Annabelle agreed with me. "So, what are you going to do, Daniel?"

I thought about her question for a moment. "I think I have to go back to the Onyx Crescent and look around; see if I can speak with anyone or maybe even speak with Olivia again, since she felt the connection, too."

Annabelle visibly winced when I said I wanted to talk to Olivia again. I felt terrible that she was upset over another woman; I assured her that my interest in Olivia was strictly platonic, and the feeling of familiarity wasn't one of love or mates.

This seemed to ease Annabelle's mind. She reached up and kissed my cheek. "When are you going to go back? I'm not going to lie Daniel, it makes me very nervous the thought of you going back there alone. What if they catch you?"

I was touched that she was worried about me. "Belle, don't worry, they won't catch me this time. I will be more careful! I need to know what's going on for my own peace of mind. I will go back within the next day or so, since they are probably on alert from today's encounter." Annabelle nodded at my answer even though I could see the trepidation in her eyes; she tried to smile for my benefit.

Goddess, I loved this woman so much. I was blessed the day she walked into the pack with her father. She didn't have an easy life before; but I promised her when I took her as my chosen mate that I would spend my life loving her, and making sure she was well taken care of. I've kept that promise every day. Annabelle as well, has gone above and beyond, making me feel like a king every day.

I wrapped my arms around Annabelle and pressed my lips to hers in a chaste kiss. "I will always come home to you and Gabriella!" I whispered in her ear.

She smiled a genuine smile and punched me in the shoulder. "You better come back, or I'll hunt you down, and you'll be in a world of trouble, Daniel." I burst out laughing at her response. I laughed until tears rolled down my face. Just as I was about to say something back, we heard Gabriella fuss from the kitchen. "I should probably finish feeding her before she gets really angry!" Annabelle blushed slightly and scampered off into the kitchen, with me right behind her.

A meal and a good night's rest would help me come up with a plan of action in the morning. I was going to find answers one way or another.

Chapter Eight

Chapter 8

D^{aniel}

I didn't end up sleeping much the night before, my mind was all over the place trying to figure out what Alpha Arnold could be keeping from me; what connection I had to Olivia; how I was going to get back into Onyx Crescent to look for information; the list went on.

I was finally able to fall into a shallow sleep right before the sun came up. Not even twenty minutes into my slumber, I heard Gabriella fuss from the other room. I knew there was no way I was going to get any more sleep at this point, so I rolled over and kissed Annabelle gently. She didn't even stir when my lips touched her. To say I was jealous of Annabelle was an understatement.

I walked quietly into Gabriella's room, gave her a big smile, and said, "Good Morning, my sweet princess. Did you sleep well?" I was rewarded with a giant toothless grin and an excited squeal.

Gaby reached her arms out to me. I walked over to the crib and scooped her up. My sweet little girl wrapped her arms around my neck and gave me the most precious hug. My heart swelled with love. I walked over to the rocking chair and sat down with her in my lap.

She looked up at me with her big green eyes, that were sparkling in the sunbeams filtering into her room from the window above the chair. "Gaby, you and Mommy are the other half of my heart and soul; Daddy has to go away for a day or two. I need you to be brave and watch over Mommy for me. She is nervous and will be sad. Don't worry, though, Daddy will always come back to you, I pinky-promise." I took her tiny little pinky and curled it around my massive one.

Gaby looked at me thoughtfully as if she was digesting what I had just told her. Seeing her so serious made me slightly sad, so I had to break the tension by tickling her and blowing raspberries on her tummy. She began to scream and laugh uncontrollably. I started laughing, too. "Well, so much for being quiet and letting mommy sleep in, huh princess?!"

On cue, Annabelle walked into Gaby's room, rubbing the sleep from her eyes and looking half-dazed. "I'm sorry, Belle, I just wanted to spend some quality time with Gaby before I leave later today. We didn't mean to wake you up." I gave her a sheepish look.

"So, you are still moving forward with your idea to sneak back into Onyx Crescent?" A shadow of worry crosses her beautiful face.

"Yes, my love, I am! What kind of life am I living if people keep secrets from me? Let's go have breakfast, and I will explain my plan to you; how does that sound?"

Annabelle gave me a half smile and agreed to listen to my plan over breakfast. "Since you're leaving me and Gaby, you're cooking for us this morning!" She giggled.

"You've got it, Belle, anything for you and Gaby." I handed Gabriella to Annabelle to change and headed for the kitchen to start breakfast.

Twenty minutes later, Annabelle and Gabriella came into the kitchen all changed. I was in the middle of flipping the last of the blueberry pancakes. "Perfect timing, my love. Have a seat, and I'll serve you both." I bowed playfully at Annabelle.

She chuckled lightly. "Thank you kindly, my sweet, sexy chef. Don't tell my mate, but you're way better in the kitchen than he is." She winked at me, and I growled lowly in a playful warning.

The mood quickly shifted, and Annabelle went serious and somber. "So, tell me what's your plan, Daniel."

I finished chewing the bite of pancake I had in my mouth, cleared my throat, and began to explain that I would sneak back into the Onyx crescent territory, and go find some omegas who were willing to get Olivia to come talk to me.

I knew it wasn't going to be easy, since most pack wolves were wary of outsiders, but I knew omegas were kind, and if I told them I had already had an audience with Alpha Olivia before, maybe they would help me out.

Annabelle took a deep breath and looked at me with worry in her eyes. I knew she wasn't happy with my plan. "Belle, I promise I'll be careful, and come back to you and Gaby as soon as I can. I won't be gone for more than two days tops."

She nodded in agreement, with tears pooling in her eyes. "Please be careful, Daniel. I wouldn't survive if anything were to happen to you." I stood up, and pulled Annabelle into my arms, and held her while she lightly cried.

She pulled away enough to look up at me, and I gently kissed away the tears from her cheeks. "I swear to you here and now Belle, that I will come home to you and Gaby. My word is all I have. I hope you can have faith in me."

Annabelle answered by giving me a passionate kiss, pouring all her emotions into it. "You better go pack a small bag now before the entire day is lost," she said, while wiping away her stray tears, and going to wipe down a very sticky Gaby. I nodded and left the kitchen to go get my stuff in order.

Olivia

I woke up the next morning feeling refreshed and excited for the first time in a few days. My life had a purpose. I was on a mission to find out who this mysterious Corey was, and I wasn't coming back until I had answers. It didn't hurt that I was getting away from my overly critical father, and getting to have fun with my best friend. This was a win-win situation for me.

Evie was in a good mood, too. She was prancing around in my mind with her tail wagging like a little pup. *"Well, someone's in a good mood this morning!"*

"Yes, I am, if you must know, I have a great feeling about this mission, and I'm never wrong." She grinned at me.

"Hahaha, alright then, I'll take your word for it!"

I finished getting dressed, and I headed down to the dining room for breakfast. On my way down, I linked Amber to meet me; she answered almost instantly that she was already in the dining room waiting for me. I entered the dining room and saw Amber sitting at the ranked table, with her father and mine.

"GREAT! I was in a good mood this morning, WAS being the operative word," I grumbled to Evie. She just shrugged her wolf shoulders at me in my mind. Well, wasn't she a great help? I thought to myself.

"Sorry, Liv, you're on your own this morning. Nothing is taking away my good vibes today!"

"Fair enough, Evie, I'll let you have your happy moment."

I walked up to the table and politely nodded to my father and Beta Shane. "Good Morning, gentlemen." Both acknowledged me and grumbled a cranky good morning back.

"Geez, who pissed in their cornflakes this morning?" I linked Amber. I saw her trying to suppress her laugh, which she ended up turning into a cough to save herself.

"Good Morning, Cupcake," I decided to say in a loud, overly exaggerated, sweet, happy tone. The very visible cringe that came from my father didn't go unnoticed; I internally patted myself on the back for that one.

I sat down and almost instantly an Omega brought me a plate of food and a large cup of coffee. My coffee was just the way I liked it, black as night. I looked up into the young omega's eyes, and thanked her warmly for bringing me my breakfast; something I knew would piss my father off even more. He believed that Omega's were beneath us, that they didn't need to be thanked and, above all, they were never to look ranked members in the eyes.

My actions hit the nail on the head. My father growled lowly at me, "Olivia, we don't allow Omega's to look us in the eyes, and why are you thanking her for doing the job she was born to do? She should be grateful we let her live and work here."

I rolled my eyes so deeply I saw the back of my head. "Oh right, forgive me, Father. I forgot they aren't living beings with hearts and souls, that work their tails off for us; how could I forget." My tone left nothing to the imagination of how I felt about his terrible view of our Omegas.

"You dare mock me to my face, Olivia?" He was starting to turn red, and the vein on his neck was beginning to bulge.

"No, Father, I wouldn't dream of mocking you." I took a sip of my coffee, signaling I was done with the conversation. Amber sputtered into her coffee, but no one was paying attention to her.

Beta Shane shifted uncomfortably next to my father as he seethed, his Alpha aura seeping out. He tried to turn things around by clearing his throat and saying, "So, Olivia, Amber is finally ready to look for her mate. She has told me you will be accompanying her on this endeavor?"

I smiled sweetly at Beta Shane. "Yes sir, that is correct. Amber is finally ready to find her true love, and I want to be there to support her on the quest," I said with such a straight face I was proud of myself, I could feel Amber dying a little inside, even though she knew my words weren't true.

My father looked at me pointedly and said, "I'm glad you're going; maybe you will finally find your mate, so I can retire."

I snorted at my father, but refrained from commenting. I simply said that the goddess worked in mysterious ways; he seemed content with my answer, then excused himself and his Beta; they had pack business to attend to.

"When were you planning on leaving?" he asked as he started to walk away.

"We will be leaving early this afternoon, Father." He advised that he had sent word to the local packs of our voyage, so they were expecting us. He then wished us both good luck and stalked out of the dining room with Beta Shane close behind him.

The moment they were gone from the room, I let out a giant sigh of relief and slumped down in my chair. I was now able to fully relax and enjoy my breakfast. "Well, that was fun!" Amber stated in a flat, emotionally empty voice.

"Speak for yourself, Cupcake. I found that to be great fun! He ruined my good mood with his presence, so I ruined his day by doing everything he hated. I think that's fair, don't you?" I smirked at her with a glint of fire in my eyes. All Amber could do was laugh with me.

"Okay, so what's the plan, Amber?" She shook her head, mind-linking me that it would be safer if we spoke in her room or mine. I had to agree with her, so we finished our breakfast in silence, and headed up to my room. Once we got upstairs and into my room, I locked the door and sighed.

"Okay, we're safe to talk. What should we do first? I was thinking, should we start with any other pack, or should we go straight for the Jade moon pack?"

Amber contemplated it for a few moments, and then said. "Honestly, I'd start with Jade Moon, I want to know what's going on as much as you do, so the sooner we get there to investigate, the better. It's also the furthest pack, so we can say we're working our way back home through the other packs. What do you think?"

I liked the way Amber was thinking and agreed that this was the best way to tackle our mission. "Alright then, we have a plan, you should go pack a bag for a few days, and we can meet down by the front door in an hour?"

"That's perfect!" Amber happily agreed.

Once Amber left my room, I took out a bag and filled it with the clothes I'd need for a few days, as well as a headlamp and gloves, in order for us to do a bit of snooping without getting caught. My bag was ready to go and I had some extra time, so I decided to hop in a quick shower to wash off my nerves that had started to bubble up a bit.

Within an hour, I met with Amber by the front door, we took our bags and headed to the garage to get my car. We put on some driving music and hit the open road. Amber and I looked at each other and smiled, we were free for a few days! This was going to be great, I hoped.

Daniel

I spent the afternoon packing a little bag, with all the supplies I could possibly need. I cuddled with Belle and Gaby one last time before I had to leave. By three, I knew it was time. I was using my patrol as an excuse to wander off, hopefully undetected; Belle would tell Alpha Arnold I was really tired and resting for the next day; all was worked out. I gave Annabelle one last long passionate kiss and hug goodbye; promising for the thousandth time I'd be back soon, safe and sound.

I headed out to my patrol post. I waited for about half an hour until I did a check-in with Alpha Arnold, then I took off at a brisk jog heading towards the Onyx Crescent. I jogged for a solid twenty minutes and started to tire. I sat beneath a tree and had some water and an apple.

Just as I was starting to relax, I heard footsteps, so I hid in the bushes. The footsteps didn't come any closer and faded quickly. I chose to continue on my way, sticking close to the tree line for protection.

Suddenly, I heard growling. I turned to see two big grey wolves baring their teeth at me. One of the warriors shifted to speak with me.

"Well, well, well, we knew you'd come back rogue; your kind are all alike. You take from others with no regard for the law, since you got nothing last time you had to come back to finish what you started, didn't you?"

I wasn't sure how to proceed. I didn't think I was on their territory yet.

It was a split-second decision, but I turned and ran, not the best plan in retrospect, but I was caught off guard again; that embarrassed me more than anything. I was so busy trying to see how close the two guards were to me, that I failed to see a third guard, who hit me on the back of the head with a large tree branch.

I hit the ground hard and the whole world was spinning. I tried to stand, but before I could I was hit again, and this time the whole world went black.

Chapter 9

Olivia

We drove for almost two hours until we finally got to the gates of Jade Moon. We slowed down at the gate and identified ourselves to the guard. His eyes glazed over and within a minute he was sending us through. "The Alpha will meet you in front of the pack house."

I thanked the guard and drove up the winding driveway towards the largest building, which I correctly assumed was the pack house. As we pulled up, there were several people standing around on the steps. I could tell instantly who the Alpha was; he stood there with a smug, Holier-than-thou look about him. I had never met this Alpha before but he was giving off the same vibes my father does, and I hadn't even spoken to him yet.

"Well, besides the Alpha, who looks like an asshole, the other men are pretty hot in this pack, don't you think?" Amber asked with a sparkle in her eyes, and a mischievous grin.

"Down girl, you're supposed to be looking for your mate, remember?" I nudged her with my elbow.

"Who's to say one of those fine specimens isn't my mate?" she asked with a huff. I laughed at her, as I pulled up in front of the group and parked my car. We steeled our expressions and got out of the car.

As I was closing the door, Evie started bouncing up and down in my mind. *"Evie, you're making me dizzy, please calm down."*

I swayed a little on my feet; "Are you ok, Liv?" Amber rushed over to me.

"Yeah, yeah, don't worry, I just got out of the car too quickly!" I didn't want to mind-link her in front of the Alpha so I just pretended I had been sitting too long. We both walked towards the group and plastered smiles on our faces.

"Welcome to the Jade Moon Pack, I am Alpha Renato Watson, pleasure to meet you both." The Alpha extended his hand to both Amber and myself. We each took turns shaking it politely; he looked at me and said, "You must be Olivia!? You look just like your father, you poor thing."

I was slightly taken aback by his sardonic tone, also being told I looked like my father was a huge insult; I never let my smile falter though. "Thank you Alpha, people always tell me how beautiful I am, I'll make sure I tell my father how good-looking you think he is!" Watching his smile falter and anger cross his eyes, before he pulled himself back together, was the highlight of my day.

Alpha Renato opened his mouth to respond but was cut off by laughter coming from behind him. I looked up to see a tall, good-looking man about my age with bright green eyes, approaching us while trying to wipe away the tears of laughter.

I was suddenly assaulted by the most amazing scent of apples and cinnamon. At that moment, Evie started to yell, *"MATE, MATE, MATE."*

This could not be happening right now. I was on a mission to find out who Corey was, not to find my mate. That was only a cover story we were using. I was internally face-palming myself. *"Evie, please calm down, you're giving me a headache, plus do you not realize that could be the Alpha's son? Meaning, Alpha Asshole over there, would be our dear father-in-law."* That horrible thought shut Evie up almost instantly and we both felt nauseous.

My theory was confirmed seconds later as the man said, "Well, Dad, she got you there!" He slapped Alpha Renato on the shoulder and extended his hand to us. "Hi, I'm the Alpha's son, Justin Watson; nice to meet you, Olivia." I stared at his extended hand, dumbstruck, not sure what to do.

"Olivia, if he's our mate why doesn't he seem fazed by our scent or excited?" Evie's question startled me into action and I shook his hand.

Nothing, I felt nothing, no sparks or tingles that are proof you're someone's mate. *"Evie, he isn't our mate!! If Justin isn't, then who is?"* I looked over Justin's shoulder and looked into the big, beautiful blue eyes of the hottest man I'd ever seen in my life. He was staring back at me with an equally shocked expression on his face.

"MATE! Liv, he's our Mate! You must go to him, please," Evie begged.

"Easy Evie, we don't know who he is yet. We have time to find out."

Justin let go of my hand and followed my gaze over his shoulder. He smiled and motioned the handsome piece of male flesh over to the group. My cheeks started to blush the closer he got, and that smell of his sent me into a tizzy. "Ladies, this is my best friend, Logan White."

I was reaching out my hand to him when Alpha Renato scoffed and cut into my daze. "Don't bother shaking his hand. He is nothing more than an Omega." The disgusted sneer was not lost on me, so this guy really was just like my father.

I looked Alpha Renato straight in the eyes and grabbed Logan's hand firmly in a hand shake. I kept eye contact, daring Alpha Renato to say something to me, which wasn't easy as the sparks flew up my arm and straight down to the tips of my toes.

I know Logan was feeling it too from the look on his face, he looked shocked and scared at the same time. He looked down at the ground and let me go. I felt the loss of connection deep in my soul and it left Evie whimpering in my mind.

Justin looked angrily at his dad. "He may be an Omega but he's my best friend and one of the greatest men I've ever met, people I know could take lessons in kindness from him." He pointedly looked at his dad, Alpha Renato's face started to get red and his Alpha aura was expanding. I saw Logan flinch back from the aura.

Amber took this moment to jump in and defuse the situation. "It's great you brought an Omega down, we're going to need help carrying our bags, please." This seemed to do the trick. Logan bowed slightly to the Alpha, and hurried to the trunk of my car with Amber. I heard him thank her for getting him out of that tense spot. I was happy Amber jumped in, but also angry and, dare I say, jealous that she saved my mate.

The first words I heard him speak were to my best friend; even Evie was lowly growling in the back of my head. *"Relax Evie, she doesn't know he's our mate yet,"* I said with a sigh, realizing how ridiculous I was being, Evie huffed and went to curl up in the back of my mind like a child.

I turned to Alpha Renato and thanked him for hosting us. I told him we were quite tired from our drive and would like to go rest before supper. He brusquely nodded and said that Justin and his Omega would show us to our rooms.

I felt Evie's hackles go up at the dismissive tone he took when speaking about our mate. *"I hate that man Liv, if I could, I'd let him have it."* I laughed at Evie, but honestly, I agreed with her completely, as far as I was concerned this Alpha was in the same category as my father, a complete piece of trash.

Once Alpha Renato took his leave, Justin turned to me with a pained smile. "I'm sorry about all that, my dad can be a bit much sometimes; you shouldn't have had to see that." He looked sheepishly at me.

I turned to him and gave him a genuine smile. "Don't worry, I've got my very own just like him at home."

That was all it took to get Justin laughing and the tense moment was over; that was until he threw his arm around my shoulder and said, "I knew I was going to like you Olivia, this is going to be a fun visit."

Before I could react we heard a loud growl coming from Logan who was standing with Amber behind my car holding our bags. "Easy buddy, I'm not trying to take your mate." He removed his arm quickly, which flooded me with relief.

"Wait, how did you know?" I gawked at him.

"It was hard not to notice the look on both your faces when you shook his hand, but I must give it to you; you've got quite the poker face, Olivia."

"Shit, do you think your dad noticed? Knowing how he felt about Logan, I didn't want to cause any trouble." I looked sadly down at Logan.

"Nothing to worry about, my dad is too wrapped up in his own warped mind to have noticed anything, if it's not to do with him he doesn't care." I let out a sigh of relief when he said this, that was one nice thing about dealing with an egotistical man.

Before I could say anything more, Amber, who had been rapidly blinking at me, exploded. "YOU FOUND YOUR MATE?" she squealed loudly, all three of us cringed at the pitch of her voice.

"Yes, Logan is my mate. Can you keep it down please? The whole pack doesn't need to hear about this," I hissed at her.

"Sorry Liv, why didn't you tell me first?" She pouted at me.

"When did I have the time, Cupcake? We were standing in front of Alpha Asshole, and I didn't mention it to Justin; he called me out on it."

"Oh true!" She looked down at the ground, a deep blush creeping up her neck and her face.

"Ok, two things." Justin broke the silence. "One, I LOVE your saying, Alpha Asshole! I will be using this moving forward. Two, why did you call her Cupcake?"

I couldn't contain my laughter at his reaction. "I'll save that story for another day if you don't mind, right now I'd like to see my room please, and have a chat one on one with Logan if he would allow that?" I looked hopefully over at Logan. He gave me a tight smile that didn't quite reach his eyes and nodded at me.

"Olivia, I'm scared. He doesn't look like he wants to speak with us." Evie was right, and I was a bit nervous now.

What if he had a chosen mate? What if he didn't like me and wanted to reject me? My heart started to race and anxiety clutched at my chest.

Logan had moved forward, and his scent began to calm me down as we walked towards our guest rooms in the pack house. *"I guess we'll have to wait and see what happens, Evie."* I could feel her unease and I knew there was nothing I could do to help, only speaking with Logan and having him accept us, would ease the tension we're both feeling at this moment.

We reached the guest rooms and Justin told us he'd come get us for supper; we would have about two hours to rest, freshen up, or do whatever else we wanted to do. He looked at me and winked at that part. I blushed and thanked him for his help. He turned and walked away.

At the same time, Amber went into her room, closing the door with a wink in my direction, as well. *"Go get him, Tiger,"* she mind-linked me with a giggle. I shook my head, not sure if I wanted to laugh or cry, I was feeling so nervous.

Logan stood there looking as awkward as I did. "Would you like to come in for a bit?" I asked him, hopefully.

He looked cautiously around the hall before he agreed and quickly opened the door to my room. As he opened the door, his arm brushed against my right breast and shot tingles straight through me, instantly making my nipples hard. I was in big trouble having Logan in my room. I took a steadying breath, and followed him in, closing the door quickly and locking it. I turned around to see Logan pacing back and forth nervously.

He stopped and looked at me. "Listen, Olivia," he had started to say, but I didn't let him finish.

"I get it, Logan, you have someone else, right? You want to reject me?" I asked, sounding angrier than I meant to sound.

"Uh no, I don't have anyone else, Olivia. Why would I reject you? I thought you wanted to talk so you could reject me!?!" He said the last part with such a deep sadness in his eyes, it broke my heart.

"So, if I understand this correctly, you're scared I'm going to reject you, and I'm scared you're going to reject me? We're both idiots," I said as I facepalmed myself and started to laugh lightly.

Logan looked at me, confused and shocked. "You don't want to reject me?"

"Goddess, NO. Why would I want to do that?" I asked, totally confused.

Logan looked at me uncomfortably. "Umm, because I'm a worthless Omega, and you're an Alpha's daughter, and future Alpha to your pack?"

My eyes flashed black, and Evie pushed forward with a low growl. *"Never call yourself worthless again, mate. You are perfect for us."* Logan took a step back out of fear as I took back control from Evie.

"Please don't be afraid; that was, Evie. She's very protective over people who are important to her; she'd never hurt you, as you are someone she deems important! I agree with her, though. Please never call yourself worthless again; you are my mate, and I will cherish you no matter what rank you are."

Plus, it didn't hurt that his being an Omega would REALLY piss my father off, which was a win for me in my books. I chuckled to myself; that part I would never tell Logan.

It took a moment for my words to sink in. Eventually, Logan rewarded me with the most gorgeous smile I'd ever seen. I won't lie when I say my knees went weak; "What is your full name, Olivia?"

"Olivia Chantal Stevens," I replied, blushing slightly, knowing what was coming next.

"I, Logan Jasper White of the Jade Moon pack, accept you, Olivia Chantal Stevens as my mate."

I felt a rush of power go through my body before I replied, "I, Olivia Chantal Stevens of the Onyx Crescent pack, take you, Logan Jasper White, as my mate."

That did the trick. I felt the bond snap into place like a puzzle, we still had to mate and mark, but there would be time for that later. I was scared of what Alpha Renato would do to Logan if he knew he was my mate and saw him marked by me.

At this moment, I was just happy to be accepted by this handsome man that the moon goddess had chosen for me. Logan looked at me bashfully and asked, "May I kiss you, Olivia?" I smiled and walked towards him, fully intending to kiss those full lips, until they fell off his sexy face.

Just as I reached for him, a loud knock sounded at my door. "Olivia, it's Alpha Renato. Please open the door. We need to talk." We both froze on the spot, not sure what to do.

Chapter Ten

Chapter 10

Olivia

Logan and I both looked at each other in disbelief. I couldn't believe my first kiss with my mate was just ruined by this asshole. Evie growled in my mind at not being able to get her paws on our man. Disbelief quickly turned to panic for Logan as he realized what getting caught by the Alpha in my room would mean for him.

"Quickly go into the bathroom and hide. I will see what he wants and send him away." He nodded at me and silently snuck into the bathroom, just as another round of banging began on the door.

"Olivia, this is my pack house and I demand you open this door at once," Alpha asshole bellowed at me.

I took off my shirt as an added effect to the story I was about to tell and swung the door open with a look of fury on my face. "I was in the bathroom getting ready to take a shower, what do you want?" Alpha Renato slid a lusty gaze down my body which made Evie and I shudder in disgust. He pushed past me into the room which I was not expecting.

Before saying another word, Alpha Renato sniffed the air, and his eyes flashed black. "Why was that Omega in your room?" he growled.

I was internally panicking about Logan hiding in my bathroom, but I didn't let that show. I squared my shoulders and lifted an eyebrow at him. "He helped bring my bags up to the room, and like a good omega he brought the bags into the room."

"Oh, I guess that makes sense! Just make sure to stay away from that boy, he is beneath you as an Alpha; you will do well to remember that. I wouldn't want my own daughter associating with the likes of that filth."

By this point, my blood was boiling, and it was taking all my power not to let Evie push forward and maul this piece of shit, but that wouldn't do us any good, so I pushed her down and settled with asking what he wanted so urgently that he had to interrupt my shower by banging on the door like a lunatic.

His face soured at being called a lunatic but he refrained from comment, he cleared his throat and proceeded to tell me that I had insulted him on his own territory by insinuating he found my father attractive and that I had better not tell my father that lie.

All I could do at that point was blink at the man. Was I dealing with an Alpha or a toddler?

Evie was howling with laughter in my head and I was desperately trying not to laugh in the man's face, knowing full well that it would cause the situation to explode. *"We need to get him out of the room, Liv, I want our mate and I can't deal with crazy man over there much longer."*

I agreed with Evie, I threw my shirt back on which gave me a moment to school my face before I apologized to Alpha Renato. I apologized for him not understanding my humour and promised not to say a word to my father about any attraction he may have towards him.

Alpha Renato's eyes flashed, knowing that I was mocking him. He was about to counter my apology, so I jumped in with a straightforward question, "I thought you and my father were friends in school?!"

"HA, me friends with that mutt? He wished he was part of our group, but we would never associate with the likes of him." He finished his statement with a sneer and his nose in the air.

"Well, well, well; it seems things weren't as rosy as your father made his life out to be!" Evie had to chime in.

"It sure looks that way, Evie! I'm not surprised in the least though." I cut my link to Evie and decided to end this ridiculous encounter. I had quite enough.

As politely as I could muster, I asked the Alpha to let me shower and get ready for supper. He hesitated for a moment, which made me nervous, but he finally agreed to leave me in peace. I told him he could tell me all the horrible tales about my father at supper; this seemed to brighten his mood. It took all my inner strength not to slam the door in his face. I reminded myself that I needed to gain access to his library, so getting kicked out now would not be a good idea.

I waited for a minute, then I locked the door and let out a deep sigh. I rushed into the bathroom to find Logan lying as flat as possible on the bottom of the sunken tub. I helped him out and wrapped my arms around his neck, crashing my lips onto his. What I wanted to do the entire time I was dealing with Alpha Renato. I wasn't wasting time anymore; who knew if we would be interrupted again?

Logan let out a low growl as he kissed me back. I felt his tongue running along the seam of my lips, which I opened to give him access.

Our tongues danced together beautifully as the sparks shot through my body.

I pulled away, eventually looking up into his beautiful blue eyes. "I am so sorry about that, Logan, your Alpha is one crazy asshole!" Logan chuckled at my accurate description of his Alpha. He looked down at me with a slight sadness back in his eyes. "Don't worry, you won't get in trouble," I told him, thinking this was why he was sad.

"I don't care about that, Olivia, I'm just a bit upset that he wasted all our time that we could have spent getting to know each other. I need to go now and help with the supper preparations. If the Alpha comes looking and he can't find me, he will know something's up." That statement hit me harder than I was expecting, I just found Logan. I didn't want to have to let him go.

Evie was whimpering in my head. *"Please get him to stay, Liv."* I wanted to be selfish and honour Evie's wishes, but I knew what was at stake for Logan if I kept him too long.

I gave him a strong hug and another quick kiss on the lips. I could feel his joy rise through our bond. At least I knew he wanted me too. That was a nice feeling to be a priority to someone for once. We walked back into my room and I unlocked the door, before checking if the coast was clear.

He whispered to me, "Meet me in the garden by the moon goddess statue at nine thirty." The thrill of a clandestine encounter sent a chill up my spine. I agreed to meet him there and asked him to be careful until we met again. Logan gave me one last dazzling smile before he checked both sides of the hallway and slipped out of my room, dashing for the stairs. With a small little wave, he ran up the stairs and out of sight.

I once again closed my door, locking it before turning to head for the bathroom. I almost made it until I heard another knock on my door. What the hell was going on here? This had to be a joke? I stalked over to the door ready to bite off the head of whoever was on the other side.

Amber was waiting on the other side of the door with a smirk on her face. I shook my head and motioned for her to come in. "So did you have fun with your mate?" she asked before I even had the door closed.

I hissed at her furiously, "Amber, wait until my door is closed, please. You never know who may be wandering the halls!" She gave me a remorseful look and apologized, before asking me the question again with a wink. I started laughing. "Yes and no if I'm being honest." She looked at me confused, so I let her know that, yes, I had fun accepting him, kissing him, and setting up a meeting later. Then, on the flip side, no, I did not have fun dealing with Alpha asshole Mc Crazy pants.

"What was all that about anyway, the door pounding and yelling?"

"Apparently he can't take a joke and wanted to make sure I never tell my father he thinks he's good looking".

Amber burst out laughing, "No way, you have to be joking."

"I truly wish I was." She could tell by my serious tone that, in fact, I wasn't joking.

"Wow, we need to get into that library as soon as we can, get the information we need so we can then grab your mate and haul ass away from this weird, angry Alpha." She was nodding to herself as she finished her statement.

"Logan asked me to meet him in the garden at nine-thirty. I'm going to ask him for his help in our quest; him being an omega is amazing because he'll know where everything is, and he can help us get our answers quicker. Amber lit up like a Christmas tree at my idea. "Now, before it gets any later, I need to shower, so please let me!" I laughed as I pushed her toward the door.

"Yeah, you do smell kind of funky!" She's lucky she's quick. She was able to dodge the punch I was trying to hit her with. She ran out of my room laughing and said she'd come get me for supper.

I didn't waste time. I ran for the shower. I was finally able to get in and wash the last few hours off of me while thinking about everything that had happened and all that was about to happen.

Logan

I gave Olivia a little wave and bolted up the stairs. I had work to do before supper and I needed to speak with Melissa. I walked into the laundry room and found my sister gathering the tablecloths and napkins we'd need for supper. "Need a hand?" My question startled her.

She jumped and screamed, sending napkins flying in every direction. "Jesus Logan, don't do that again. You're going to give me a heart attack." She was clutching her chest dramatically, which made me laugh; Melissa was always over the top when we were growing up. I think she was meant to be an actress.

"You can't be mad at your big brother. You won't be seeing me for much longer." I gave her a mysterious look, and it didn't take long for her to take the bait.

"What are you going on about? Did Justin finally get sick of you and is letting his dad throw you out of the pack?"

Now it was my turn to be dramatic as I clutched at the invisible knife Melissa hit me in the chest with. "Funny girl, I guess if you don't want to know your brother found his mate, that's fine." I turned around and started to walk away, knowing full well I wouldn't get far; I didn't even make it through my five-second countdown before she shrieked louder than anyone I'd ever heard before. "Keep it down, will you, Mel! You're going to get us in trouble." Lucky for us, it seemed like no one was around,

"How am I expected to not freak out when you're telling me you found your mate! Who is she? Do I know her?" She was bouncing up and down with excitement. This made my heart swell with love, knowing my little sister was happy for me.

"Before I tell you anything, I need you to do me a huge favour in exchange for information." She nodded at me to go on. "Can you please take my shift on the cleaning crew? I asked my mate to meet with me in the garden so we could get to know each other better."

Melissa's face dropped in mock horror "NO not the cleaning crew, you know how much I hate those tasks!" I brought out the big guns at this point, aiming my big sad puppy dog pout at her, I knew she couldn't resist this tactic and it worked! "FINE, I'll do it, stop with the sad puppy eyes! Now tell me who she is!"

I gave her a big hug, and spun her around; she smacked me upside the head, so I put her down. "Her name is Olivia. She is one of the guests who arrived this afternoon."

"Is she the tall Alpha with the light brown hair and stunning hazel eyes?" I confirmed that, yes, that was Olivia. Melissa's jaw was on the floor at this point and I could see her coming to realize what I was worried about. "Oh my god Logan, that means you're going to be an Alpha!!!! My big brother, the Alpha." Her eyes shone with love and admiration which brought tears to my eyes.

"I'm not an Alpha yet! I was lucky she accepted me for being an omega."

"She would have been very stupid not to accept you Logan." I growled lowly at her for insulting my mate. "Easy, big guy, I said she would be stupid! You said she accepted you, so clearly, she's smart. I can't wait to meet her!"

I gave Melissa a hug and told her I'd introduce them soon, but for now, I wanted to get to know her, and we had to be careful that the Alpha didn't find out. Melissa agreed, knowing how terribly the omega's were treated by him and especially me, because I dared to be best friends with his son.

"Come on, we better get these tablecloths and napkins down to the dining room before we get in trouble." We linked arms after picking up all the linens and headed downstairs, I had a huge smile on my face. For once, life was looking up for me. I was so excited to see where this was going to lead and I couldn't wait for nine thirty when I would get to see my Alpha beauty.

Chapter Eleven

Chapter 11

Olivia

I felt much better after the shower. I was sitting on the bed, trying to decide what to wear for supper. I felt the need to dress up a bit for Logan, which was odd since I knew I didn't have to impress him. *"Olivia, you could go down there in a paper bag, and he'd be happy to see you."* Evie chuckled,

"You're right Evie! I'm just going to be myself." So, I threw on a little blue sundress, that made my ass and breasts look fantastic.

"Careful Liv, that dress is playing with fire! Logan might jump over the table and mark us on the spot...which I wouldn't mind." The grin I could see on Evie's face in my mind made me smile.

"Just remember, my crazy horny wolf, we need to be careful around Alpha Renato; he can't suspect Logan is our mate; I fear for his safety."

As I was finishing getting ready, there was a knock on my door. I swung it open to find Justin and Amber waiting for me. Justin let out a whistle as he looked me up and down approvingly. "Damn Olivia, you clean up nicely, Logan is going to cream himself when he sees you!"

"Did you really just say that Justin? What are you sixteen?" I shook my head at him, all he could do was chuckle and blush furiously. Well, at least he had the decency to be embarrassed, if nothing else, for that cheesy line.

"Let's go for supper, I'm starving". Amber cut through the awkwardness.

We made our way downstairs to the giant dining hall, and I was shocked to see only Alpha Renato sitting there, no other pack members. Justin saw the look on my face and leaned in, whispering to me that the rest of the pack would eat later after his father. His father didn't like mingling with people that he considered below him; he said that last part with disgust dripping from every word.

My eyes flashed black, not only because of the injustice that this Alpha was inflicting on his own people, but Evie and I were both bitterly disappointed we wouldn't get to see Logan until our set meeting time. As we walked closer to the table, Alpha Renato looked up at me, and then took another entirely too-long gaze over my body, as he did earlier in my room.

This not only turned my stomach but made me extremely uncomfortable. Justin noticed this and stepped in front of me. I whispered a quick thank you and sat down across and to the left of the Alpha. Justin took the seat directly in front of his father. "Glad you all could join me; I was starting to get hungry and almost started without you." The Alpha sounded less than impressed as he admonished us.

I looked over at Justin and Amber, who both rolled their eyes in unison; that's all I needed to know about how they felt. I was suddenly startled by Alpha Renato banging the table, while bellowing at the omegas to bring him his supper. I was seething at this grown man's behaviour, when all of a sudden I smelt apples and cinnamon.

My mood instantly perked up at the thought of seeing my mate again. Evie was bouncing around my head with her tail wagging. I looked over to the doorway of the dining room to see Logan, but all I saw was a beautiful petite blonde omega carrying supper.

My hackles instantly went up and Evie was growling viciously in my mind. *"She was with our mate, Olivia, she touched him, let me out I am going to tear her apart."* I had never heard Evie this angry before.

I clutched the edge of the table so hard I was worried it was going to snap off. I was trying so hard not to shift that it was becoming painful, and I started to shake.

At this point, Justin noticed the state I was in, and saw me burning holes in the back of this omega's head. Thank the goddess, he put two and two together quickly and said out loud, "Hey Melissa! How's my best friend's baby sister doing tonight?" He looked over at me with a wink and my jaw hit the table. Sister?! Logan had a sister?

"Oh, thank the goddess, Liv, I didn't want to have to kill anyone tonight; well except, maybe Alpha Asshole over there, if he looks at us like a creeper again." Evie collapsed in a heap, thankful that our mate was still ours, and he hadn't lied to us about having another woman.

Melissa turned towards us after serving Alpha Renato, she blushed as she got closer to Justin; I would have to remember to ask him about that one day. She started to serve me my supper but wouldn't look at me, so I put my hand on her arm, stunning her into looking at me with wide blue eyes that looked exactly like Logan's.

"Thank you so much for serving me my supper, Melissa! You have beautiful eyes by the way." Her face broke into a bright smile at my words, but that quickly faded away as Alpha Renato's angry Alpha aura made its way across the table.

"Olivia, you are a guest in this pack and I would hate to have to ask you to leave. This is your last warning. You are not to speak to them. They are not worthy of speaking with you, and they know their place in this pack. The next omega I catch you engaging with, I will snap their neck and their death will be on you." Fury instantly flowed through my entire body; I was about to make Evie's wish come true and let her maul this monster to death, but just as I was about to let Evie out Amber mind-linked me.

"Liv, remember we need to find that info! We can come back and get rid of this jackass another day." This sobered me up quickly. I cleared my throat, swallowed my pride, and submitted to this prick who dared call himself an Alpha.

He seemed quite pleased with my submission and subsequent apology, he continued to eat his supper as if he hadn't just threatened me and all of his pack members. I would not forget this moment and in the future, it would make me very happy to make him pay for this night. Within five minutes after the incident, Alpha Renato spoke again. "So, Olivia, you wanted to hear all about your father's pathetic and feeble attempts at a social life in school?"

I choked on the water I had been drinking, but managed to squeak out, "Sure." This set him off on a two-hour-long tirade of his glory days! I learned that my father was not popular or well-liked in school. Kids thought his name sounded sissy and would tease him mercilessly about it.

They told him he would never amount to anything, even though he was of Alpha blood. They apparently even locked him in a broom closet, saying that's where he belonged with the tools of his future trade, since he was too weak to be an Alpha. I stayed quiet the entire time Alpha Renato was telling us his tales, not that he would have given me a spare second to say anything anyway; he seemed to be in love with listening to himself speak.

I looked over to see Amber and Justin half asleep on their plates, and it was then that I realized it was past nine o'clock, and I needed to find a way out.

I elbowed Justin, who jumped a little, and dared to cut his father off when I gave him a look pleading to get me out of here. "Hey Dad, I think the girls are tired from their drive. I'm going to take them back to their rooms."

Alpha Renato abruptly stopped babbling and turned his nose up at us, "Fine if that is what you wish, but I must say, I have plenty more stories to entertain you with tomorrow."

I internally groaned. "Oh, I'm sure you do! Thank you for supper." I bowed my head towards him and got up, before he could trap us with any more useless drivel. Once we were out of earshot, I let out a huge sigh. "Thank you, Justin, for saving us!! I can say I'm not the biggest fan of my father, but after hearing the way your father was speaking tonight, I can understand why he is the way he is." I shook my head in despair now knowing how my father became the monster that he is, he could have chosen to be better, but he ended up being just like his tormentors; sad really.

"Well, Liv and Justin, I'm just happy neither of you are like your fathers!" Amber linked her arms with both of us, and we headed towards the stairs together, laughing in relief that we were decent people.

As we got to the stairs, I removed my arm from Amber, and whispered to them both that I was going to meet up with Logan in the garden. Justin gave me a huge shit-eating grin and told me to have fun. Amber did the same.

I laughed to myself as I headed quietly out into the garden. I remembered seeing the goddess statue when we arrived earlier in the afternoon, so I headed in that direction. Evie and I were starting to get a bit nervous, wondering if he would actually be there waiting to see us.

All our fears were banished as I rounded the corner of the garden and was hit with his intoxicating smell of apple cinnamon. I picked up my pace, and he turned around just in time to catch me as I threw myself into his arms and kissed him. I definitely caught him off guard because he stumbled back two steps before steadying us and wrapping me in his strong arms.

I let out a content sigh and smiled up at him. "Thank you for being here!" I couldn't help but say.

Logan looked surprised. "Of course, I'd be here. There is nowhere else I'd rather be. I've been counting down the hours until I could see you again!" He lit up the garden with his beautiful smile. This time he bent down and kissed me with such a heated passion I had to press my thighs together to give myself some friction.

Logan

I couldn't wait to meet up with Olivia. I went to the goddess statue over fifteen minutes early to wait for her. I was slightly nervous she wouldn't show up.

"Come on now, don't be silly, human. She already accepted us!" My wolf, Norman, boasted.

"You're right, buddy, she did accept us! But you know how our luck goes. To me, this all seems too good to be true."

Before either of us can say anything else, I get hit by the most beautiful smell of lilacs and fresh summer rain. *"Mate is here. She came! I told you that you had nothing to worry about!"* I smiled at Norman, and turned to face Olivia just in time to be mauled by her.

She jumped at me, and I barely caught her as I stumbled back a few steps. I wrapped her in my arms, managing to steady us both without falling over and embarrassing myself. The kiss she gave me made my head spin as the tingles coursed through my body, and the content sigh she gave me, combined with that beautiful smile and killer sundress, made my cock jump in my pants.

Olivia surprised me by thanking me for meeting her. I told her that, of course, there was no other place I'd rather be and that I had been looking forward to our meeting for hours. I gave her a bright smile and bent down to claim her full pouty lips in a heated kiss. I felt her squeeze her thighs together and could smell her arousal.

This made Norman growl in my head, but now wasn't the time or the place to claim our mate; we had many things to discuss first. I broke the kiss and smiled down at her. "You look absolutely stunning in that dress, Olivia." She beamed up at me with a blush creeping along her cheeks. "Will you come with me? I've got a little surprise for you."

She looked up at me bashfully and slid her hand into mine. I led her a little further into the garden, where I had set up a tiny picnic for us, in a part of the garden where there were beautiful fairy lights twinkling like stars. Olivia gasped when she saw where I had brought her. "It's so beautiful, Logan, thank you."

I kissed her on the forehead and let her know I would do anything to make her smile at me the way she did. We sat down on the little bench, and I handed her some cream-filled pastries. "I'm not sure how hungry you are after your supper with the Alpha, so I got a few small treats for us." She shook her head and told me that she barely ate. She was too nauseated by the Alpha's attitude.

She went on to tell me everything that happened; from how she met my sister to the Alpha threatening her and the omegas; to finally, the terrible stories about her father. I was shocked and pissed off on her behalf. I'm not our Alpha's biggest fan, but this just pushed me over the edge.

I was glad Justin was there to save them in the end, which made Olivia laugh. "Oh yes, I owe him one for getting us out of there, you kind of owe him too!" I looked at her quizzically. "Had he not gotten his father to shut up and take us to our rooms, I wouldn't have made it to this meeting. We'd still be sitting there listening to him go on about himself." Olivia faked a vomiting motion which made me laugh.

"I'll make sure to thank Justin in the morning for getting you to me." I reached out and cupped her cheek; she leaned into my touch which made my heart swell with happiness. I silently thanked the goddess for bringing me this angel of a mate. I leaned over and kissed the tip of her nose, making her blush. I could get used to making her do that every day, all day.

We talked for what seemed like forever. She told me about her childhood and how she didn't really want to be Alpha. I found that to be very brave of her, knowing what she wanted out of her life and not wanting to compromise. I can't say I wasn't a bit relieved. Maybe if she renounced being Alpha I wouldn't have to be either.

"We can be an Alpha," Norman huffed in my head.

"Buddy, I know you like to think that, but we're lovers, not fighters or leaders." Norman turned his back on me and curled into a ball; I knew he'd get over it eventually.

Olivia gave me the cutest little yawn that made me want to take her to bed and tuck her in, but before we parted, I had two more important questions to ask her. "What is the real reason you came to our pack Olivia?" She looked momentarily caught off guard, but told me the truth, that she and Amber were trying to solve a mystery and needed to look through our archives.

"Oh, I love a good mystery, can I help?" Melissa whisper yelled as she jumped out of the bushes, scaring the hell out of both Olivia and I.

"Mel, what the hell are you doing here? How long have you been listening to us?"

"Oh not long, I came to warn you both, Alpha Renato is heading this way for an evening stroll and I didn't want you to get caught." I gave Melissa a quick appreciative hug.

"I guess that's the end of our night," I said sadly, looking at Olivia. She looked sad as well but knew this was for the best; at that moment, we caught a whiff of the Alpha approaching. Shit, we were going to get caught. Melissa grabbed the basket of picnic food and Olivia's hand.

"Quick, come with me, I can get you back to your room. Logan, stay here and pretend you're working! You were on the cleaning crew tonight anyway and garden cleanup is part of it."

Thank the goddess for Melissa's quick thinking, I gave them both a nod, and Melissa pulled Olivia through the bushes that she had come out of not moments before. I had just enough time to grab some nearby hedge clippers when the Alpha came into the area.

I bowed my head to him, and he sneered at me, walking by me as if my existence pained him too much to be close for long. This didn't bother me, I wanted him away from me as quickly as possible. As soon as the coast was clear, Norman piped up and insisted we go to Olivia.

We needed to make sure she was safe in her room before we could rest for the night. I put down the clippers, and headed toward the pack house as fast as my legs could take me. The whole way, I was praying that Melissa got her to her room safely without any hiccups.

Chapter Twelve

Chapter 12

*L*ogan

It took me about five minutes to get from where we were in the garden up to Olivia's room. Once, I was in the guest wing, I was hyper-vigilant and as quiet as possible, since I had no business being there.

I knew Alpha Renato was outside, but if anyone else caught me, I was done for. I carefully approached Olivia's door and knocked gently. There was no answer. I knocked again, a little harder, in case my first attempt wasn't heard. I waited holding my breath, still nothing; I was beginning to panic slightly.

"I don't smell mate or hear her," Norman whined in my head; he was right, I didn't hear a damn thing.

I took out a pocket knife I carried and picked the lock to her room, the door flung open and I was greeted by a dark empty room.

My stomach dropped and I started to sweat, fear rose up and clutched my heart.

What if Melissa went the wrong way and they ran into Alpha Renato? What if he snapped Melissa's neck like he promised he would and he's got Olivia trapped somewhere? My head was spinning with what ifs and I was starting to get short of breath.

"FIND MATE NOW," Norman boomed in my head, breaking me out of my panicked state.

I closed Olivia's door and ran for the stairs. While I ran, I tried to mind-link Melissa; but to my dismay, she didn't answer me. I made a split-second decision to go quickly to my room, to put on black clothes so I could blend better with the shadows.

I was going back out to the garden to hunt down my mate, and my sister, who I prayed was still alive! As I got closer to my door, I heard whispering and giggling on the other side. I recognized Melissa's giggle instantly, which made me hope the other sweet sound I was hearing was Olivia.

I burst into my room, which made both girls jump and squeal in unison. "What the hell, Logan? You scared the shit out of us," Melissa hissed at me while clutching her chest.

"I scared the shit out of you?" I gritted out between clenched teeth. "Why the hell are you in my room Melissa, and not in Olivia's like you said you would be?! I went there right after Alpha Renato walked by, and was scared to death when neither of you were where you said you would be. I thought that asshole caught you and snapped your neck; I even mind-linked you with no answer! I truly thought you were gone and Olivia was trapped by the Alpha. I came back here to change so I could go hunt you both down." I was seething at this point and flailing my arms in exasperation.

I had never freaked out like this before, but the thought of losing my mate and my sister simultaneously was just too much for me. I let out a long loud sigh as I tried to compose myself; Olivia got up quickly from where she was perched on my bed, walked over swiftly and pulled me into a bone-crushing hug.

I buried my face in the crook of her neck and took deep breaths of her sweet lilac and summer rain scent. This almost instantly calmed my nerves. My heartbeat slowly started to even out, my breathing was less shallow, and I could barely hear myself think over the deafening purring sound coming from Norman in my head.

"Mate smells so good, and she feels even better holding us close." I could see the heart shapes forming in Norman's eyes as he spoke; all I could do was chuckle at him.

"I'm sorry if we scared you, Logan. I felt bad for cutting your date short, so I figured I'd bring the date to you. Alpha Asshole won't come looking up here for Olivia, so you'd both be in the clear. Please don't be mad at us." Melissa looked at me hopefully as she apologized and explained the situation, I couldn't stay mad at her with that reasoning.

I accepted her apology and asked that she at least warn me next time she decides to do that. "I'm sorry I wanted to surprise you, and I put the block up because I was talking with Olivia and didn't want to be interrupted, I didn't think what would happen if you tried to link me." She looked sheepish for a split second before a huge smile split her face wide open, "By the way, what do you think of the new nickname Olivia taught me for the Alpha?" She started laughing hysterically.

"It is funny, Mel, just don't ever accidentally let that slip within earshot of the man! I truly fear what he would do to you if he ever caught you calling him Alpha Asshole." Fear passed through Melissa's face, and she nodded at me, in a silent promise that she would be very careful about when and where she would say that amazing new nickname.

"Well, kids, I hate to love and leave you, but I don't like being a third wheel." Melissa giggled as she walked towards my door. "Oh, Olivia, don't forget tomorrow to meet me after lunch by the grandfather clock in the main hallway. Just tell Alpha Asshole you always take an afternoon nap after lunch to help you digest. He believes in that kind of crap and will leave you alone." She winked at Olivia, who nodded back to her and bid her good night, thanking her for her help escaping the garden. With one last smile, nod, and wave Melissa closed my door, leaving Olivia and I alone in my room.

The realization that I had my mate alone in my room sent a shiver through my body and made my cock twitch, which I knew Olivia felt, since she was still pressed tightly against my body. She looked up at me with hooded eyes and a Cheshire cat grin. "Does someone want to say hello?" she asked coyly.

I blushed six shades of red at her words; I never had a woman be so upfront with me. I'm not a virgin and didn't expect Olivia to be either, but in my experience, I had to do all the chasing. All my prior rendezvous meant nothing compared to what I would have with Olivia. "I won't lie to you, Olivia; I want you very much but I won't do anything, you aren't ready for."

Her answer was to reach up and kiss me deeply as her other hand cupped my cock through my pants and began to rub it softly. I let out a throaty moan which led to her squeezing me a bit harder; the feeling was incredible and I didn't know how long I would last if she kept that up.

I broke our kiss and picked her up, bridal style, which made her squeak like a cute little kitten. I carried her to my bed and placed her down gently. I reached and took off my shirt in one go. Olivia's eyes darkened as she took in the sight of my bare chest; she reached for my pants, with a low growl she undid them and let them drop to my ankles.

Olivia's eyes lit up, a sexy smile curved her lips which she started to lick, as if she were starved and staring at a snack. "I can work with that," she told me in a breathy tone.

My cock jumped at her words, and I shuddered as she trailed a soft finger from my root to the tip. I wanted her so badly that I was about to embarrass myself. Before that could happen, I grabbed Olivia's arms and put them over her head, leaning her down on the bed as I kissed her passionately.

Olivia

When Logan's pants hit the floor and his cock sprang in my face, Evie let out a joyous howl in my head, *"Liv, we hit the jackpot with our mate. He's not too long, just the right thickness, and look at the curve...oooh it's going to feel so nice!"* She was panting and drooling in my head like a rabid dog.

"Easy, Evie, or I will have to block you. Please don't overdo it; this is our first time with Logan. I don't want to scare him off; you can get freaky with him later, I promise." Evie calmed down and retreated slightly, giving me the clarity to continue my fun.

I told Logan I could work with what he's got and licked my lips. I couldn't wait to enjoy my snack, if he let me. I trailed a finger from his root to his tip, which made him shudder with pleasure. Before I could grab him, he took my hands and shoved them over my head, kissing me passionately and pushing me into the bed.

Alright, he liked to dominate. I liked this side of him. He broke off our kiss leaving me gasping for air, before I knew what was going on he had hiked up my dress, so my pussy was now on full display. "Oops, did I forget to put on underwear?" I gave Logan a wink as I said this and he let out a growl as his eyes turned black; his wolf clearly pushing to the surface, it took a moment for his eyes to go back to those amazing pools of ocean blue.

I couldn't help but laugh a little at him. "Oh, so, you're a naughty little kitten roaming around the pack house without underwear, your bare pussy enjoying its freedom?" He gave me a hungry look, "You know I didn't have supper tonight before meeting you; I think it's time I have a snack."

Before I could say anything remotely cute back to him he had started to lick my pussy from my slit to my clit; I shivered from the feeling of his tongue making contact with my sensitive clit. I let out a moan as he swirled his tongue around it and sucked it into his mouth. This made my pussy start to leak juices onto my thigh.

"Now, now, we can't waste any of your sweet nectar my naughty little kitten," Logan purred at me. He moved down and curled his talented tongue into my slit, lapping up all my juices. He was licking me like a man who hadn't eaten in a week.

The feeling of Logan eating me out was like heaven, the sparks enhanced everything to a new level, one I had never experienced with any other partner. This is what makes our mates so special; everything is heightened.

My stomach began to tighten with his tongue dipping into my slit, then back up to suck on my clit. The sensation was incredible. He added to my pleasure by inserting two fingers into my pussy and slowly working them in and out, adding a come-hither motion every couple of strokes. He continued rubbing my G-spot, and finally nipped my clit lightly, sending me over the edge into a leg-shaking orgasm.

Logan helped me ride it out and before he could say anything I hauled him up onto the bed, flipped him over, and straddled him. The look of shock on his face was comical. "I want you inside of me now, I can't wait," I told him as I slowly lowered myself onto his amazing cock.

Logan let out a mighty groan as he grabbed onto my hips tightly. I enjoyed how wonderful his cock felt pulsing inside me. Evie was right, that curve was pure bliss. Once I had Logan deep-seated inside me, I slowly twisted my hips and tightened my pussy muscles, giving his cock a massage. He let out a sensual moan, and that's all it took for me to go buck wild, bouncing up and down on him.

Logan was hanging onto my hips for dear life, but was keeping up with me nicely, meeting me with his own hard strokes. We were both moaning messes and I wasn't going to last much longer; from what I could feel, neither was Logan. I couldn't finish this way though. I managed to hop off Logan's cock, which left him stunned.

I got on all fours and winked at him over my shoulder. "I need you to spank me and then take me as hard as you can, that ok with you?" The poor man looked equal parts aroused beyond belief and scared. "It's ok my love, I like it rough, don't be scared to spank me."

I didn't have to wait long before his large warm hands made contact with my round ass, he spanked my right cheek first which sent a swirl of pleasure through me, I let out an approving moan. My left cheek spank was a bit harder, which was amazing, and I almost came right then and there. He quickly plunged his cock back into me and, like the wonderful man I knew he was, he took me hard and fast just as I asked.

Logan and I didn't last long like this. With one last thrust, he came hard; I could feel him convulsing against my ass. I wasn't quite there so I quickly pinched my clit and threw myself over the edge, so that my pussy could milk his cock as he came down from his high. Logan collapsed onto my back but rolled us at the same time, so I ended up nestled in his arms. It took us a few minutes to catch our breaths.

Once Logan could breathe again, all he could say was, "WOW, I've got a wild sex kitten as a mate! I am in heaven." I burst out laughing.

This was the start of what was going to be one hell of a wonderful partnership. I knew I would never be bored with Logan. We truly were each other's perfect match. I thanked the goddess as we snuggled together and drifted off to sleep. I would never have thought this morning when we left my pack that I was going to end the day like this.

Chapter Thirteen

Chapter 13

Daniel

My eyes slowly and painfully fluttered open. Wherever I was, it was pitch black, cold, damp and I felt like I was lying on the ground. Did they leave me in the woods? It didn't smell like I was outside, it actually smelt mouldy and like urine. I scrunched my nose at the rancid smell as I tried to sit up.

My whole world started to spin so I curled back into a ball. I had a splitting headache, although I guess that's what I got for being hit in the head at least twice, which I can barely remember, by a giant tree branch. I groaned at the pain radiating through my head and about my foggy memories. How the hell could I be so stupid and let myself be caught like that?

"Well, it got us into the pack didn't it?" Xander piped up with a light chuckle.

"Oh my goddess Xander, are you ok?"

"Yes Daniel, I am quite tired from healing us, that took many hours, the branch did a number on your head. I'll be alright with a bit of rest. I'm here if any danger presents itself, but for now, I'm going to take a nap." With that, I saw him curl up and start to snore loudly in my mind.

I shook my head, his snoring caused my brain to pulse, but relief washed over me. Xander was still with me, albeit tired, he was thankfully unharmed. I let out a loud sigh.

Suddenly, bright lights came on, blinding me and causing severe pain to shoot through my skull. I cursed out loud and hissed at the light.

"Oh boys, come see! The pathetic fleabag is finally awake." I recognized the voice as one of the guards I faced off in the woods with. I opened my eyes slightly for confirmation and was greeted with a sneering face. "Did you have a good nap, rogue? Enjoying your accommodations?" He and two other guards who had sauntered up started to laugh at me.

I tried to sit up again, ignoring the pain. I couldn't let them see me weak. "I want to speak with Alpha Olivia," I demanded in the most authoritative voice I could muster. Their laughter stopped instantly and the first guard's face hardened as fast as lightning. That little Bitch is NOT our Alpha nor will she ever be. It makes sense that a weak, pathetic rogue like yourself wants to speak to a woman. You will be speaking with our Alpha very soon, don't you worry! Before he comes down you need to take a bath rogue, you stink."

As he said that, he threw a full bucket of freezing cold water at my face, drenching me from head to toe. All three guards started laughing like fools and walked away, leaving me to wallow in my self-pity, pain, and now, soaking wet clothes.

I sat on the hard floor of the cell for I don't know how long, there were no windows and obviously no clocks in this dungeon. All I knew was I was starving, my stomach was growling loudly and I had dried off from the earlier water attack. By that alone, my guess had to be several hours I'd been waiting.

I was drifting in and out of sleep when finally I heard a door creak open down the hall; I heard muffled voices and then finally footsteps coming towards me. I stood up shakily to face whoever was coming to see me. The person's scent hit me before they came into view. It was familiar but foreign all at the same time.

Xander's hackles went up instantly and he jumped up in my mind, taking an attack position. *"Xander, do we know this person?"* He didn't have time to answer me as the person in question came into view. What I saw made my jaw hit the floor and left me speechless.

Olivia

The first rays of light started to filter in through the curtains in Logan's room. I was lying on his hard chest in a puddle of my own drool; I groaned internally at myself. *"Way to stay classy there Liv, mate might not want to keep us after he wakes up to a lake on his chest."* Evie mocked me.

I slowly pulled the blanket up to mop the drool. As I did, one beautiful blue eye opened to watch me, and a giant smirk spread across Logan's face. He let out a deep chuckle that vibrated his entire chest, and I knew I had been caught. "So you're a drooler?" he said through his chuckling, "I'm really happy I'm finding this out now." My heart stopped, and my blood ran cold.

"What do you mean Logan?" I looked up at him with a mix of fear and anger boiling up in my veins, depending on what he said next he was going to start the morning off with a black eye.

Logan saw my clenched fist and gulped. He knew he had poked the wolf too hard. "Easy, my wild kitten! All I meant was, I'm glad to see that you're not perfect! You drool like the rest of us. I was worried you were too good for me."

I let out a breath I didn't know I was holding and shook my head at him, telling him not to be stupid. Of course, I'm just a regular girl and we're equals, so he had better knock it off. He gently kissed the tip of my nose and hugged me tight, I managed to roll out of his hug and stretch. "In all seriousness Logan, last night was beyond amazing; you are a dream come true."

He blushed at my words. "I've never had a woman be so forward with me, I really liked that!"

I gave him a sly smile. "Oh we will do many more things you will like; just not now! I need to get back to my room. Hopefully, no one noticed I was missing." I gave him a gentle kiss on the lips and jumped off his bed. I rummaged around his room for my shoes since I had slept in my dress that was all bunched up.

"I should probably roll this down before wandering around the pack house, shouldn't I?" I giggled. Logan let out a warning growl and his eyes flashed black. "Ooohhh so possessive; I love it!" As I walked towards the door I winked at him.

I had my hand on the doorknob when he stopped me. "Olivia, one thing before you go, why are you meeting Melissa after lunch by the clock?" I smiled at him remembering last night we really didn't do much talking after Melissa left, Evie started to purr and flash scenes from last night in my head which made me shiver in pleasure.

"Not now, Evie!!" I chastised. She smirked at me while mumbling about how I lied, I didn't let her have her way with Logan before promptly turning her back on me. I shook my head at her. *"Cranky wolf,"* I called out to her before noticing Logan looking at me expectantly.

"Sorry Logan, my wolf was being a cranky diva! I'm meeting Melissa after lunch because she is going to help me and Amber get the information we are looking for. She said she knows a secret way into the archives and has a way to conceal our scents."

His eyes lit up with recognition and he nodded at me. "Melissa is very good at getting around the pack house undetected. I'm happy she's going to be helping you."

I ran over and gave him a big hug. "Thank you for being an amazing mate and not going all caveman on me; insisting I don't do this."

He looked puzzled for a moment. "Why would I stop you? This is something that is important to you, so I want to help and support you in whatever way I can." I couldn't help but swoon with those words, I really did get lucky with Logan.

"Alright my prince charming, I've got to go before I get caught! I'll see you later, I'll have Melissa mind-link you when we're out of the archives and we can hopefully meet up."

Logan gave me his million-dollar smile and off I went to shower and get ready for the day ahead. I was feeling light and excited about what was to come later today; I would hopefully be getting the answers I needed. I made it to my room without running into anyone, I was happy that I woke up early.

Just as I was unlocking my door a loud voice boomed out, "OOO-HHHHH, someone's doing the walk of shame; wild night, Liv?" I whipped around to see Amber standing in her doorway with the biggest shit-eating grin on her face.

"Shut up!!" I hissed at her as I ran into her room and shut the door. "Are you crazy, Cupcake? Did you want to wake up the entire pack house?"

"Relax Liv, no one else but us are on this floor, and I can promise you that no one will tell a soul; good news travels fast and everyone knows you're Logan's mate."

I blushed furiously at what she said, "Oh shit, really? EVERYONE knows?"

"Yup! Everyone and their mother knows, except Alpha Asshole." She laughed hysterically at herself. "I really do enjoy that nickname Liv, thank you for that." I nodded at her as that was all I could do. I was slightly shocked and worried that everyone knew. "Don't worry Liv, I was talking with some of the omegas after you left Justin and I last night. I even met up with your new sister-in-law, Melissa. She's a great girl, by the way! Anyway, they are all very excited for Logan and they all hate the Alpha, they are biding their time until Justin takes over."

I'm not surprised in the least by what Amber just told me. Alpha Renato has a god complex and thinks he's hot stuff, and above all the members of his pack, good thing Justin is nothing like him. "So, you and Justin huh??" I poked Amber with my elbow and wiggled my eyebrows at her with a giggle.

"Oh, hell no! He's cute and all but not my type, plus who wants Alpha Asshole as their dearest daddy-in-law?" She put on a look of horror which made me double over with laughter.

"I truly feel bad for Justin's mate wherever she is." Amber agreed with me. "Speaking of unknown people, Melissa has offered to sneak us into the archives after lunch so we can go digging for Corey's information! We are meeting her by the grandfather clock after lunch."

"Oh, that's great news. Make sure you bring down the headlamps and gloves you brought and we'll hide them behind the clock." I had completely forgotten I had brought that gear.

I thanked Amber for reminding me and then excused myself to freshen up and get ready for breakfast. I told Amber I would pick her up once I was ready and she sent me on my way. I jumped in the shower feeling pumped about what was to come in the next few hours. Today was going to be a great day!

Chapter Fourteen

Chapter 14

Olivia

The morning went by rather quickly. Once I finished my shower and got dressed, I went to pick Amber up across the hall and we headed downstairs. We met up with Justin halfway down the stairs on route towards the dining hall. As we got to the doorway of the hall we were stopped by two warriors. "What is the meaning of this?" Justin asked with an angry edge to his voice.

"Alpha ordered that only he is allowed to eat breakfast this morning." The guard shrugged his shoulders at Justin like he was asking the dumbest question in the world.

"But I am his son, your future Alpha, and these two women are invited guests." Justin's face was turning red by this point and his lips were curling up into a snarl.

"You'll have to take it up with the Alpha, I'm just following orders," the guard said dismissively.

"Oh, you better believe I will be having a word with my father," he gritted out, and turned on his heels heading for the kitchen, with Amber and I following closely behind him.

"Don't worry Justin, we can grab something from the kitchen and eat in the garden, it's a beautiful day. I'd much rather eat in peace and quiet outside with the both of you, than have to listen to your asshole father."

Justin gave a slight nod, but I could tell he was mind-linking as his eyes were glazed over. He started to growl and shake violently as we walked into the kitchen.

"Justin, are you ok?" Melissa rushed over and put her hand on his arm which seemed to break him out of his rage; I found this very interesting.

Justin let out a huge sigh. "Yeah, I'm fine! Sorry for the outburst of anger, I was linking my father and he's being a dick. Apparently, we didn't appreciate his hospitality enough at supper last night, so he chose to eat breakfast in his own company this morning. I tried to tell him what an insult that was to you both as our guests, but he just shut the mind-link down."

I didn't want to insult Justin since he was sticking up for our honor, but his father did us all a huge favour. I gave him a kind smile and thanked him for sticking up for us. By this point, he had calmed down enough to go speak with the head kitchen omega, to sort us out with a picnic breakfast.

I smelled the apples and cinnamon before I felt the sparks wrap around my waist. Logan hugged me from behind and nuzzled my neck, peppering it with butterfly kisses all its length. I leaned into his embrace, enjoying the feeling of being in Logan's arms.

He bent down and whispered in my ear, "I missed you very much."

I tilted my head to look up at him and smiled. "It's only been four hours since the last time we saw each other."

"So what? I'd miss you even if you were only gone for a single minute," he whispered back into my ear.

I gave him a peck on the lips as Justin came back over to where we were standing. "Get a room, you two." His eyes were sparkling with mischief as he heckled us.

"Just wait until you find your mate, Justin. I'm going to take great joy in embarrassing you!" Logan chuckled wholeheartedly, a shadow passed over Justin's face that only I seemed to pick up on.

"Ask him about it over breakfast, Liv!" Evie suggested, I told her I most definitely would; something is up with Justin and today seemed like a good day to solve mysteries.

"Will you join us for breakfast, Logan?" I asked with a hopeful look, I wanted him to get to know Amber, since she is my best friend and Beta.

Disappointment passed over his handsome face. I knew the answer at that moment before he told me. "I wish I could, Olivia, but I have work to do around the pack house. Maybe I can meet up with you guys later, and go for a walk around the pack grounds? I'd love to show you where I grew up!" It was Logan's turn now to look hopeful and I loved it.

I could never disappoint him; he was so sweet and gentle, so I said yes. I would love for him to show me around where he grew up. Truth be told, I was looking forward to it! "Logan? Am I going to have to meet your parents?" The thought of meeting his parents so soon made me slightly nervous. He stiffened around me, and his heart rate accelerated.

I was about to ask what was wrong when Melissa said in a soft voice, "We don't have parents anymore, Olivia, they died several years ago."

I noticed Justin started to rub Melissa's back in comfort and I turned around in Logan's arms to fully hug him.

"Logan, I am so sorry. I didn't mean to bring that up and upset you." He thankfully hugged me back, which made me feel a little less anxious.

"It's not your fault, Olivia, how were you supposed to know? We hadn't talked about it yet! No harm done, I promise. Yes, it still makes me sad to think about them, but they are both in a better place together."

Amber walked up to us at this moment with a picnic basket full of breakfast and asked if we were ready to go out to the garden, completely unaware of what had just happened. I smiled and told Logan I would see him soon, giving him one last sweet kiss.

Justin bid Melissa a good day, the heated gaze that passed between them did not go unnoticed by me or Amber; she raised an eyebrow at me and all I could do was shrug.

"Lead the way, kind sir." Amber playfully bowed towards Justin, and he led us out of the kitchen laughing.

We ended up in a new part of the garden I hadn't previously seen the night before. It was full of fragrant lilac bushes, which were my favorite. I sat down with a content sigh, waiting for Amber to pass around the food from the basket she was carrying.

There was a lull in the conversation, so I took a chance to see if my theory was correct. "So, how long have you and Melissa known you were mates, Justin?"

"Not long, only a couple of weeks. She just turned twenty-one." He quickly threw his hands over his mouth and looked at me wide-eyed in fear.

"You caught him off guard, and he spilled his secret instantly without even thinking. Good job, Liv. I'm impressed!" Amber chuckled through our mind-link.

The look on Justin's face broke my heart though; I understood the fear, we were both in the same boat. Not wanting to prolong his suffering, I let him know that Amber and I wouldn't tell a soul.

"Thank you, Olivia, I was so excited to find out she was my mate. Melissa is Amazing! We haven't even told Logan yet." He looked at me sheepishly; knowing that was a bit of a harder ask, keeping that from my mate. I hesitated for a moment but gestured that my lips were sealed.

I did ask him to consider telling Logan soon though. He's his best friend and he would be so happy for them; it would also get me out of the tough spot they were putting me in. "I will talk to Melissa later and I promise we'll tell Logan soon. Thank you for your discretion. We need to keep this under wraps until my father makes me Alpha, then I can claim her officially as my mate and Luna! If my father tries anything, he will be sent to the cells."

I admired Justin's sense of duty and protection towards Melissa. I promised him I would try and help in any way I could. "Thank you, Olivia. I guess this makes us family! I'll be your brother-in-law through marriage."

This revelation brought a huge smile to my face. I went from an only child yesterday to gaining a new sister and brother; I was so excited. "Now, sis, since I told you my secret, it's your turn to share yours with me!" Justin gave me a pointed look, and Amber let out a loud laugh.

"Are we that obvious?" she asked.

"No, not really. To any regular person, your cover story makes sense, but to someone like me who knows all the inner circles and keeps up with the gossip, then yes, you are obvious. I know both of you weren't interested in looking for your mates." I was very impressed by Justin's powers of deduction and how he came to that conclusion.

"Alright, if you really want to know, I owe you that much for tricking you into spilling your secret; buckle up."

I launched into the whole sordid tale, starting with overhearing my father and Beta's conversation about someone named Corey, who was meant to be killed. Down to my mother and Omegas acting really weird when Corey's name was mentioned; I told him our plan to search his pack's archives for an answer.

Justin looked at me thoughtfully as I ended my story. "Well, I must say that really is a weird situation, Olivia, hopefully, the archives will give you the answers you need. Whoever had the idea to check our archives, you're brilliant."

Amber beamed at his praise. "I'm the brains, and she's the brawn of this operation." She giggled as she pointed at me.

"One thing that concerns me though, girls, is that you can't just waltz into our archives; I can't, even if I wanted to. Appropriate channels need to be navigated in order to gain access and it's not like you can tell anyone what you're looking for." Justin looked pensive as he tried to think of a solution to our problem.

"Don't worry Justin we've got that covered, your beautiful mate has kindly offered to help us; she knows a secret way into the archives and I brought gloves and headlamps so we can go in undetected." The look of worry that crossed his face didn't surprise me, we all knew the stakes if Melissa got caught. I promised him we would make sure she was safe and well-protected while we were there. Justin thanked me and gave us information on where to find the birth and death record books that we would need to search through.

"Thank you, Justin. That information is really helpful. It will make things go a lot quicker." I happened to look at my watch and saw it was getting late. "Justin, would you be able to link Logan, please? I think it's time we took that walk around the pack all together, then go get ready for lunch and our after-lunch activities." I winked at Amber and then turned as I smelled my mate approaching.

Daniel

At three years old, not having any siblings or parents around who looked like me always made me sad. I was happy to have had Alpha Arnold and Julie taking care of me. I was lucky, a lot of orphans didn't make it out in the wild by themselves. I was well taken care of by the two of them. It just hurt to see others who had the same eyes or facial features as family members, and know I was alone.

I always wondered what happened to my family. Did they love me? Did something terrible happen to them?

I asked a lot of questions as a young pup, which Julie always patiently answered as best she could. In the end, though, she never managed to satiate my curiosity and, over time, it was forced to the back of my mind. Something there to think about once in a while, but knowing it would just cause pain and more questions if thought about too long.

I was brought out of my flashback by a disgusted scoff, and there I was, looking into the eyes that sent me into the flashback in the first place. Eyes that were identical to mine, the same size, shape, and unique honey hazel colour that I had never seen on anyone else ever.

From the eyes, it went to a similarly shaped nose, albeit slightly wider at the base. Our mouths were completely different, but we had the same face shape and bone structure, including the same wavy light brown, almost blonde hair. It was like looking into a mirror twenty years into my future, my mouth remained agape, and all I could do was blink at this angry-looking man.

"Xander, do we know him?" All Xander was doing was growling and I couldn't get an answer out of him. I was on my own, it seemed.

I didn't have time to think of anything to say before the man spoke. "I am Alpha Francis. What made you believe you could come onto my territory? Are you trying to claim this pack for yourself? You have no right to this land anymore. You should have died a very long time ago, he sneered at me. An error that I fully intend to rectify, today."

I was so lost over everything he was saying to me. Why would I want to claim his land? Why was I supposed to die?

"I don't even know you, Alpha Francis. Why would you need to kill me?"

He let out a humourless laugh. At this point, I started feeling weak, and my head started to spin from all the questions as well as a lack of food and water. I was so overwhelmed I fainted, falling back into the darkness.

Chapter Fifteen

Chapter 15

Olivia

Logan came into the garden, and I jumped into his arms, giving him a quick kiss.

"Okay, do you guys need a moment alone?" Amber shot at me. I slid down his body and stuck my tongue out at her.

"No, we're good!" I shot back playfully. "I can't wait for you to see where I grew up." Logan was beaming at me, which melted my heart on the spot. I interlaced our fingers together, until Justin apologetically warned us that wasn't a good idea, since we would still be crossing paths with pack members who were loyal to his father. I kissed the back of Logan's hand and let it go. He looked crestfallen but nodded in understanding.

The four of us walked out of the garden and toward the village. The pack may have had its flaws in the way of its Alpha, but the territory itself was beautiful, lush, and green with mountains further back. We made our way down to the schoolhouse, which was very cute. I could imagine little Logan and little Justin playing there, which led me to ask them how exactly they became best friends.

Justin started to laugh. "You wouldn't believe our story, Olivia."

"Oh, try me." I smiled back.

Justin went on to tell me that on the first day of kindergarten, he was being bullied because he was smaller than all the other kids. Even though he was the future Alpha, the kids didn't care. Logan was shy and quiet but when he saw the other kids picking on Justin, he ran over and beat them all up. Logan got in a lot of trouble, especially with the Alpha, who was less than pleased that his son had to be protected by an Omega.

From that day on, Justin and Logan were inseparable and best friends. Logan continued to run off the bullies at school until Justin finally hit his growth spurt in seventh grade.

"Logan was my gentle giant protector," Justin said while fanning himself in a joking way. We all had a good laugh at both of them.

"Well, Liv, your mate is a protector like you! I love it," Amber told me with a giant smile on her face. I had to admit I was surprised Logan beat people up. He seemed so quiet.

"I guess it's true what they always say; to watch out for the quiet ones. They are the wildest," Evie chimed in with a wild grin on her face. *"Mate is so perfect. I can't wait to meet his wolf; he must be wild, too."* I ended up laughing out loud at Evie and caused everyone to look at me funny.

"Evie, my wolf said something funny, sorry guys." My cheeks heated up in embarrassment. At that same moment, a giant chill ran up my spine, and I felt instantly uneasy, as if I was being watched. I looked around, but there was no one in sight.

I tried to shake it off as we continued to walk around and get the pack tour from Justin and Logan. I was trying my best, but I just couldn't shake the feeling of being watched, and it was starting to make my skin crawl. I didn't want to cause a scene, so I mentioned that it was getting close to lunchtime and we should probably head back so we wouldn't be late.

Justin agreed and took a moment to link with his father to make sure we were actually welcome for lunch. This made his jaw tick, and I saw his eyes darken in anger. A few moments later, it was confirmed that we were, in fact, invited for lunch. Amber and I rolled our eyes at the same time and started to giggle.

We headed back to the pack house to get changed for lunch. It didn't take us long to get back, and I thanked Logan and Justin for the tour. They both wished us good luck with our afternoon endeavours. Justin promised to meet us in the dining room for lunch. We all went our separate ways.

Before Amber went into her room, I asked her if she had felt anything weird while we were on our tour. She looked at me with a blank expression,

"No Liv, I didn't feel anything. Why? Did you feel something weird?"

I shook my head and just said, "Never mind. I thought I did, but I must just be tired and imagining things." I gave her a smile and went into my room to get changed. I walked into my room to find the window open, which I knew when I left that morning it hadn't been. I started to get that uneasy feeling again.

"Evie, is there someone here?" She gave a low growl but then shook her head.

"No, Olivia, not right now there isn't, but someone was in here. I can smell them faintly; they smell slightly familiar, but I can't put my paw on it." I relaxed slightly, knowing that the person was no longer in my room, but knowing someone had been there made me quite anxious.

As I approached my bed, something caught my attention. There was a folded piece of paper on my bed with my name on it. I walked over and picked up the note, unfolded it, and read. What it said made my jaw drop, and my heart race.

'I know the truth! It *will come out, and then we must talk.'*

There was no signature, nothing. Did this person know why we were here? How? There were so many questions. My head started to spin. I linked Amber to come quickly, which she did within thirty seconds. I showed her the note, and she was as freaked out as I was. She said we needed to tell Justin. I agreed, but I wanted to find out who this was from first and not risk scaring the person away.

Amber stayed with me as I changed, and we both went down for lunch. We stopped at the clock and hid the bag of supplies behind the clock like we told Melissa we would do. We met Justin by the door afterward. He gave me a grave smile like we all know what we're walking into, and he was trying to apologize in advance. I patted his shoulder and told him not to worry. I had a plan to make it as quick and painless as possible.

We walked into the hall and sat down in front of the Alpha. I thanked him so much for giving us a second chance to enjoy a meal with him. Internally, I wanted to vomit from my words, but I managed to speak with a straight face, no emotions showing.

I could see Alpha Renato puff out his chest, so I knew I had him on the line. I continued by saying I had spoken to my father the night before, and he couldn't believe I had been lucky enough to eat supper with Renato.

"Liar, Liar, pants on fire," Evie shot at me. I shushed her with a giggle; I needed to stay concentrated.

This ploy fully worked because Renato took my bait and went off on a tangent about how my father only wished in his youth that he could have meals with him and his friends, blah, blah, blah. This continued for the entirety of our lunch. Alpha Renato stopped to take a sip of wine, and that's when I took my chance to get us out.

"Thank you so much, Alpha Renato, for letting us spend this lunch with you. I am feeling slightly under the weather. It's my terrible genes and all. Would it be okay with you if we took our leave and I went to rest?"

Alpha asshole scoffed at me. "But of course, dear child, being burdened with subpar genes, I can only imagine what ills you face. Please go lie down, and I will see you all at supper. I have some great stories to tell you about when your father met your mother."

It took everything in my power not to roll my eyes and snarl at the man. I managed to keep my composure and thanked him for his kindness and told him I couldn't wait to hear all about it at supper. The three of us got up rapidly and made our escape into the hall,

"Liv, you are so strong! How you made it through that with a straight face and not having punched the man, you are my new hero." Amber breathed out.

Justin looked like he had seen a ghost; he just kept shaking his head. I reassured him that nothing his father did or said reflected badly on him. He isn't his father. He gave me a look of thanks as if my words helped heal some of the broken pieces; that broke my heart seeing him feel so bad for his father's transgressions.

As we walked up to the clock in the hall, Melissa was already waiting for us with a big smile on her face. "I linked her that we were free when we were leaving the dining hall." Justin beamed. He walked over carefully, making sure the coast was clear, and gave her a sweet kiss.

"Thank you, Justin, for your help. It is truly appreciated." He wished us good luck, and he set off to work on patrol schedules.

Melissa showed us that she had found the gloves and headlamps that we had hidden. She gave us each a pair of gloves and whispered to us to follow her. We followed Melissa down a secondary hallway, and under a staircase, we stopped at a dead-end wall. She pushed two stones and pulled a third, causing a click to be heard and the wall to move.

"Ohhhh, a secret passageway!" Amber loudly whispered in excitement. Melissa and I both spun around to shush her. "Sorry, I get excited too easily, you know that, Liv," she said, as her cheeks turned bright red.

Melissa handed us each a headlamp and motioned for us to follow her quietly. We tiptoed through the wall and into the back of the archive room. We looked around cautiously and let out a small sigh of relief that there was no one in the archives at that moment.

We had to be very quiet, though, since there were guards outside the door. We turned on the lamps and headed for the section Justin had told us would contain the ledgers we needed to search for. I told Melissa and Amber to start with the birth ledgers, and I would start with the death ones.

I started my search five years before I was born since I didn't know when Corey was supposed to have died, and started to work my way up to the year I was born. I was beginning to lose hope of finding anything until suddenly, there it was, four months before my birthday.

Corey Stevens, three years old, died of a rogue attack. Body never recovered.

I couldn't believe my eyes. This couldn't be right; my hands were shaking so hard I dropped the ledger, and it made a terribly loud thud on the table. Melissa and Amber looked over, and we all froze, holding our breaths in case the guards rushed in. After what seemed like an eternity, no one came in. Melissa and Amber hurried over to me.

"Liv, are you okay? You're chalk white, and shaking." Amber was looking at me with a worried expression. I couldn't get the words to come out, so I pointed at the page.

Amber let out a huge breathy squeak. "Holy shit, you have a brother?"

Chapter Sixteen

Chapter 16

Daniel

I was small, and my legs couldn't keep up. I tripped and scraped my knee. I cried out in pain, and a gruff voice told me to shut up and started dragging me through the forest. I couldn't stop crying, and a wild fear coursed through my little body. I didn't know where I was being taken, and I couldn't see the face of the person dragging me.

Next thing I knew, I was being thrown onto the ground and told to never come back, forget this place, I am not worthy of ruling this pack. As I fell, I smashed my head on a rock, and the whole world went black.

I'm shocked back into consciousness by a bucket of cold water. I sputtered and sat up, holding my head as it spun. I looked up into the cold, unforgiving eyes of Onyx Crescent's Alpha as he threw the bucket down and let out a vile humourless laugh.

"You're so weak and pathetic. Clearly, I made the right choice by getting rid of you! Now, if only you had died like you were supposed to," he finished with a sneer.

That voice, it was the voice from my nightmare; I started to shake in anger and jumped to my feet.

"Who the hell are you, and why were you trying to get rid of me as a child?"

A wicked smile played on the Alpha's lips. "Come now son, you don't even recognize your own father?"

The world stopped at that very second, and I fell to my knees, clutching my head as memories flooded back to me. I cried out in pain as the realization hit me. This man was my father, he wasn't dead, and he clearly didn't love me. He tried to kill me, which didn't work in his favour.

"Why would you want your son dead?" I managed to choke out.

"You are no son of mine. You were born weak, and you were cursed to only get weaker and die, thanks to your mother's terrible genes. This pack will never be passed on to someone as unworthy and pathetic as you. How you survived is still a mystery, but one I never intend to find the answer to. I will end your miserable existence later today," Alpha Francis snarled at me as he spun around and headed for the door.

He stopped momentarily and let me know that my time was coming to an end. He wanted me to suffer as greatly as possible, so he left me to rot until he came back to finish me. I cursed him at the top of my lungs as he slammed the dungeon door behind him. The noise echoed through the room, drowning out my angry scream.

How could I be related to that horrible excuse for a wolf?

"Well, it's very simple, you see, your mom met your dad...had sex, and boom, you were born," Xander cut through my angry haze.

I stopped and just blinked at his words. *"Xander, this isn't the time to be funny. This is serious. My so-called father is going to murder us if I don't find a way out of here,"*

"I think this is the perfect time to be funny! It got you out of your blind rage, did it not? You need to be level-headed in order to get out of here. You're welcome!" He smirked at me from the back of my mind, and I couldn't argue with his logic. He was right. I couldn't let my anger and disappointment get the better of me.

I took a deep breath in order to center myself. As I was doing that, a thought crossed my mind. If Alpha Francis was my father, that meant I was an Alpha too, and better yet, I have a sister! Olivia was my sister! No wonder I felt an odd familiarity with her when we met.

I asked Xander if he thought Olivia knew about me being her brother? A twinge of anger ran through me at the thought of my own sister choosing to pretend she didn't know me.

"Daniel, I'm a hundred percent positive Olivia had no clue you were her brother. She had the same odd feeling of recognition as well, but she was nice to us and let us go. If she knew and was crazy like our father, she wouldn't have done that."

"You're right, Xander. Thank you for the dose of reality." I let out a small sigh of relief before the panic started to set in all over again. I got back to my feet and walked over to the bars, giving them a shake. To no one's surprise, they didn't budge.

"Great plan, genius!" Xander sighed at me,

"Well, do you have a better idea?" Before Xander could answer me, we heard the door swing open and hurried footsteps coming towards us. Xander's hackles went up, and I instantly knew it wasn't the Alpha by this person's scent. Who was it then?

Olivia

This can't be true. How could I have a brother? There would have been signs of another child or mentions from people in our pack? My mind was reeling. I was suddenly snapped out of my shocked state by tingles coursing through my whole body as strong arms wrapped around me.

"What are you doing here?" I whispered breathlessly,

"I felt your sorrow and shock through our bond. Melissa linked me and told me where all of you were; I came right away to help you." I collapsed onto Logan's chest and thanked him for being there for me. He asked what happened, and I proceeded to show him the death ledger entry I had found.

While I was lost in my own little shocked world, Amber had found the matching birth announcement for Corey in the other ledger, which confirmed he was, in fact, my brother and was only three years old when he was supposedly killed by rogues.

"That makes sense, Amber!" She looked at me with a puzzled expression. Before I could explain further, Logan whispered that Justin couldn't keep the guard's attention outside the door any longer without arousing suspicion, so we should probably close up the books and leave quickly. I should have known Justin was helping us in whatever way he could. I owed him one.

I pulled out my phone quickly and took pictures of both ledgers as proof for any future needs. We put the books away and quietly crept out of the archives the way we came in.

As soon as Melissa closed the secret door, I told everyone to meet up in my room in five minutes so we could talk. I asked Logan or Melissa to let Justin know of the plan. Amber and I made our way carefully upstairs and into my room,

"Liv, are you sure you're okay? You went catatonic on us down there. If it weren't for Logan, I fear we'd have lost you forever." She rubbed my arm gently with a sad look on her face,

"I'm fine, Cupcake, I promise! It was just a huge shock, that's all. I'm fine now, thanks to Logan and our bond."

Amber smiled at me as we heard a gentle knock on my door. I rushed to open it, and Melissa quickly came in. I started to close the door, but it was blocked by Justin and Logan, who were right behind each other.

"Room for two more?" he teased. I ushered them in quickly and locked the door behind them.

"So, was your expedition fruitful then?" Justin asked anxiously,

"You can say that." I sighed while shaking my head.

I went on to tell Justin and the others that I had found out I had a brother who was supposed to be dead from a rogue attack at the age of three. A brother that, oddly enough, no one in my pack had ever spoken about, including my mother. Justin looked puzzled at this information, so I continued on with my train of thought that had been interrupted in the archives.

"Amber, if, in fact, what I overheard our father's talking about is true, then Corey is alive! He is living as Daniel, the rogue that we let go the other day."

Ambers' face lit up in recognition but then dropped just as fast. "Liv, do you think he knew you were his sister and was playing you? Maybe he was on our territory to try and take over the pack, to reclaim his birthright."

"That thought did cross my mind, but he didn't seem more familiar with me than I was with him, and it seemed genuine. Evie even confirmed it." I went on to tell Amber I think her dad couldn't go through with killing an innocent child, so he must have given him to the rogue pack. Amber seemed grateful that I was willing to have mercy on her dad and not consider him a murderer.

"If your father finds out he is still alive and that my dad didn't do what he was supposed to, he is going to be so beyond pissed, and my dad's life is going to be in danger." Amber looked terrified as she came up with that conclusion,

"Don't worry, Cupcake. We will leave this afternoon and go home to make sure your dad is safe!" I knew it was of little consolation, but it was the best I could do at that moment. Logan looked sad at the mention of me going home, but I had a plan for that.

"Logan, you and Justin will travel to my pack in the next two days. Justin, you will tell your father you were inspired by us and want to find your mate." Melissa growled at me for saying that, and I gave her a sympathetic look as Justin wrapped his arms around her.

Logan looked between his sister and Justin with his mouth wide open. Justin cleared his throat awkwardly and Melissa just smiled before they both looked at Logan sheepishly. "I guess now is as good a time as any to tell you Melissa and I are mates". Justin exclaimed proudly, "now we really are brothers."

It took Logan a moment to process this information, but once he did, he reached over and hugged Justin and Melissa with tears in his eyes. " I am so happy for the two of you. I couldn't think of anyone better for my little sister than my best friend." Justin and Melissa both relaxed and smiled, knowing their secret was now out in the open amongst their closest family member.

I looked at everyone before continuing on with my plan. "So you see, it's obviously just a cover story to get Logan out of this pack and over to Onyx Crescent, where I will mark him as mine." I don't think I had ever seen a more beautiful smile light up anyone's face before, but the smile Logan gave me as he whipped around made my heart soar.

We agreed that I was going to tell Alpha Renato that my mother had fallen ill, and I was needed back at home immediately. Justin felt there wouldn't be an issue since his father hated having to 'babysit' guests, as he put it.

We were finishing up our plans when suddenly a giant gust of wind blew into my room from the window that had just been swung open. A strange woman with a cloak over her head was standing in the middle of my room.

Everyone instantly jumped into action. Justin pushed Melissa behind him, and Logan tried to do the same for me. Everyone was growling at this stranger. I gently pushed past Logan and stood in front of the she-wolf, demanding to know who she was.

The only thing she said was, "Do you want to know the truth about your brother?" Leaving us all stunned.

Chapter Seventeen

Chapter 17

*A*nnabelle

I woke up with an uneasy feeling in my stomach. I hadn't heard from Daniel in two days, and I was starting to get worried that something bad had happened to him. I trusted my chosen mate with my life and didn't want to feed him to the wolves, but I felt like he needed help. I decided that Alpha Arnold needed to know what was going on; he could help. First things first, I needed to get Gabriella up and ready for the day.

I walked into her room, and she gave me the most beautiful smile, the same smile as Daniel's. My heart squeezed at the thought of possibly never seeing his handsome face ever again.

"Good Morning, Princess. We're going to get your Daddy some help today," I told her as I changed her diaper and outfit. Gabriella cooed at me as if agreeing that it needed to be done.

When Gabriella was all ready, we went downstairs so I could feed her some breakfast. She was a good eater, so it didn't take long before we walked over to Alpha Arnold's. I knocked on the door, and Luna Julie answered with a bright smile.

"Annabelle, and my little sweet pea! To what do we owe the pleasure of this visit? Is everything okay?" I loved how caring Julie was. I nodded and asked her if she would mind watching Gaby for a few minutes, because I needed to speak with Alpha Arnold. She happily agreed. She took Gaby from me and headed for the living room. "Arnold is in his office. I've linked him that you're going to see him."

"Thank you, Julie, you are truly wonderful." I smiled at her as I walked down the hall toward the Alpha's office.

I took a deep breath and knocked. I heard him say come in, so I pushed the door open and walked in with a smile. "Good Morning, Alpha Arnold, how are you?" I bared my neck in respect.

"I'm good, Annabelle; please come in and have a seat." My nerves got the better of me, and my hands started to visibly shake. "Is everything okay, my dear? I've never seen you agitated like this before." Alpha Arnold looked at my shaking hands with a concerned look on his face. I took a giant gulp of air as I sat in the chair facing him and just started spilling out my entire story. Alpha Arnold kept his face neutral the entire time, only nodding every now and again.

As I came to the end of my tale, I apologized again for lying to him about where Daniel was, and told him I would take whatever punishment he saw fit. Once I finished my story, I unconsciously wrapped my arms around myself, trying to soothe my anxiety that had risen to an alarming height, while I told the Alpha what was going on. Alpha Arnold cleared his throat before he spoke.

"There will be no punishment, Annabelle. You did nothing wrong. I should have anticipated that he would do something like this after the last time we spoke." I blinked at him in shock. I was sure I was in so much trouble, but his words and his aura told me he wasn't lying, and I began to relax a bit.

Alpha Arnold let out a sigh and scrubbed his hands down his face. "To be honest, this is probably my fault. I had information that he needed to know, and I kept it from him for selfish reasons." I was confused by what he said.

So, he went on to tell me that when Daniel was three, Julie had found him unconscious in the forest near the pack grounds. He was completely alone, and his hand was bleeding. Alpha Arnold knew he belonged to another pack, because he didn't smell like a rogue.

When Daniel regained consciousness, he had no memory of who he was or where he was from. Since they couldn't have pups of their own, they decided to name him Daniel and raise him as theirs. A few days later, they caught wind that the Onyx Crescent's heir, a three-year-old little boy named Corey, had been murdered by rogues.

Alpha Arnold knew there weren't any rogue attacks in the area, so he dug around and came to learn that Daniel was Corey. He didn't understand why the Onyx Crescent Alpha would try and murder his own son, but he knew he needed to protect him. He told me Julie had a friend who was a witch; the witch gave Daniel a potion to change his scent, so as to protect him in case he ever came into contact with Onyx Crescent pack members. I was flabbergasted by the whole story.

"Why did you never tell him this information?"

The Alpha's cheeks started to redden. "That is where I became selfish," he said sheepishly. "I wanted Daniel to grow up strong and be well-trained. When the time was right, I was going to reveal who he truly was and let him challenge his father for his pack, so we could broker a peace deal and live without fear anymore of those entitled assholes."

I couldn't believe Alpha Arnold was keeping that from Daniel his whole life for such a selfish reason. I was disappointed at how deceitful he was and told him as much. Alpha Arnold apologized, saying he would gather a few of his best warriors and work on a plan to go find Daniel. I thanked him and got up abruptly. I needed to go for a walk to clear my head and calm down.

I went to find Julie and Gabriella in the living room. I thanked Julie with a quick hug and took Gabriella to our house to grab the stroller. We walked for a good twenty minutes or so. Gabriella had fallen asleep by this point.

Suddenly, I picked up the sound of approaching guards. It could only be the Onyx Crescent assholes since they acted as if they owned all the land around them; knowing how aggressive they were, I started to panic. I was in neutral territory; there was nothing they could do to me technically, but they wouldn't care. I knew what they were going to do if they found me. I had to act fast; I was too far from the pack, I couldn't mind-link, and our warriors would never make it in time anyways.

I couldn't let them get their hands on Gabriella. I walked a little further into the forest and found a thick patch of bushes. I gently took her out of the stroller, careful not to wake her up,

"I love you, my sweet angel. We will meet again one day-" I choked back a sob as I kissed her head. As gently as possible, I put her on the ground in the thickest part of the bushes and backed out quietly. I knew I had to get those jackasses away from Gaby. I grabbed the stroller and ran in the opposite direction, talking loudly to myself as if I were talking to a baby.

"Hey you there, rogue, stop walking and come here," one of the guards gruffly commanded. I turned to him and gave him a look like I wasn't from this planet,

"I can't stop. I'm walking my baby; my baby needs to be walked, or else he will cry. I hate it when he cries. I want to throw him out a window." I cringed at how unhinged and drunk I sounded, but I needed them to believe I was crazy for this to work.

There were three guards, and they all started coming toward me. One yanked my hands off the stroller as another one looked inside.

"There is no baby in this stroller. Are you crazy?"

I started to shriek and claw at the guard holding me. "No, no, get away from my baby. He can't be disturbed." The wolf holding me shook hard to get me to stop shrieking

"This bitch is crazy, we need to teach her a lesson." He pulled me closer to him, and I took my chance. I elongated my claws and sliced through his neck. The blood splattered everywhere as he went down on the ground, gurgling. It didn't take long before he was gone.

The other guards shifted instantly, smashing the stroller and coming at me in full force. I begged the goddess to look after Gabriella and Daniel as I shifted into Erin. I jumped at the closest wolf.

I managed to get a few good swipes in, but they were too strong for me, and I knew that this was the end. They were going to rip me to shreds. I pictured Gabriella sleeping peacefully and wished that she would have a wonderful life. Erin shed one single tear as they dealt the final blow.

Olivia

I blinked at the woman and regained enough of my composure to ask her who she was. She smiled at me as she removed her hood.

"Hey, that's Margot!" Justin said from behind me. "She lives on the outskirts of the pack, not very social. Margot, what is the meaning of this?" he demanded.

Margot looked slightly embarrassed as she bowed her head at Justin. "I'm sorry I didn't mean to cause a kerfuffle. Please let me start from the beginning. Olivia, I am your aunt Margot," she said the words, and they caused me to stumble back. Logan caught me and held me tight. "That's impossible. I don't have an aunt. Both my parents are only children."

"Are you sure about that? Half an hour ago, you thought you were an only child!" She looked at me pointedly, and I had to admit she was right. Clearly, there was a lot I didn't know and a lot I was being lied to about.

I asked her to continue with her story. I needed to hear everything before I had a complete meltdown. "Your mother is my older sister. We were happy that she was mated to an Alpha until we met your father, and then we were scared for her well-being. He was obsessed with perfection, and our family, sadly, wasn't perfect. Your mother wasn't worried about telling your father how imperfect our family was until she had to."

"We found out she was pregnant with your brother, and our mother accidentally let it slip to your father about the illness that runs in our family. You see, every male that is born has this illness that will kill them if they are not mated before they turn twenty-five."

I couldn't believe what I was hearing from this woman who claimed to be my aunt. I urged her to continue. She went on to say that my father was so enraged by the news of his son dying, that he refused to listen anymore and took off in a fit. He left before hearing the baby could be saved.

There was hope for the males, they just needed to find their mate or take a chosen mate in time. "Which, clearly your brother managed to do, since he is twenty-nine and still alive." I nodded at Margot as I tried to absorb everything she was telling me.

Margot continued by saying my father started treating my mother like a pariah, after finding out her family history. "He was not happy about the birth of Corey and stayed far away from him. He never acknowledged him or did anything with him, really. He forced your mother to try for another heir and was marginally happier to find out she was having a girl."

She looked at me with apologetic eyes. I smiled back at her, knowing what she was referring to. My father was a misogynist through and through.

"I was banished from the pack after Corey's untimely demise by the supposed rogues. I knew your father had something to do with it, and I confronted him about it. He did not take kindly to that and banished me, as well as putting an Alpha command on the entire pack, so that they could not talk about my existence or Corey's; as far as the pack was concerned, neither of us existed. Since I'm no longer part of the pack, I can speak about him without problems." I looked over at Amber, and we both nodded.

That explained the Omega's reactions and my mother's reaction to the mention of Corey; they were under Alpha command. I knew my father was a piece of work, but this just brought him to a whole new level of douchebag.

I turned back to Margot and asked her what made her reach out to me. She told me that she had been in the garden tending to the lilacs when she overheard me telling Justin why we were here. She knew then that she needed me to know the entire truth about my family.

Margot did apologize for following me around and leaving the mysterious note on my bed. I accepted her apology, knowing that at least she wasn't some crazy stalker; the information she relayed today was very important, and I was eternally grateful to her.

"What are we going to do now, Liv?" Amber asked.

"We are going to move forward with our original plan. We are going home, and we need to find Daniel as soon as possible." Margot looked at me, puzzled, and I let her know that Corey was now known as Daniel. He had been taken to the rogues and raised by them.

"Margot, I would like to formally invite you back to Onyx Crescent. By me doing this, you will be allowed back onto the pack lands. I want you to travel with Justin and Logan, but please stay concealed. I will reveal you when the time is right." Margot agreed; she wanted to help us in any way she could. She missed my mother and wanted my father to be brought to justice for his terrible actions.

We convened our little meeting, and I took Justin with me to his father's office, to get Amber and myself out of the pack. Alpha Asshole didn't look overly sad to find out I needed to leave urgently; he even looked amused that my mother was ill.

"Liv, can I please knock him out before we leave? I promise I'll make it quick and very painful!" Evie begged me; I wouldn't lie, I thought long and hard about her request.

"Evie, you'll have your shot at him one day, I promise,"

"FINE, be that way!" She sulked into the back of my mind. I didn't have time to deal with a pouting wolf.

I took my leave from Alpha Renato's office, and ran back to my guest room to pick up my bags and Amber. Logan looked depressed as I packed up my car. I wrapped my arms around him, not giving a damn who could see us, and gave him a deep kiss.

"I will see you in two days, and when I do, I am making you mine!" He smiled at me and said he was holding me to that promise. I winked at him and climbed into the driver's seat as Amber said her final goodbyes to Justin and Melissa. With one last wave, we were on the road back to Onyx Crescent, both lost in our own thoughts, trying to process the last few hours.

Amber

The ride home was uneventful. We were both quiet; only the radio softly sang to us as Olivia drove. I felt so bad for Olivia. She found out some crazy truths about her family today, and honestly, I'm not sure how she was still functioning; if it were me, I would have fallen into a deep, dark pit of despair.

Her father truly was an evil piece of shit. I couldn't believe he treated his son like that and tried to kill him! My father was on my shit list as well. I knew he was the Beta, so serving his Alpha was mandatory, but willingly going along with such a convoluted plan made me truly sick to my stomach.

There was only a slight consolation that he didn't go through with the murder and chose to hide the child, but not much. We were about half an hour away from the pack when Lana started to whimper in my mind and get very agitated,

"What's going on, Lana? Are you okay?"

"Amber, you need to tell Olivia to pull over. You need to get out of the car right now!" I was so confused as to why my wolf wanted me to get out of the car at that exact moment, but I've learned to never question Lana; she is my intuition.

"Liv, please stop the car right now! Lana needs me to get out immediately." She looked super confused but pulled over as I had asked, and I jumped out of the car.

"What now, Lana?"

"Walk straight ahead forty paces, and listen carefully." I did as I was told, and when I'd almost made it the forty paces, I heard crying, not an adult crying but a baby crying. I surged forward and stumbled across a thick set of bushes.

The crying was coming from the middle of the bushes. I pushed through them to find a small baby, maybe around five or six months old. I couldn't really tell. She was red in the face from screaming. I scooped her up immediately, and she stopped crying almost instantly.

"There, there, little one, you're safe now." The baby nuzzled into my chest and passed out almost instantly. The poor thing must have exhausted herself with all the screaming. I started to walk back from where I came and ran into Olivia,

"Oh my goddess, Amber, where did you find that precious angel?"

"She was hidden in the bushes back there crying her heart out, what kind of monster would leave their young pup in the bushes alone in the forest?" Olivia motioned for me to follow her.

"Not a monster, Cupcake, a mother trying to protect her pup!" She pointed to a gruesome scene ahead of us. There was blood splattered everywhere, a smashed baby stroller, clothes, pieces of flesh, and fur everywhere. We walked a bit further and saw an Onyx Crescent patrol guard mangled on the ground. Olivia and I were instantly furious.

"What the hell was one of our guards doing all the way out here? This is neutral territory!" Olivia growled. Evie was close to surfacing.

"I don't know, Liv, but we need to find out. If our men attacked this pup's mother, that makes them murderers." She agreed with me as she continued to seethe.

We looked but did not find the woman's body, meaning either her own pack found her or the rest of the guards took her back to our pack. Olivia and I rushed back to the car, and sped the rest of the way home as I held tight to the little bundle in my arms. Lana was purring in my head, content that we had saved her.

I had a few questions for Lana; like how did she know the baby was there? The questions could wait for later, though. We had bigger problems to deal with.

Daniel/Corey

The man came into sight. He was someone we had never seen before. Xander continued to growl.

"Who are you?" I demanded.

"Keep your voice down, will you!" The man hissed at me. "I am the Beta of this pack."

I cut him off before he could say anything else. "So, you've come to finish me off for the Alpha, or should I say my father," I spat out in disgust. The Beta looked at me and blinked several times.

"You know who you are then?" I nodded at him as I crossed my arms over my chest. "Corey, I'm not here to finish you off. I couldn't do it then, and I won't do it now." I was frozen where I stood.

What did he just call me? Corey? Was that my actual name?

"Talk about an identity crisis," Xander threw out randomly,

"Now's not the time, Xander..." I sighed at him.

"Noted, just trying to lighten the mood!" Of all the wolves, I had to get the comedian. I internally facepalmed.

"I can tell by the look on your face you aren't used to the name Corey. That was your name, son." The Beta's demeanor softened, I could tell he was nothing like my father, and don't ask me why, but I felt like I could trust him; Xander approved.

"What did you mean by you couldn't do it then?" I asked him.

The Beta sighed and told me that he was in the forest with my father the day he tried to kill me. After I had hit my head on the rock and passed out, my father walked away and commanded his Beta to finish me off.

He couldn't bring himself to harm an innocent child, so instead, he carried me close to my current pack, that he knew existed there at the time; made a small cut on the palm of my hand to smear my blood on himself; he wrapped my hand and left me half hidden under a tree hoping someone would find me soon.

He said he smeared dirt on his shoes, hands, and clothes in order to make my father believe that he had killed and buried me. Clearly, the ruse worked. I was mad that this man didn't stand up for me more, but I understood he was caught between a rock and a hard place. I was grateful he gave me a chance at life and said as much to him.

"I only wish I could have done more. That is why I snuck down here. I am going to get you out!" I was shocked that he'd just said that, knowing if he got caught, it would cost him his life for sure.

The Beta slipped on a pair of gloves and unlocked the cell. As I stepped out, he bent the lock mechanism as if I had done it to escape.

He led me to the back of the dungeon and pushed me into the corner, moving the wall inwards.

"Listen to me. Once you're inside the passage, push the wall closed and follow the tunnel; it will lead you out into the forest near the stream on our land." I knew where that was; it was where Olivia and I had met for the first time a few days ago.

I thanked him profusely and ran into the tunnel. I turned and closed the wall as instructed. The tunnel became very dark once the wall was closed, but I used my wolf's sight to guide me to the end. I came out near the stream as the Beta said. I made sure the coast was clear and bolted for the border.

By some miracle, I made it over the border, but I dared not breathe a sigh of relief, since I knew the Onyx Crescent guards liked to patrol and control the neutral territory.

I shifted into Xander and ran like the wind, for my pack. I made it back as the first stars started to pop up in the night sky. I shifted and ran into the house, excited to see Annabelle and Gabriella.

"Belle, Gaby, I'm home! I missed you both." I yelled happily, but I did not get a response.

I should have found it weird, but I thought maybe Annabelle was giving Gaby a bath and didn't hear me. I ran upstairs to be met by silence and darkness. A twinge of fear crept into my chest.

Where could they be?

"Maybe they are at Alpha Arnold's house?" Xander suggested.

"Good call, buddy!"

I went into my room, put clothes on, and then ran over to Arnold and Julie's house, excited to see the loves of my life. I knocked, and within seconds the door flew open to reveal Julie with a tear-stained face. She looked at me with relief and something else that I couldn't place.

"Oh my goddess, Daniel, you're back. We've been so worried." She wrapped her arms around me in a giant hug.

Arnold came into the foyer and gave me a massive bear hug, as well. "We were worried sick, Daniel. How could you do something like that without telling us?" he admonished.

I looked sheepishly at Arnold and apologized. "I'm sorry, Alpha, it was something that needed to be done, and I found out a great deal that I need to discuss with you. However, right now, I really want to see Annabelle and Gabriella. Are they here?" I looked between Julie and Arnold, hopefully. The looks on their faces, though, gave me a huge sinking feeling in the pit of my stomach.

"Come with us into the living room, Daniel," Julie said gently. She pulled me towards a couch.

I instantly became nauseated and began to sweat. "Arnold, where are my mate and daughter?" I said more brusquely than I meant to. Arnold bowed his head, and Julie started to sob.

"They're dead, Daniel, those assholes killed them!" Julie was barely able to choke out between sobs.

My heart stopped, and I started seeing spots behind my vision. I held onto the arm of the couch for dear life, or fear of flying off.

"What do you mean, they're dead? Is that some kind of sick joke?" I felt my anger rising with the panic as shock was setting in.

"It's true, Daniel. We would never make a joke about something as serious as that. Annabelle came to me this morning and told me everything that was going on, because she was terribly worried about you. We had a discussion, and she needed some fresh air, so she took Gabriella out in her stroller." Alpha Arnold shook his head, and started to cry as he told the story.

"Supper time was growing near and she wasn't back yet, so Julie and I went to go look for them and found the most horrifying scene.

Gabriella's stroller was destroyed, there were body parts and blood everywhere, Annabelle put up a good fight, because she managed to kill one of the assholes that attacked them, but ultimately they got her and Gaby."

He hung his head in shame. "We brought back what we could of them for a proper burial, but, Daniel, there isn't much; I am so sorry." Tears were now flowing freely down my face.

Xander began to keen in my head for the loss of our chosen mate and our pup. The sorrow had me in its icy grip, and I began to feel like I was drowning.

I couldn't breathe.

Julie came over and started to rub my back. "You're having a panic attack, Daniel. Please try and take deep breaths." She talked me through the attack until I was able to breathe a bit easier.

I felt completely numb thinking about my sweet little girl whose bright smile I would never see again. My sweet Belle, with her soft heart and playful soul that made every day bearable, the more I thought about it, the angrier I got!

I finally jumped up, with a rage I had never felt before, and ran for the door at full speed. "Those assholes need to pay for what they have done!"

Julie tried to stop me, but I was too quick for her. I had a mission, and no one was going to stop me!

All of a sudden, Arnold's Alpha aura expanded, and he boomed. "Halt!" I was fighting his Alpha command with everything I had. Since I was an Alpha myself, it was easy. That shocked Arnold, so he tried again. "Daniel, I said halt, please!"

This time Xander took over and froze us in place. *"We need to listen to our Alpha, we can't go running back angry like this. We will get caught again and this time executed. We need a plan."* Xander's words took the edge off my anger; he was right. If I went charging back into Onyx Crescent, I wouldn't be able to avenge Annabelle or Gabriella.

I turned to Alpha Arnold with fire burning in my eyes. "Okay, what's the plan"?

Chapter Eighteen

Chapter 18

Olivia

We arrived back at the pack just after supper. Amber was still holding the little orphaned baby.

"What are we going to tell my father and yours?" I asked her as we were driving up to the pack house.

"I planned on telling my father we visited the orphanage at Jade Moon, and I fell in love with this little angel, so I adopted her," Amber said matter-of-factly.

"Perfect! Just one question I'm sure people are going to ask; what is her name?"

Amber looked pensive for a moment and then snapped her fingers. "I've always loved the name Charlotte, I think it suits her. What do you think?" I looked over at the sweet little girl and agreed that Charlotte was a beautiful name, and I thought it would work well.

"Listen, when we get in there, once the hype over Charlotte dies down, I'm going to try and suss out if the guards brought her poor mother back as a prisoner. If not, then we know she was sent back to the goddess."

Amber agreed that would be the best course of action, even though I could see it pained her to think of giving the baby back. She seemed to have grown attached and protective of little Charlotte in the hour since we found her.

I parked the car, and we got out, leaving our bags for now. I would ask an Omega to come grab them for us later. Right now, we needed to get Charlotte inside and find stuff for her to use.

As we walked into the front hall, a few Omegas stopped and stared at us, then quickly walked away, whispering to each other.

"Well, that didn't take long!" Amber linked me as she rolled her eyes,

"To be fair, it's not every day the Beta's daughter walks into the pack house holding a baby, when they know she went out in search of her mate!" I linked back.

"Touché," she said out loud and nodded with a grin on her face.

I stopped the next Omega I saw walking by and asked her if she knew where my father was. She said he stormed up to his office after supper with his Beta, and that he seemed to be in a terrible mood. Nothing new there, I thought to myself.

I thanked the Omega and started to walk up to my father's office, with Amber following close behind. As we approached the office, Charlotte started to fuss and whine.

"Wow, children really can sense evil, can't they!" Evie laughed in my head.

I burst out laughing out loud, which caused Amber to stop and look at me like I was insane. I told her what Evie had said, and she started to laugh out loud as well.

This helped lighten the mood, and Charlotte settled down again, which I was grateful for; my father was a pain to deal with on a good day. If he was in some sort of bad mood, it was going to make things more difficult. As I was about to knock on the door I caught the tail end of my father whispering angrily at Beta Shane, that it was impossible for him to escape. He'd had that dirty-no-good son of his locked up and guarded. I knocked quickly and threw the door open without being invited in.

"Olivia, what the hell is the meaning of this intrusion?" My father growled at me.

I took a deep breath, bracing myself for the shit show that was about to unfold. I had been shocked hearing what he was saying before I walked in, but I quickly schooled my face, pretending I hadn't just heard that little tidbit of information.

My father didn't let me answer, he only glared at Beta Shane and continued talking. "Olivia, it's quite a surprise that you're back so early! Didn't find a mate, so you gave up and came home with your tail between your legs?" he snickered at me.

I bit the inside of my cheek until I tasted blood before I answered. "Yeah, something like that."

Amber and her ever-perfect timing chose this moment to step forward and announce she didn't find her mate either, but fell in love with the orphaned Charlotte and thrust her into her father's arms. "Congratulations, you're a Grandpa!"

Beta Shane's mouth fell open, and he started stammering as he looked down at Charlotte, who had woken up by this point and was blinking up at him.

"A baby, Amber, really?" my father asked her, barely concealing the contempt and distaste in his voice.

"Yes, a baby, Alpha. She was all alone, and we connected. I couldn't just leave her there, so she is my daughter now." She looked my father directly in the eyes, challenging him to say something more about

Charlotte to her. This is why I loved Amber, and why she was my best friend. She never backed down, even if it was up against my father.

"Very well then, I guess congratulations are in order," he said dryly.

Beta Shane came out of his stupor long enough to mumble, "I will link the Omegas, to gather any baby things we have hanging around the pack, and bring them to your room. You will need a crib, blankets, diapers, formula." He was lost in his listing of baby necessities.

As if she knew that he had said formula, Charlotte started to fuss and cry. We didn't know when the last time she had eaten was, so we needed to take her to the kitchen and get her fed.

Beta Shane looked shell-shocked as he handed Charlotte back to Amber. "We will talk more about this later," he barely whispered. I couldn't tell if he was happy or upset about the whole thing. I guess we'd find out later.

I bid my father good night, and we promptly left the office. You could tell he was happy we were leaving because we barely made it out the door, before he started telling Beta Shane that he didn't care if he now had a grandchild. He still had a job to do and the first thing he needed to do in the morning was find out how the rogue escaped. I shook my head as I closed the door.

"Damn, that man is insufferable and such a giant douche! All it takes is one little accident, and the world is a better place, Liv!" Evie offered her words of wisdom.

"I'll have to think about that one, Evie. Thank you for the idea, though." I chuckled to myself as we went down to the kitchen to get ourselves and Charlotte supper.

The head kitchen Omega was smitten with Charlotte, and almost immediately, baby cereal and formula appeared on the counter for us. We sat down and fed the baby. To our delight, she loved to eat and wolfed down two bowls of baby cereal.

"The poor thing must have missed a few feedings. She's starving," Amber said sadly, as she spooned more cereal into Charlotte's eager mouth.

By the time we finished feeding baby Charlotte, the Omegas had brought us a quick dinner, which we inhaled in no time. While we waited for dessert, we overheard two young Omegas washing dishes and whispering to each other.

One asked the other if she heard Dwayne had been killed that afternoon. The second Omega confirmed she had heard the two remaining guards speaking about the crazy bitch who killed him, and they were happy that they gave her what she deserved by ripping her apart.

Amber and I looked at each other with sorrow in our eyes and then looked at Charlotte, who was so innocent. Her mother died protecting her, and now we had an answer.

Both Amber and I were in our own little worlds when the dessert was brought to us. We both got a much-needed laugh out of it. The dessert was two chocolate cupcakes. As soon as Charlotte saw them, her eyes got round, and she reached for them with drool running down her chin.

"Well, I'll be damned, Cupcake. She really is meant to be your pup!" I barely got that out, I was laughing so hard, and we both had tears rolling down our faces. Charlotte looked between us like we were a bunch of wackadoodles.

"Oh, little one, Mommy and Auntie are going to make you give us that look a lot in your lifetime," I whispered to her and was rewarded with a big gummy grin that melted my heart. We finished in the kitchen and ran up to Amber's room.

Once inside, we found a crib and a changing table stocked with everything she would need to care for Charlotte. It had been so long since we had a baby in the pack house, I was impressed they were able to get all this stuff so quickly. Amber walked over to the changing table and started to change Charlotte's diaper, and put her in some jammies.

"So, what is our next move, Liv?"

"Did you hear what my father was saying to yours as we entered his office earlier?" Amber shook her head no, so I continued on and told her about him, saying he had Corey or, rather, Daniel locked up in the dungeon, but it seemed he escaped. That's why my father was royally pissed.

"No way!! I wonder how he escaped?" Amber asked with a look of awe on her face.

"I know! It's almost impossible to get out of there. Anyways, however, he did it, he's lucky! I think our next move is to go to Daniel's pack, and either speak with him if he's there, or the Alpha of his pack." I needed Daniel to know that I was his sister if he didn't already know, and that I supported him. Amber agreed it was the best course of action.

"We could take Charlotte out for a stroll as our alibi, then I can slip away and go to the other pack seeking out Daniel or the Alpha." That part Amber wasn't too happy about. She didn't want me to go alone, but I refused to let her take the baby; it would be too dangerous.

We left on good terms a few days ago, but who knows, now? If Daniel didn't know I was his sister, he could see me as a threat, the daughter of the Alpha who imprisoned him.

We decided to turn in for the night, and we'd refine the logistics of our plan after breakfast. I hugged Amber goodnight and gave baby Charlotte a kiss on the head, wishing them both a lovely sleep.

As I got back to my room, my phone pinged, and I looked to see a message from Logan.

'I miss you already.' It read. My heart melted as I typed back.

'Only two days until you are mine forever. Sweet dreams, my amazing mate.'

I changed and flopped onto my bed with a huge grin on my face. I couldn't wait to make Logan mine. I closed my eyes and drifted into what I hoped would be a peaceful sleep.

Sadly, that wasn't meant to be.

Chapter Nineteen

Chapter 19

Daniel

"What's the plan?" I snarled at Alpha Arnold, my blood pumping so hard it felt like I was buzzing.

"Can we please go to my office? I have something you need to know, and I would like to hear what you found out while you were at Onyx Crescent." Arnold motioned me towards his office.

I agreed and started to follow him down the hall. I was taking some deep breaths in an attempt to calm myself down; the adrenaline was starting to make me dizzy. We walked into the office, and Julie joined us.

"I need to be part of the first half of this conversation," she told me meekly, almost as if she were embarrassed, which piqued my interest in what they were about to tell me.

"Please have a seat on the couch, Daniel. This isn't a formal meeting." Arnold went and sat on the chair facing the couch; Julie sat on his lap.

A pang of sorrow gripped my chest at the thought of never having my beautiful Annabelle sit on my lap ever again, a stray tear ran down my face. I tried to wipe it inconspicuously, but Julie was sharp and noticed. She understood instantly and hurried to sit on the couch with a guilty look on her face.

"I'm sorry, Daniel. I never meant to make you feel bad like that."

"It's okay, Julie, it can't be helped. You were just acting as you normally would. It will take me a while but I hope the pain will lessen in time. People are allowed to love their mates even though I no longer have mine."

I hung my head and took a few deep breaths as pain radiated through my chest. I looked up at Arnold with tears shimmering in my eyes and asked him what he needed to talk to me about.

Before he had a chance to say anything, Julie blurted out, "We knew you were the Alpha's heir from Onyx Crescent when we found you." She chewed her lip, her brows tugging together. "Well...not the day we found you but a few days later," she amended.

"We had heard whispers of your quote-unquote death by rogues." Her face looked pained and I didn't know if it was because of her memory or her own guilt.

"And this never came up in conversation...over the past twenty six years?" I shouted. I had never raised my voice at her but I couldn't even process what she was trying to say.

Hurt flashed across her face, she looked at her lap and said, "We never told you because we loved you and wanted to keep you as our own and keep you safe from your psycho father." I kept silent, unsure of what to say. "We are so sorry, and we hope you can forgive us for deceiving you." Julie finished with a huge sigh and choked back a sob.

To say I was shocked by her admission would have been an understatement.

"So, for all these years, you knew I was Corey, and you didn't say anything to me?" I was trying to remain calm even though that was the last thing I felt at that exact moment. Arnold and Julie both looked taken aback by me using my real name.

"Yes, I know my name was Corey; I found that out from my dear old dad as he berated me for being alive while I was locked up in his dungeon." Julie looked sick to her stomach, and Arnold looked furious that I had been locked up and treated so terribly by my father.

"I can explain why we didn't say anything for so long, Daniel," Arnold replied. I nodded at him to go ahead.

Again, before he could get a word in, Julie blurted out, "Would you prefer if we called you Corey?" Her big, sad eyes probed mine. I had to laugh to myself. Julie was so cute interrupting her mate; she meant well, and I appreciated the love and kindness she showed me.

"No, Julie, please continue to call me Daniel. Corey has no meaning to me. It died when the man who was supposed to love me tried to kill me and couldn't even be bothered to do it himself, I might add!" Both Julie and Arnold nodded at me.

Then Arnold was able to proceed with what he wanted to tell me. He said the reason he didn't tell me right away was, first and foremost, to protect me, but then, as the years went on, he thought it would be a good idea to make sure I had the best training and was skilled enough.

So when I was ready, he would tell me everything, and I could go challenge my asshole father for my birthright, then hopefully broker peace between our two packs. Or, at the very least, have our pack recognized as such, instead of being called rogues, which we weren't.

As Julie had previously asked, Arnold also requested my forgiveness for keeping this from me. This was quite a revelation from my Alpha. I wouldn't lie; it hurt to know they knew who I was and kept it from me, but the more I thought about it I knew I couldn't fault them for it.

Like the Onyx Crescent Beta, who couldn't do more than what he did for me, the same can be said for Arnold and Julie. They kept me safe, clothed, housed, fed, educated, trained, and, most importantly, loved.

I looked between the two of them, and with a big sigh let them know that I had forgiven them. However, under one condition, which Julie eagerly asked for, she wanted to make it up to me so badly. "The one condition is you can't keep anything from me anymore. I want full transparency from the both of you, please."

I thought my request was fair, and it seemed so did Arnold and Julie as they both agreed within seconds. Julie launched herself at me and hugged me tight with tears streaming down her face.

"I don't know what I would have done if you never wanted to speak to me again," she sobbed.

I wiped away her tears and gave her a kiss on the cheek. "You have been a mother to me for the last twenty-six years. I could never stop speaking to you." She gave me a beautiful smile as she blew her nose. I chuckled at her and turned to face Arnold, who was asking me what I had found out when I was captured.

I proceeded to tell him that my father had told me who he was by bemoaning the fact I was still alive. He had told me he refused to give me HIS pack and that he wouldn't let me get away with living much longer. Telling the story hurt almost as much as hearing it the first time, but I continued on.

I told them about meeting the Beta, who confessed to being the one who had saved me in the woods and left me near our pack to be found. They were impressed that he had the thoughtfulness to leave me close to help as well as pretend to have done the task by smearing himself with my blood.

"Remind me to thank that man if we ever meet in the future," Julie said quietly. I smiled at her and squeezed her hand, which I had reached out and taken hold of.

"How did you escape, Daniel, if that asshat, Alpha Francis, had you locked in the dungeon?" Arnold asked curiously.

"The Beta let me out. He showed me a secret passage to escape that led into the woods, deep in their territory, after he told me all his sins; it was his way of making things right." Arnold looked approvingly at me when suddenly something struck me like lighting.

"How was I able to be on the Onyx Crescent territory multiple times in my life, even meeting my sister the other day and they didn't recognize my scent?"

Julie gave me a sheepish look. "I had a witch friend make me a potion that you took as a child to change your scent. That way, you would be protected if ever you came into contact with members of your old pack. The spell, however, will wear off the day of your thirtieth birthday, so you will go back to your familial scent soon."

I blinked at Julie a few times until I realized that my birthday was, in fact, in two days' time. I was so wrapped up in trying to find out what was going on and being captured I forgot.

Another sharp pain hit my chest as the thought of not getting to spend my birthday with my love or my baby girl crossed my mind. Arnold said that I should go to bed and get some rest; I had been through a lot. He offered me my old room in their house, so I didn't have to be alone in my own home with the memories so soon. I accepted their gracious offer, but before leaving for bed, I wanted a plan for tomorrow.

Arnold responded, "I myself will take a few of the men to scout out around Onyx Crescent under the pretense of a hunt. I will try and get a message to Olivia to meet with me since you said she was nothing like your father and she felt your odd connection as well."

I shook my head forcefully. "You aren't going without me! I need to be there in case you get attacked."

Arnold looked at me pointedly. "You need to stay here and rest. We will find a way to contact Olivia. I promise on my life; please trust me, son. I don't want anything to happen to you, and Alpha Francis will be out for blood in order to protect his dirty secret." The look of sadness he gave me as he silently pleaded with me to listen was enough to sway me into agreeing.

"But at the first sign of trouble, you need to link me or shoot a flare if you're out of range to link; anything so I can come help if need be! Deal?"

Arnold took my hand in a firm handshake and shocked me by pulling me into a strong hug. "You really are my son, Daniel. I'm sorry for all the pain you're going through right now. I am here for you, and we'll get through this together." I hugged him back tightly and thanked him while choking back a sob.

I was hit with a wave of fatigue and decided to call it a night. I hugged Julie and headed upstairs to my old room. I fell into bed like a stack of bricks, falling into a deep, nightmare-filled sleep.

My dreams were a loop of Annabelle begging for me to save her and Gabriella crying for her mom and me, so much for the restful sleep I so desperately needed.

Chapter Twenty

Chapter 20

Daniel

All I could hear was Gabriella crying without end. Annabelle looked at me helplessly as the Onyx Crescent wolves tore her apart in front of my eyes. I couldn't move from where my feet were seemingly rooted to the ground. I could only watch on in horror as the love of my life was taken away from me over and over again.

After what felt like hours, I blinked, and suddenly it was silent, and the scene around me had changed. I was now in a beautiful garden surrounded by waterfalls, and a sense of peace hung heavily in the air. I could feel I wasn't alone, but I couldn't see anyone just yet.

"Hello, is anyone there?" I shouted.

"Please don't shout, come sit with me, Daniel," a beautifully melodic voice spoke to me.

I looked around again and, this time, noticed the most beautiful woman I had ever seen with silvery white hair sitting by a waterfall to my left. She was gently stroking the head of a wolf that looked exactly like Erin, Annabelle's wolf. I swiftly walked over to the woman and bowed my head in respect.

"Moon goddess?" I asked in awe.

She gave me a secretive smile and said playfully. "Just call me Selene."

I knew for sure that I was in a dream because there was no way our much-adored Moon Goddess had just told me to call her Selene like I was her personal friend.

I sat on the grass next to her and tried not to stare. This made Selene giggle like a schoolgirl.

"It's okay to look at me, Daniel. I know you weren't expecting this! I couldn't let you torture yourself anymore with that horrible nightmare you were having." I nodded, and a single tear rolled down my face.

Selene reached down and wiped it away; her touch was calming, her skin smooth and cool. I leaned into the touch as a child would with their mother's tender, healing touch.

Selene proceeded to tell me that she had brought me to her garden to let me have one last moment with Erin. Annabelle's body was gone, but her wolf spirit would live on in Selene's garden.

Erin came forward and nuzzled my hand while she whimpered. "I'm so sorry, Erin, that I wasn't there to protect you both. I will make the assholes who did this to you pay dearly." She licked me as if she agreed and trotted back over to Selene's side.

"You will be waking up soon, Daniel. Please know you've still got quite a mountain to climb, but I promise if you stay true to yourself and don't give up, everything will fall into place for you. You will know true happiness once again. I will always be watching over you and your family." I thanked Selene for her kindness as I let her words sink in.

I bid her goodbye, and everything slowly went black around me. I woke up with the sun's rays shining in my eyes. I went to rub them and found traces of tears running down my face; it really wasn't a dream.

I got to say goodbye to Erin and met Selene, our moon goddess.

"She is wonderful, isn't she?" Xander sighed happily in my mind.

"You were there with me, Xander?"

"Of course, silly human, I'm the other half of your soul! I just couldn't say anything since you were technically sleeping, but I got to say my goodbye to Erin as well. She told me that Annabelle fought until the bitter end and asked Selene to watch over you and Gabriella." It gave me comfort knowing she was brave and fought to the end.

A thought crossed my mind at that moment; why would she want the moon goddess to watch over Gaby if she had already been killed?

The thought was gone quickly, though, as I stretched and saw the time on the clock next to my bed. I hadn't realized that it was so late. I wanted to speak with Alpha Arnold before he left on his expedition.

I rushed downstairs and found Julie sitting in the living room, drinking a cup of tea. "Where is Alpha Arnold?" I asked.

"Oh honey, he's gone already. He left hours ago!"

"Shit!" I swore under my breath.

Julie patted the couch next to her and told me to come relax a little; he would be back soon enough. I didn't have much of a choice, so I threw myself down on the couch with a sigh, hoping Alpha Arnold would get back soon.

Olivia

I woke up feeling like I had been hit by a truck. I barely slept more than twenty minutes at a time. Every time I closed my eyes, I had visions of my father trying to kill Daniel or our guards ripping apart Charlotte's mother.

It was a never-ending nightmare of people in my life being terrible. It killed me to know how truly evil my father was and how much pain he had inflicted on others.

I got up and used the bathroom to freshen up. After changing, I jogged down to find Amber and Charlotte for breakfast. I entered the dining room and saw Amber sitting by herself at a smaller table with Charlotte bouncing on her knees.

Amber was smiling at the baby, but I could tell from her eyes that she was upset. I walked over, gave her a big hug, and whispered to her that whatever it was that was bothering her we'd hit it head-on together. Amber looked up at me with a grateful look in her eyes and gave me a small, genuine smile.

I then picked up Charlotte and tickled her tummy until she squealed. Her squealing caused everyone in the dining room to stop and stare at us. This included my father and Beta Shane, who were at the ranked table looking over at us disdainfully.

I loved to piss off my father, so I kept little Charlotte squealing for a solid two minutes and reveled in every cringe or growl that came out of the asshole. I finally handed Charlotte back to Amber and sat across from her to eat my breakfast that had been brought over.

I thanked the Omega with a big, bright smile as I looked her in the eyes. This was the final straw for my father, who slammed his fist on the table and shouted my name.

I turned to him with a syrupy, sweet smile on my face.

"Yes, Daddy?" Another dig because he hated it when I called him daddy; he said it was a mockery to be called that and preferred me to call him Alpha or Father.

I knew I was playing with fire and poking the big bad wolf this morning, but after the shitty night I had, I was willing to go all in and push every button to piss this excuse of a man off.

"You know what, Olivia? I don't even have the patience to deal with you right now! We'll be having a talk later," he gritted out as he pushed away from the table and stormed out of the dining room with his Beta chasing after him like a lost puppy.

"Well, now that the black cloud of our lives is gone, we can enjoy our breakfast in peace." I smiled at Amber and dug into my breakfast, satisfied that I managed to piss my father off more than usual.

I looked over at Amber and asked her why she looked so upset. She told me she had a great night and early morning with Charlotte. I cocked my eyebrow at her. That didn't sound like a reason to be upset. She understood my look and continued on with her story and the reason she was upset.

Her father had come to her room right before breakfast and told her that Charlotte had to go back to the orphanage; she could not be a single mother to a pup that wasn't even hers. It was a disgrace to her Beta blood. They apparently argued for half an hour, and it ended with him telling her that if she didn't take Charlotte back herself, he would do it.

"Oh, HELL NO," I blurted out. That got me a few sideways glances from other pack members, but I didn't give a shit at this point. I was so pissed off on behalf of my best friend.

"Listen, Cupcake, he will not be taking your pup anywhere. I promise you that! Justin and Logan are coming tomorrow. We can have him tell your father it's an insult to return a pup; that will scare him off his warpath."

Amber considered my idea and smiled.

"That could very well work, Liv! Thank you for having my back."

I reached across the table and squeezed her hand.

"I'll always have your back, Cupcake, just like you'll always have mine! Speaking of which, don't we need to go change the baby?" I gave her a conspiratorial wink and nod towards the stairs.

"Absolutely, she needs to be changed right now. Can you help me, Olivia?" She went along with my charade nicely. I couldn't help but laugh to myself about how absurd this was as we got up and made our way to Amber's room.

Once we got upstairs, I told Amber that we were moving forward with what I had said last night. We would take Charlotte out for a stroll, and when we got to the stream, I would take off for Daniel's pack and see if I could speak with either him or his Alpha.

Amber still wasn't happy with this idea, but she sighed and agreed, knowing she'd never win this argument with me. I thanked her for not fighting me, and we changed the baby together and left her room for our walk within fifteen minutes.

It didn't take long to get to the stream. I gave Amber a quick hug, telling her I'd be back as soon as possible and, if need be, to cover for me. She told me to be careful and wished me luck talking to Daniel. I nodded as I stripped off my clothes and shifted to Evie. Amber took my clothes and put them into a bag she had brought, then attached the bag to my back.

I took off running for the border, which didn't take me long to cross. I ran for a solid twenty-five minutes before I smelled a familiar scent. I stopped abruptly as the two guards who killed Charlotte's mom came into view.

"What are they doing out this far again, Evie?"

"I don't know, Liv, but I don't like the feeling these two give me!" instantly, her hackles went up, and she let out a warning growl.

One guard stepped forward with a twisted smirk on his face.

"Well, well, what do we have here? Lost wolfie? Shift, and I will show you what I do to lost she-wolves."

Evie let out one terrifying howl.

I shifted back immediately into my human form, standing in front of him naked, and I couldn't care less. The second guard had the sense to look slightly scared when he realized who I was, but the first one clearly had a rock for a brain.

"Oh well, look who it is, it's the Alpha's little bitch; oops, I meant daughter. The wannabe future Alpha." He laughed to himself as if he were the funniest man alive.

"He won't be alive for long, Liv. Let me at this fucker." Evie was chomping at the bit in my head to be let out and end this waste of life.

"I'm glad you think you're so funny; it will make ending you so much more satisfying." My lip curled into a snarl as I spoke. "What are you doing out this far past our border? You don't belong out here."

"That's where you're wrong, sweetheart. We own all of this land. The other scum around us just don't want to acknowledge that fact; we're teaching them one by one who the real owners are!" He sneered at me, and I'd had quite enough at this point.

"This land is neutral territory, and I will defend it. You are both in the wrong."

I shifted back into Evie as the two guards shifted as well. The loudmouth of the two lunged at me, but Evie was ready. She swiped at him and sent him flying against a tree.

He shook himself off and came right back for more, which made Evie smile; she couldn't wait to beat the hell out of this fucker.

We knocked the first guard around quite a bit before the second one decided to join the fight. He managed to sneak up behind us and bite Evie's back leg. She let out a pained howl, which was answered with four other howls we had never heard before.

The distraction was all I needed to whip around and break guard number two's neck with a loud crunch. This pissed the first guard off, so he chose to jump at me.

I spun and kicked him in the face with my back paws. I then pounced on him and ripped his throat out just as the four other wolves reached the scene.

I shifted instantly and put my hands up to show I meant no harm. I must have looked quite the site completely covered in blood.

Chapter 21

Alpha Arnold

I had gotten up early and prepared myself and the three men I was taking with me to recon Onyx Crescent. Before I left, I went to check on Daniel and found him sleeping with a serene look on his face.

I didn't have the heart to wake him, so I let him sleep. I knew he would be mad at me, but this was for the best, and he would forgive me eventually. I kissed Julie goodbye and told her to get Daniel to rest if she could.

The four of us took off at a good trot and made it to Onyx Crescent just as the sun was beginning to rise. We circled around the perimeter without coming across anyone. We saw two guards at one point leave the territory and head towards our pack. I wondered to myself if those were the two who killed Annabelle and Gabriella?

A rage I had never felt before bubbled up inside me, but I needed to tamper it down; I was here for a reason. Even though killing those two assholes was warranted, it would have to wait for another day, especially since I couldn't confirm they were the culprits.

We did recon for a solid two hours but came up empty-handed. We decided to head back to our pack and regroup. I had to come up with another way to get a message to Daniel's sister, Olivia.

As we got closer to our pack, we heard a pained howl ring out up ahead. All four of us howled back and sprang into action; someone was in trouble, and we needed to help.

We showed up just as a large she-wolf ripped the neck out of another large wolf she was pinning to the ground. The wolf looked up at us as we came closer and instantly shifted into a beautiful woman who was dripping in blood.

She put her hands in the air, showing us she meant no harm. Despite her wild appearance at that moment, I knew instantly she was an Alpha by her aura and not just any Alpha, the Alpha we were looking for; Daniel's sister.

She confirmed this by introducing herself. "My name is Olivia Stevens. I am the future Alpha of the Onyx Crescent pack. We are your neighbours. I mean you no harm. These two wolves were guards of my pack that were doing unlawful things, and I brought them to justice."

I liked her immediately; she had the same moral compass as Daniel. I shifted and quickly threw on the pants I had been carrying. "Olivia, I am Alpha Arnold of the Blood Viper pack."

Her eyes lit up instantly before I could even say another word. "This is amazing!! I'm out here because I was looking to speak with you or your pack member, Daniel; it's a really long story. Is he here?" Olivia looked behind me at the three other wolves.

"No, Daniel is back at the pack. He had quite an ordeal yesterday. Please allow us to escort you to our pack, where you can clean yourself up, and we can all talk."

Olivia agreed and shifted back into her large wolf. She grabbed a bag that had been thrown off to the side and walked over to us, ready to follow. I linked Julie as we were running to let her know we had succeeded and were coming home with Olivia.

Daniel

Sitting on the couch was the most boring thing in the world. *"Want me to sing you a song to pass the time?"* Xander laughed in my head.

"No, thank you! Your singing is worse than your jokes," I scoffed at him.

"Well, that's the last time I offer to entertain you!" Xander turned his back on me in my mind and pouted. What a drama queen, I thought to myself.

Just then, Julie jumped off the couch, scaring the hell out of me. "Julie, what is it?" I asked with concern.

"Arnold's coming back, and he has something for you." This was good news. Maybe he had found a way to get Olivia a message. I couldn't wait to hear what he had to say. We didn't have to wait very long.

Fifteen minutes later, Alpha Arnold came through the front door, followed by none other than my sister, Olivia. I was shocked, to say the least, seeing her standing there, even more so that she was naked and covered in drying blood. Xander instantly became alert and agitated in my mind, which I found off, but assumed he was worried that his sister was hurt.

"Oh dear heavens, you poor girl," Julie shrieked as she ran up to Olivia. "Come with me. I will get you to a shower so you can clean up." She ushered Olivia towards a guest room.

"Thank you very much for your kindness," I heard Olivia say to Julie as they went upstairs.

I turned to Alpha Arnold with a stunned expression on my face. "How did you get her here? What happened to her?"

He chuckled lightly. "I asked her to follow me, and she did! As for what happened, we stumbled across her ripping her own guard's throat out close to our borders. She was on her way here to see you!" I didn't think my face could look any more shocked, but apparently it could, because Alpha Arnold started to laugh at my expression.

He went into more detail and told me they had heard a pained howl on the way back to regroup, and they went to help whoever was in trouble, that's where they found Olivia dripping in blood, having just killed the guard. She then told Arnold she was on her way to this pack to see me.

"I guess we'll just have to wait and see what else she has to say once she's cleaned up." I shook my head in disbelief, this girl was wild.

Arnold agreed with me and said he was going to go freshen up, he needed to put some clothes on before Olivia was ready to talk. Julie came back downstairs as her mate was going to change. "That poor, brave, sweet girl, she reminds me a lot of you, Daniel! You're definitely siblings." Julie giggled as she walked to the kitchen to prepare tea and a snack for our meeting.

Half an hour later, we were all sitting in Alpha Arnold's office. I looked at Olivia and gave her a guarded smile. "Nice to see you again."

"It must be nice to know she isn't going to kick your ass this time, huh?!" Xander crawled out of the back of my mind to burn me.

"Really, Xander?"

"What? It's true! Last time we met Olivia, she handed you your ass on a platter." He burst out laughing, and I blocked him. I had more important things to concentrate on and was not in the mood.

Olivia smiled back at me and then asked me if she could give me a hug? I found this a bit odd, but agreed. She got up and launched herself at me; I was able to catch her as she wrapped me in a bear hug, practically crushing me.

"I've always wanted a sibling," she whispered to me. I pulled back and looked her in the eyes.

She knew!

This news helped shine a bit of light into my current dark reality. I broke into a real smile and hugged her back hard.

Olivia

I confirmed with Daniel that I knew he was my brother. I was rewarded with a huge smile and a giant bear hug; he was as happy about the news as I was. This was a huge weight lifted off my chest. I sighed happily as we released each other, and I took my seat again.

"So, I told your Alpha that I was on my way here, when they found me taking care of those guards." Daniel nodded at me to go on. "I was coming here because I've recently stumbled across the fact that you're actually my brother!"

Daniel smiled at me and said he knew we were brother and sister after our father told him, while holding him captive in our dungeon. I looked down at the floor, so embarrassed that our father was such a monster,

"Don't be sad, sis. You're nothing like him, and neither am I! We should celebrate!! His actions don't define you." I looked at Daniel with awe and gratitude. That was an amazing, empathetic answer.

He was the perfect Alpha that our pack needed at this moment in time, to replace the toxic sludge we currently had. We spent the rest of the afternoon telling each other our stories of how we came across the secret.

Daniel was very impressed with my detective skills and was very excited that I found my mate and our aunt in the process. He asked me if I knew the reason why our father tried to kill him as a child; he was totally confused by this.

I told him that I had been just as confused by our father's actions, before I found out the real reason from our aunt. I told everyone the story Margot had told me, about the illness in the family that killed unmated males past twenty-five.

"Our father didn't know there was a cure, so he set out to get rid of the flawed heir, who would have shown other packs we weren't perfect."

I gave Daniel an apologetic look, as he stared at me blankly.

"Oh, so daddy dearest is a narcissist and perfection whore, is he?" Daniel hit the nail on the head with that comment, and made me laugh.

"Oooh, I really like your brother; he's funny!" Evie was swooning in my head and made me smile.

THE LOST ALPHA

I had a brother!

I wasn't alone anymore, and the best part of it all was that he was the legal heir to Onyx Crescent. He could challenge our father and be Alpha, relieving me from that Hell. I was so excited I could cry.

"Clearly, you mated and survived; I'm so happy about that," I said excitedly to Daniel, but was met with a wave of sadness coming off of him.

"I was mated. She passed away recently." That was all he said.

"Oh, I'm so sorry." I got up and gave him a quick hug. I felt awful for bringing that up, so I tried to change the subject. "Daniel, you're going to have to challenge our father, and take the pack back as the rightful heir!"

The sadness suddenly faded, and he looked stunned at my comment.

" Aren't you set to be the next Alpha? I could never take that away from you," he stammered.

I told him I had no desire to be Alpha, I was a place filler as the only heir.

"Okay, if you don't want to be alpha, couldn't you just take over the pack and then transfer it over to me?" He asked, hopefully.

I looked at him sadly and shook my head. "Our father refuses to give HIS pack over to a woman, he will only give the title to my mate."

I knew for a fact once he found out Logan was an Omega, he would lose his ever-loving mind and refuse to ever give over the pack to me. "Unfortunately, Daniel, you're shit out of luck. My mate is an omega. Daddy dearest hates omega's almost as much as he hates women, so you'll have no choice but to challenge the man." I gave Daniel a sympathetic look. "He did try to kill you, this is pretty good revenge if you ask me!" Daniel looked at me thoughtfully as I went on, "You get to discredit him in front of HIS beloved pack by coming back from the dead. You get to kill him and save the pack from his terrible ways. Your take over was destined, brother. It's a win-win for everyone."

He didn't look convinced by what I had to say until I mentioned it was perfect revenge for what he did to him.

Suddenly his eyes began to burn with a fire, that made me gasp at the intensity.

"I will absolutely use this to avenge all that he has taken from me." His fists were twitching as he clenched them tightly.

I was happy he was on board with taking over as alpha. I didn't want him losing that fire to challenge our father, but I did ask him to wait an extra day before issuing the challenge. I wanted to torture him first with my mate, who was arriving tomorrow.

Daniel agreed and couldn't help but smirk at me. "You are perfectly evil, and I'm here for it! You'll do anything to get under his skin, won't you?"

I gave Daniel a devilish smirk. "You bet! He's been putting me through Hell all my life. I have to have fun somehow."

We both burst out laughing, and that's when we realized Alpha Arnold and Luna Julie were still sitting there watching us both with expressions of awe on their faces, which only made us laugh harder.

Daniel

Challenging our father was not really what I wanted to do. I could fight if I had to. Arnold had made sure I was well-trained, but I was more of a lover than a fighter.

The thought of being Alpha of my own pack also terrified me, but I knew I was born to fulfill that role, and I would do my best for the people of the Onyx Crescent Pack. Olivia had made a good point; I couldn't be worse than what they had now as an Alpha. Thinking of how awful my father was made me cringe and thank Selene that I wasn't raised to be anything like that asshole.

Once our laughter subsided, I got serious and asked Olivia what was the best way to go about this. We needed a plan. I didn't want anyone getting hurt in this process. She told me about Justin, the future Alpha of the Jade Moon Pack, and her mate Logan, who was coming to visit her with our aunt, incognito, due to arrive tomorrow.

She said to give them tomorrow to discuss things and not to arouse suspicions from our father. The day after, she would bring them all over here to finalise a plan if that was okay with Alpha Arnold?

Alpha Arnold agreed fully, and then our meeting was over. Olivia had been gone for quite some time and had to get back before they sent out a search party. We exchanged phone numbers, so if anything changed, she would let me know.

I walked her to the border and gave her another big hug, wishing her a safe return home. She shifted and took off at a sprint. I stood there watching the spot where she disappeared for quite a long time.

I was thinking back to what Selene had said about there still being a mountain to climb, but I could be and would be happy again. I knew now that she meant challenging my father. It was going to be the mountain climb, I was going to be missing Annabelle forever, but now that I found my sister, I did believe I could have some happiness in my life again.

Before I went back to Alpha Arnolds, I looked up at the night sky and thanked Selene for watching over me and thanked Annabelle and Gabriella for loving me.

It wasn't going to be an easy road, but I felt it was worth it. I was going to give it my all and take back what was rightfully mine.

Chapter 22

Alpha Francis

I stared at my Beta with unadulterated hatred, the one person who was supposed to have my back and do everything I told him to do, had completely screwed me over.

"Rip his throat out, right now," my wolf, Sheldon, snarled in my mind.

"Patience, old friend, patience. He will get what is coming to him soon enough."

Shane and I were never very close growing up; he was a loner and pretty much stayed to himself like a loser. I did not like to associate with losers. MY pack was going to be the most powerful pack around and needed only the best at the top!

I was better than him, and now, looking back, if I had the chance, I would never have chosen him as my Beta. My mate, Angela, was Shane's only friend, and she convinced me to choose him as my Beta.

Angela insisted that because we were a fated pair and our bond was stronger, it would work the same with her friendship bond for Shane. Their friendship bond was strong, so it would carry over to the pack; she said we would be an unstoppable trio. Angela swore he would be loyal and do everything for us.

"Ha, if she only knew what a back-stabbing low life he has been," Sheldon scoffed.

I agreed wholeheartedly with Sheldon. The more I thought of how badly Shane screwed me in this situation, the angrier I got. I needed to get away from him.

I stood up swiftly and told him I needed to go find Olivia; she needed a good stern talking to about this morning's behaviour. Shane looked at me with a stupid bewildered look on his face, that I wanted to punch off so badly.

I slammed my office door and marched over to Olivia's room. I pounded on the door and was met by silence. I tried to link her and found there was a block up, so I couldn't reach her. That sent me over the edge, and I flew down the stairs, fully intending to turn the pack house upside down to find her. She will answer for this insubordination.

As I got to the bottom of the stairs, Olivia waltzed through the front door without a care in the world." WHERE WERE YOU, OLIVIA?" I roared, the walls shook, and she looked at me.

A wave of shock passed through her eyes. Good! Be scared of me, little girl, then maybe you won't think of crossing me again, I thought, as I stalked towards her.

Olivia

As I ran home from the Blood Viper pack I couldn't help thinking how amazing it was that I now had a brother. I wasn't alone anymore. My heart felt full. I was smiling to myself as I quickly pulled on my clothes and walked through the front door of the pack house.

My good mood was instantly shattered as I heard my father roar out my name. I hadn't heard him angry like that in a long time and I had a moment of fear pass through me that I hoped he didn't catch.

"Geez, someone is extra grumpy tonight!" Evie scoffed in my head, I quickly looked down as if submitting to my father, but in reality, I was quickly linking Amber.

"My father seems to be on a rampage. Have you told him anything about my whereabouts today?"

"No, he was holed up in his office all day with my dad! I was going to tell him you were out buying baby stuff for Charlotte." I'm grateful for Amber's quick thinking. The only issue is I'm empty-handed at the moment, so that won't fly.

I tell Amber as much, and she tells me to just tell him it's being delivered tomorrow. She then let me know she made some online purchases today, under my name, in anticipation of needing the alibi. I could honestly kiss my best friend right now.

I wished her a quick goodnight, and looked up at my father so he didn't suspect what I was doing. "Good evening, Father. What can I do for you?" I asked in a low voice.

Now wasn't the time to poke the wolf. I didn't want him going feral and possibly hurting an innocent pack member, as they were scurrying around the main floor, finishing their jobs before bed.

"I asked where you were, Olivia! I tried to link you and you didn't answer," my father seethed at me.

"I wasn't on pack grounds when you linked Father. I was on my way back from the mall."

"The mall? What the hell were you doing there, mingling with trashy humans?" He looked like he was about to hyperventilate, at the very thought of me being around humans.

This made my blood boil, but I kept my composure. "I went to get stuff for baby Charlotte that she was missing!" He looked at me skeptically and knew what he was thinking. So, before he said it, I blurted out, "I'm having it all delivered. It will arrive tomorrow." He nodded at me, but I could tell he still wasn't a hundred percent certain I was telling the truth.

"We can tell him I told you so tomorrow, when the stuff Amber ordered arrives." Evie chuckles, indeed she is right, and tomorrow will be a new day to piss my father off.

I take the lingering silence as a chance for me to escape, and I start to walk towards the stairs, when my father blocks me. "Where do you think you're going? I'm not finished speaking to you yet."

"I'm tired and was going to head off to bed! Tomorrow is a busy day of deliveries, and we also have guests coming. Don't forget about Justin and his entourage from the Jade Moon pack."

This revelation seemed to snap my father out of his anger as he mulled over my words. "Ah yes, the future Alpha is coming to visit! We must make sure to show him why our pack is far superior to the shit hole his father runs."

If I could have rolled my eyes at that moment without being beheaded, I would have. *"Don't worry, Liv, I've got you!"* Evie rolled her eyes for me as deeply as she possibly could.

"Fine, go to bed. I want you to look decent for our guests, but make sure, Olivia, when you address the omegas, you don't look them in the eyes! You know damn well they are beneath us."

I clenched my fists and suppressed a growl. "Good night, Father." I nodded at him as I rushed up the stairs to my room. I need to get away from him and shower. Speaking to that man was revolting, and I needed to wash away his horrible words and toxic presence.

As I locked my door, my phone pinged. I looked at it and smiled; it was a message from Daniel.

I am so happy to know I have a sister as kick-ass as you! See you tomorrow.

I sent him back a quick thank you. It warmed my heart that he was as excited as I was to have a sibling. I started to strip so I could go take a shower when my phone pinged again. This time, it was Logan;

'Tomorrow is the day! I can't wait to hold you in my arms. Sleep well, my beautiful angel.'

If I told you, I melted like a puddle onto my floor. I wouldn't be kidding, *"Don't forget Liv, you promised I could get freaky with our mate!"* Evie was panting in my mind.

"Way to kill a moment, Evie". I facepalmed. *"Don't worry, you will have your time with Logan and his wolf. Just let me mark him first okay?"* Evie huffed, but agreed to let me do it my way for the time being. However, she threatened to take over if I didn't get on with it quickly enough for her liking.

Of all the wolves I could have gotten, I got the sassy horn dog; *"Hey! At least I have personality and I'm beautiful to boot."* Evie started strutting in my mind, and I just blocked her out so I could answer Logan.

I shot him off a quick text and then took an even quicker shower. I really was exhausted after the day I had. Having to kill two of my own guards was not a highlight of my day. I had a lot of digging to do. I needed to make sure the poisonous corruption ended with them. If not, I had to clean house, so Daniel could win a healthy, loyal pack.

I threw myself into bed with a tired sigh and fell asleep almost as soon as my head hit the pillow. Tomorrow was going to be an epic day. I'm getting to claim my mate; introduce him to my brother; finalize the plan to take my father out of power and then flaunt my fated omega mate to my father.

I fell asleep with a huge smile on my face.

Chapter Twenty-Three

Chapter 23

Logan

I woke up early in anticipation of heading to Onyx Crescent today. Olivia said she was going to claim me, and we would mark each other. I was excited. *"I hope I get to meet Olivia's wolf today. We spoke briefly when they were here, and Evie is amazing."* Norman was swooning in my head.

I chuckled at my love-struck wolf. *"Please, you're no better, Human! The way you drool over Olivia, and don't forget what you did in the shower last night!!"* Norman was looking at me pointedly.

"Okay, okay, you've made your point, buddy." I couldn't help but laugh at both of us. Two pups head over heels for their other halves.

"Let's get changed and go find Justin." I wanted to get there as soon as we possibly could. I was just pulling on my shirt when there was a knock on my door.

I opened it to find Melissa smiling at me. "I came to wish you a great time at Onyx Crescent. I can't believe my big brother is going to be an Alpha! I'm so proud of you." She gave me a huge hug, which I returned and Norman puffed out his chest in my head.

"I'm not Alpha, yet!" Hopefully, I never will be, I thought to myself.

"I know this whole trip is set up for you, but under the guise of Justin finding his mate, I need you to make sure no she-wolves hit on him, please!" She gave me a pleading look and my heart broke a little for her, that she needed to be that insecure.

"Mel, you know how much Justin loves you. He would never do anything to hurt you."

"I'm not worried about him dingbat!" She punched me in the shoulder "There are a lot of she-wolves who feel entitled to throw themselves at any high-ranked member." I rubbed my tender shoulder; Melissa had a mean right hook!

I saw her point and told her as much. I promised I would do everything in my power to keep the crazy she-wolves off of Justin, while we were at Onyx Crescent. Melissa thanked me and gave me one last hug, before swiftly leaving my room to get to work.

I grabbed my bag and hustled out to find Justin. I found him in the dining room having a conversation with his father. Alpha Renato looked over at me and sneered. "Ah, it looks like the trash is ready to go. Son! Make sure you don't embarrass me while you are at the Onyx Crescent, or you will live to regret it." This was directed at me.

I balled my fists, but nodded. "I would never dream of embarrassing you, Alpha Renato," I said as calmly as I could muster.

"Did I ask you to speak to me? Get out of my sight before you ruin any more of my day." He waved a dismissive hand at me, and I gladly stalked out of the room.

I waited for Justin by the front door, and it didn't take long for him to join me. He had a mortified look on his face, and before he could open his mouth to apologize, I told him not to; it's not his fault his father is the way he is.

"Come on, my man, let's go get you marked by your beautiful mate." He smiled and threw his arm over my shoulder, as we walked out of the pack house towards his car.

When we approached the car, Margot appeared as if out of thin air with her bag slung over her shoulder. "Are we all ready to go?" she asked with a half smile. I could tell she was nervous about going back to her old pack. I couldn't blame her after the things she told us her brother-in-law, Alpha Francis, did.

We got into the car and headed for Onyx Crescent. After what felt like the longest ride in history, we finally arrived. I was so excited, and so was Norman. He was prancing in my mind with a goofy grin on his face.

"Mate, mate, mate, mate," he kept chanting; I had to laugh.

We rounded a curve in the driveway, and the pack house came into view, with Olivia and Amber standing on the stairs waiting for us. Amber was holding an adorable baby, her sister, maybe?

I wasn't so concerned about Amber or the child. I only had eyes for my beautiful mate. The wind was blowing her hair as if she were a regal queen from a fairy tale.

"Who is the love-struck pup now?" Norman snorted. I felt my cheeks heat up. Norman was right. I was head over heels for this woman.

Olivia

I woke up at the crack of dawn with a pep in my step and full of excitement. Today was the day I claimed and marked my mate! *"I can't wait to get my paws on him; once you have, of course,"* Evie said casually. I said nothing to her as I got dressed and headed down for breakfast.

Amber and Charlotte were already eating, and waving me over to the corner table where they were sitting again. "Haven't made up with your dad yet?" She gave me a dark look that I dared not comment on.

"The man is insisting on sending Charlotte back to Jade Moon with Justin." She growled.

I let out an exasperated sigh. "Even when you told him it would offend the other pack?"

She scrubbed her hands down her face before saying anything, which made me hold my breath for the answer. "I didn't get the pleasure of an answer from my dad; your father answered for him!" She looked at me and just blinked.

I facepalmed myself and let out the breath I was holding. "Oh, for fuck's sake. Let me guess, he said he doesn't care if he insults them?"

"Something like that." She glared at the ranked table where our fathers sat, as she aggressively took the last bite of her toast. "I'm so sorry, Cupcake. I won't let them touch her. You know that, right?" Amber gave me a sad smile and nodded; she knew I had her back.

I stood up to go give my father a piece of my mind, when he let out an annoyed growl. "Olivia! It seems your delivery has arrived." For the first time ever, I saw a defeated look pass across his face.

"Thank you, Daddy, for letting me know." I sang out sweetly. "I'll direct them to where all the packages need to go." The vein on my father's neck bulged as his jaw ticked from my words.

"Take that, asshole," Evie cackled to herself. I left the dining room with a large grin on my face. Phase one of piss off daddy dearest, had commenced.

It took about an hour to get all the packages unloaded and up to Amber's room. Once I was done, I went back to have my breakfast. I didn't get to eat very much, before the guard at the gate linked me that Justin had just driven through.

"He's here, he's here, he's here". Evie was jumping up and down like a kid in a candy store.

I told Amber they were here, and we took off to the front to meet them. The car pulled up, and I saw Logan's gorgeous blue eyes glued to me. I couldn't help but blush at his intense stare.

He got out of the car first, and started walking towards me. I let out a happy little squeak and rushed down the stairs, throwing my arms around his neck.

Suddenly a mighty roar came from behind me. "GET YOUR WORTHLESS HANDS OFF MY DAUGHTER!"

Oh shit, I hadn't heard him come outside, I was too wrapped up in my happiness bubble seeing Logan again. I had to think quickly before my father killed him on the spot.

Justin was thinking quicker than I was. He walked around the car and saved the day. "Alpha Francis, it is my great honour to finally meet you. My father speaks highly of you!"

I saw my father look at Justin and blink, as if he couldn't register what he had just said. I took this moment to let go of Logan and take a step back.

Justin continued, "Please forgive my omega if he overstepped, but he saved Miss Olivia's life. She was rushing down the steps and tripped! Had Logan not caught her I fear what would have happened. He's a hero."

My father knows better than to insult a guest directly by calling them a liar, so he looked at me for confirmation. I looked down at the ground and confirmed Justin's telling of events.

"Very well, omega, you saved my clumsy daughter. Now you can remove yourself from her presence." Logan, being a smart man, rapidly retreated back to the car.

My father then turned to Justin, "So, I hear your father speaks highly of me? Too bad he's such a terrible Alpha. I would have been inclined to speak highly of him as well, but sadly that isn't the case."

I stared at my father in disbelief, I couldn't believe he had just said that to Justin. My father and Alpha Renato were truly the same person, it made sense now why they hated each other.

Thank the goddess Justin was easygoing, and knew from my stories that my father was a major asshole, so he took the comments in stride.

"I'll be sure to tell him you said that!" he chuckled lightly.

"Very well, I hope you do!" My father looked indignant as he started to walk away.

I was truly mortified by this interaction, but knew we'd have a good laugh about this later.

"One more thing, young Alpha, before I get back to running my large and successful pack," he puffed out his chest at Justin. Evie rolled her eyes for me, since I wouldn't dare change my current facial expression, and risk my father's wrath. "There is the matter of the orphaned baby that you thrust upon my Beta's daughter. You need to take her back with you, no questions asked, and that's final."

He looked menacingly at me and Amber, we were both staring at him in horror.

"Ah yes, the baby, we will discuss her return later on. For now, we are tired from our drive and would like to go rest in our rooms, please." Goddess, this man was impressive. He had no clue what was going on but was rolling with the punches, and saved our asses.

"I can't believe we forgot to tell Justin about Charlotte and her back story." I quickly linked Amber. She looked at me with a pained expression on her face and agreed that we were idiots.

To avoid any further issues, I spoke up quickly, "I will show them to their rooms, Father."

"Very well, Olivia, run along and do your duty." Damn, could he be any more condescending, I huffed to myself.

Thankfully, my father bid us farewell and left us all lost in our own thoughts. I was the first to snap out of it and went to see Logan and Margot, who had managed to stay hidden the entire interaction. "Well, I see someone hasn't changed one bit! I dare say he's even gotten worse," she scoffed.

"Is that even possible?" I looked at her in bewilderment.

"Sadly it is possible, my dear," Margot confirmed.

I sighed in frustration, turning towards Logan. "I am so sorry he spoke to you that way, my love, but don't worry. Once you wear my mark, he can go to Hell, and will have no choice but to respect you." My eyes blazed with fire from anger I'd never felt before.

"I'm not so sure about that, Olivia, we'll have to wait and see," Logan said while rubbing the back of his neck anxiously.

I reached out and squeezed his hand. "We will get through this together, I promise!" A genuine smile lit up his face. He nodded and went to get the bags out of the car.

"So, is anyone going to tell me what's up with this baby your father wants me to take back?" I whipped around to look at Justin.

"Oh my goddess, yes! Thank you so much for just going along with that and not asking questions."

"I'm used to my asshole back home, so I know better," Justin said with a sad chuckle.

We grabbed all their bags and headed up to the guest rooms. On the way, Amber and I told them the story of how we found Charlotte, and what we told our fathers.

"Wow, that is heavy, Olivia. Don't worry, I won't let anything happen to this cutie pie." Justin's eyes were serious as he gently petted Charlotte's head. Charlotte cooed at him, and I could tell he was smitten.

"You will make a great father one day," I told Justin.

"I truly hope so! I didn't have the best role model, as you know". His sheepish look said it all, and I commiserated with him on not having the best role model as a parent either. We got to his room first, and he told me to have fun and take good care of his best friend.

He gave me a sly wink, which I punched him for. "Ow, you're strong, Olivia, that hurt!" I laughed at him and continued on to the next room, which was Margot's.

Finally, we got to Logan's room. I opened the door and practically pushed him inside, bolting the door shut. Amber linked me that we'd meet up later, as I hadn't even bothered to say anything to her before shutting the door in her face. I apologized, then put up a block.

I needed my mate that instant with no interruptions. I turned around and sashayed over to Logan, who was sitting on his bed. I gave him my most dazzling smile as he looked up at me. "Hello mate, are you ready to be mine for always and forever?" I purred into his ear.

He wrapped his arms around my waist and pulled me towards him. I instinctively straddled him and encircled my arms around his neck.

I bent my head down and slowly licked the perimeter of his ear, stopping at the lobe to slowly suck and nip at it.

This action sent a visible shiver through Logan, and he let out a soft moan, the sound of his moaning sent a wave of heat down to my core that made me tingle.

Sitting on Logan's lap the way I was, I could feel his cock harden and pulse every time I sucked his ear lobe into my mouth; his breathing was beginning to quicken.

"Does my sexy man like that?" I purred in his ear as I ran my left hand through his thick, wavy hair.

He responded by grabbing my hips and pushing me down onto his rock-hard length, which was painfully bulging out of his jeans.

"Does that answer your question, my little minx?" he rasped out.

I smiled and took his mouth in a hot, passionate kiss that made me moan. Our tongues danced with each other beautifully.

I started to kiss his neck, making my way to his marking spot; I lightly sucked and nipped on it, which made his head fall back.

I worked his shirt out of his jeans and pulled it over his head, continuing my quest down his chest to his rock-hard little nipples. I pinched the left one, slowly licking and sucking the right one as my free hand worked on Logan's belt.

I wanted what I wanted, fast, but without seeming desperate, so I was multitasking in a sexy way. Once his belt was off, I slid down his body and took his jeans off with his boxers, leaving his gorgeous cock to spring free in my face. I dropped the jeans to his ankles and quickly kissed my way up his leg.

I stopped to suck on his balls, which made him jump in surprise, but he settled down with a moan. I took his balls in my hand and slowly started to roll them around, while my tongue snaked up the sensitive underside of his throbbing cock.

Once I reached the head, I slowly took him into my hot mouth, swirling my tongue all the way down. I took his full girth down my throat and hummed, creating a luscious vibration.

Logan bucked his hips and let out a shocked moan. I continued by bobbing up and down his length. He wrapped his hands in my hair to guide me. I picked up the pace and hollowed out my cheeks. I knew he was close to cumming, as he was panting at that point. I squeezed his balls and gave him two more heavily suctioned bobs. That was all it took for him to release down my throat. I took all he had to give me and swallowed it.

"Sweet and tangy!" I told him as I sat up, wiping the corners of my mouth. Logan looked at me with a half-dazed smile. I was enjoying watching the blissful smile on Logan's face, and wasn't expecting him to grab me. He threw me onto the bed in one swift motion, I landed on my back with my legs spread.

His eyes had gone black. *"Hello, my sweet mate, Logan is too dazed to be useful right now; I'm Norman, his wolf."* He gave me a look that said I was going to be his next meal.

"Well, hello there, Norman. It's nice of you to come out and play." I gave him a seductive grin. Next thing I knew, he had shredded my dress off my body.

"You won't be needing that anymore," he chuckled as he slowly kissed his way down to my core. He got to my thong and took a long lick before tearing it off my body. *"You taste divine, Olivia."* That was the last of the talking he did as he dove face-first into my wet pussy, like the ravenous wolf he was.

He stroked his fingers in and out of my pussy at a rhythm I had never felt before, using his incredible tongue on my clit. I could feel my orgasm coiling deep in my stomach. The moment his tongue started to take long, broad strokes from slit to clit, it was game over for me.

My orgasm washed over me hard and fast. Norman helped me ride it out by lapping up all of my juices. Leaving me a satisfied, twitching, mess on the bed. *"We will meet again soon, I hope."* He winked at me before Logan's eyes went back to their brilliant blue that I loved so much.

"I am so sorry, Olivia. Did he hurt you?"

"Hurt me? Oh goddess, no, Logan. Norman was a true gentleman, he gave me a hand and a tongue!" I giggled.

Logan looked relieved but annoyed that his wolf had overtaken him, while he was dazed. "Don't worry, love, you're just in time for the main event!" I winked at him and rolled us over, lowering myself onto his newly hardened cock.

Logan moaned and grabbed my hips, as I twisted them all the way down to the base of his cock. Once he was fully seated inside me, I contracted my core muscles and gave his cock a wonderful massage.

He looked quite taken by the sensation, so I started to roll my hips and slowly lift myself up and down. The feeling was fantastic, and I let my head fall back. Logan's eyes were rolling in the back of his head, as I was enjoying the slow pace.

Suddenly, I was thrown into the backseat of my mind. *"Evie, what are you doing?"* I asked, shocked.

"You promised you'd be quick, and you lied. I wanted a turn with my mate. Sorry, Liv. Our deal is off." I couldn't believe this was happening.

All I could do was watch as Evie hopped off Logan's cock and rolled him over. He let out a surprised squeal, which was nothing compared to the sound he made as Evie spanked him! At first, he didn't seem to enjoy it, but after the third time, he moaned and got into it. Evie spanked him multiple times before flipping him over and licking up his entire body, stopping to suck and bite his nipples.

"Hello, Logan, I'm Evie, and I am going to ride you so hard, we're both going to see stars." Logan nodded as Evie climbed back onto his cock in reverse cowgirl.

Staying true to her word, she went buck wild, bouncing, twisting, and meeting all of Logan's thrusts with hard, pounding bounces. As they were both nearing climax, Evie twisted around and grabbed Logan by the back of his head, exposing his neck. She licked his marking spot, elongated her fangs, and bit him.

Logan screamed, and came so hard his body was convulsing beneath us. Evie kept riding him at the same pace as she licked her bite mark closed. After a moment, Evie gave me back the reins with a satisfied glint in her eyes. She had done what she needed to do.

Logan was ours now!

I felt like I was about to cum and saw Logan's eyes darken instantly. Norman pushed forward at that moment, marking me. His bite caused intense pain to shoot through my body, which quickly changed to wild pleasure.

Stars burst behind my eyes, and made my head spin. We both slowed as I came down from my high; Logan licked his bite mark closed; I fell beside Logan on the bed panting and gasping for air.

I managed to roll over and smile at him. "You're mine now, my love, Forever."

He leaned over and kissed me, pulling me onto his chest, where I fell asleep quickly after all that exercise.

Chapter Twenty-Four

Chapter 24

Logan

I woke up about an hour later. Olivia was lightly snoring on my chest with the smallest puddle of drool escaping the side of her mouth. I smiled to myself at how lucky I was. She was all mine.

I wasn't delusional. I knew there was still a massive hurdle to overcome; her father was just as bad as my own Alpha. As long as he didn't kill me, I knew Olivia and I could make it work.

"I won't let the crazy Alpha hurt us or Olivia, don't worry," Norman growled fiercely. Maybe he does have some Alpha wolf in him after all, I thought to myself.

I shifted slightly to regain some feeling in my arm that was wrapped around Olivia, it had gone numb. She stirred and looked up at me with a sweet, lazy grin. "Hey there, my sexy mate! That was fun. I can't wait for round two later." She stretched like a little cat next to me. "I'd love to spend all day in bed with you, but I have a surprise for you and Justin."

"A surprise?" I cocked my eyebrow at her.

"Yes, I didn't tell you, but I met up with my brother Daniel yesterday."

"You did?! That's great, how did it go?"

"He was as happy as me to know we're not alone in this world, we're going to meet him and his Alpha today at their pack to discuss how he will take over Onyx Crescent." I was stunned by what she said, I hadn't even thought about what would happen if her brother came back into the picture.

He was obviously the rightful heir to the pack, meaning I was off the hook for needing to be Alpha. I was so excited by this and instantly felt the stress leave my body.

"So, we won't be the Alpha?" Norman asked, sounding dejected.

"No, I'm sorry, buddy we won't be. We'll still be important but with less stress." This seemed to mollify him for now.

"Are you okay with not being alpha Olivia? I know you've trained your whole life for this." I looked at her with concern.

Olivia gave me an odd look before answering, "If I am being honest, I am better than okay with not becoming alpha."

I was shocked by her answer, "You don't want to be alpha?" The expression on my face made her laugh.

"No Logan I never wanted to take over this evil pack from my father, he would never let me run it properly and would always be breathing down my neck. He's even said I will be Luna only."

I nodded at her words as I tried to digest everything she had just said. I looked up to see an odd expression on her face, so I asked her what was wrong.

"Judging by the look on your face, are you disappointed you won't be Alpha Logan? Knowing my father wanted to make my mate the Alpha?"

I couldn't contain the smirk that formed on my face. Before I answered her, I leaned forward and planted a kiss on her open lips with all the love I had put into the kiss.

"I think you are misreading my facial expression, my love, I am beyond happy to NOT have to be Alpha. The thought of that was stressing me out, you just lifted a huge weight off my shoulders. I thank you for that."

She smiled and let out a laugh as she gently cupped my cheeks.

"I'm happy to hear that we're on the same page and neither of us want this. I would never want you to feel uncomfortable or out of place by my side." She looked at me with all the love she had on full display.

"We can stay here and just be regular happy wolves." She beamed, with that being said I pulled her into a big hug and kissed the top of her head.

"You are my right now, my future, and my forever! As long as you're by my side I know everything will be alright."

Olivia looked up at me with tears brimming in her eyes. "That's all I've ever wanted Logan, to know I'm important to someone and that someone has my back."

"Well you don't need to look any further, I'm here!"

I wiped away a stray tear that had fallen and kissed the tip of her nose affectionately.

"Come on, let's get up and make our way to your brother's pack, we don't want to keep him waiting."

Olivia agreed reluctantly and climbed out of my bed, she followed me into the bathroom where we rinsed ourselves off, ending in front of the large mirror admiring our beautiful marks.

They were identical, both onyx-coloured moons with a howling wolf at the base. I touched my mark, and a shiver ran through me.

"It's beautiful, Olivia."

She looked up at me with a bright smile. "Logan, I have a slight problem."

"What kind of problem love?" I looked at her in confusion as we walked back into my room.

"Norman shredded my dress and my panties earlier, how am I supposed to leave your room?"

My cheeks turned bright red, and I cursed Norman under my breath. "Here, you can wear my shirt and shorts." She took them from me and put them on, seeing her wearing my clothing made my cock jump, which did not go unnoticed by Olivia.

Her eyes darkened "Later, my love. We need to get to my room so I can change." I agreed and finished getting dressed, we carefully made our way back to Olivia's room where she threw on a pair of tight jeans and a tank top that showed off her beautiful breasts, this afternoon was going to be torture I sighed to myself.

Olivia

The way Logan looked at me when I finished getting dressed sent heat straight to my core, again. We didn't have time right now though, so I pushed down my desire, and we headed to get Justin and Margot from their rooms.

I linked Amber and let her know I was gathering the group, and we'd be heading over to the Blood Viper pack. The plan was Amber would stay behind with Charlotte and be our back up if my father came looking for us. We needed to be careful leaving the pack house. I didn't want to spoil the surprise and have my father see our fresh marks so soon.

Justin and Margot were waiting for us, and we all quietly left through the side door without interruption. I took us the long way to the border, avoiding any possible patrols, and before we knew it, we were at the border of Blood Viper, having crossed no one on the way.

Daniel and Alpha Arnold met us there. I was so excited to see Daniel that I ran and threw my arms around him in a giant hug. I wasn't thinking because Logan let out a sharp angry growl, which stunned Daniel and made him take a defensive stance.

"I'm sorry, Logan, please come here, let me introduce you." I waved Logan over to where I was standing, he was a bit hesitant as he knew he was being jealous. He also knew he had just growled at an Alpha male, his future Alpha to be exact. "Daniel, I would like to introduce you to my mate Logan White from the Jade Moon Pack."

A knowing and understanding look passed over Daniel's face and he reached out to shake Logan's hand. "No hard feelings? She's all yours, after all, she is my sister." He made a grossed-out face and we all laughed, which diffused the situation.

Logan visibly relaxed and shook his hand back with a sheepish, yet, thankful expression on his face. "It's nice to meet you Daniel, or would you prefer I call you Alpha?"

Daniel looked taken aback by being referred to as Alpha. He thought about it for a moment and replied, "I would prefer if you called me Dan or even Brother since we are family now."

A huge smile lit up Logan's face, and it made my heart melt that Daniel accepted him so easily. "I would happily call you brother." Logan nodded at Daniel.

I couldn't believe I went from feeling alone most of my life, to my family growing so quickly in a matter of days. I was so happy I felt like my heart was going to burst.

The sound of a throat-clearing brought me back to the present. It was Alpha Arnold. "I hate to break up this happy family moment, but I think it would be best if we moved this inside. We never know who is lurking in the forest."

We all agreed and followed him back to his house. His mate, Julie, was waiting for us in their living room, with snacks and tea. She greeted everyone warmly, and gushed when I introduced her to Logan.

"Oh, you're freshly marked. I love it! Have you had a chance to celebrate with your parents yet?" Julie was so innocent and full of love that I couldn't bring myself to burst her bubble, that my parents wouldn't be happy at all. Maybe mom would be since she wasn't evil like my father, she just went along with him to keep the peace. Deep down I believed she would be happy for me.

I gave Julie a sad smile and told her that we hadn't had time to speak with my parents yet, but would share the wonderful news later. Julie studied me and nodded in understanding. I think she realized that my father, being the monster he was, wouldn't accept Logan; she could smell that he was an omega wolf, and put two and two together.

Julie gave me one last hug before going to sit on Alpha Arnold's lap. I then introduced Justin to Daniel and Alpha Arnold. When it was Margot's turn to be introduced she stood up, and walked over to Daniel. Kneeling in front of him, she told him who she was and begged his forgiveness for not realizing how evil our father was, and not being able to adequately protect him.

I watched as every emotion possible crossed Daniel's face, it ended in love as he smiled down at Margot. He asked her to please get up and asked if they could hug. He didn't blame her for anything and was happy to know she tried to stand up for him, and was sorry she had been banished for it. Margot was crying happy tears as she vowed to make our father pay for what he did.

"Margot, we will all work together and make sure he gets what's coming to him. He has hurt a long list of people." Both she and Daniel agreed with me.

That segued into us discussing a plan for Daniel's upcoming challenge against my father. Justin offered us a dozen of his loyal men who had no love for his father, and who were under Justin's command. As we talked, Justin came to understand that I didn't have any guards at the moment whom I could trust.

As far as I was concerned, they were all loyal to my father or out for themselves, like the guards I killed yesterday. Justin said he would go home in the morning, and tell his father he wanted to bring the men for a training program that we were offering. I had to admit that was a pretty great idea.

Alpha Arnold offered us four of his best fighters. They only had ten and he didn't want to leave the pack vulnerable, especially since he'd be there with Daniel as well.

Daniel looked at that moment like he was trapped on a boat stuck in a storm. "Are you okay? I know this is happening fast, but our father is angry and is looking to remove you from this life. You need to strike now while we have the upper hand."

Daniel agreed with me. "I know I have to do this, I've just lost a lot recently and I'm scared of losing more."

"Daniel, you've got everything to gain from this! You've already gained a sister, a brother-in-law, a long-lost aunt, and new friends. Everything will work out, we've got your back!" He gave me a warm smile.

Julie piped in just then, "What a wonderful birthday gift, Daniel!"

We all looked at Daniel who was just blinking with a sad expression on his face.

"It's your birthday, Daniel?" I jumped up and gave him a huge hug wishing him a happy birthday.

As I was hugging him I noticed that his smell had changed and he now smelled like my family. I mentioned this and Alpha Arnold let me know how that was possible. I had to say I was impressed with the lengths they went to protect Daniel as a child.

Everyone else wished Daniel a happy birthday and we finished up our meeting not long after.

We agreed that Daniel, Alpha Arnold, and their men would meet me at our western border the next day at two in the afternoon. Justin promised to be back by then with his men and, at that point, the challenge could be issued. I was smiling to myself about how well things were working out when my phone pinged.

I looked to see a text from Amber.

EMERGENCY get back here quickly, Charlotte hasn't stopped crying all day and your father is going ballistic looking for you and Justin. He insists Justin needs to take the baby back right now. I'm trying to hold him off but you need to hurry!

"Oh shit, we need to go right now guys, my father is on a rampage and looking for us."

I quickly hugged Daniel and Julie, wishing them a great night. We thanked Alpha Arnold for his hospitality and ran out the door. We chose to shift and carry our clothes back, since that would be the quickest way back.

We got back quickly enough and ran into the pack house, not thinking about anything. I was about to link Amber to see if she knew where my father was.

I didn't need to because a moment later the walls and windows shook with the growl that ripped through the entryway. "WHAT IS THAT MARK, OLIVIA"??

"Show time," Evie chirped with a wicked grin.

Chapter Twenty-Five

Chapter 25

Olivia

I turned towards the roar with a snide, satisfied grin on my face, ready to rub salt into the wound. What I did not expect was that my father would run full speed into Logan, and tackle him to the floor.

He was furiously punching Logan and smashing his head into the floor, screeching like a madman.

"No dirty, worthless, piece of shit omega will EVER take over my pack! You will never be part of my family. I will burn those marks off the both of you," he roared, his voice blending with Sheldon's as he began to choke Logan.

Everyone was so shocked that they were frozen in place. No one could believe what they were seeing. My father had completely snapped and gone feral; his eyes were crazy and he was foaming at the mouth.

Justin was the first to snap out of it, and ran over trying to get my father off of Logan, but my father turned and slashed Justin deeply across the chest, sending him flying with blood gushing.

I heard Amber scream, but felt as if I were trapped in a bubble floating elsewhere. She ran over and started applying pressure to Justin's chest to stop him from bleeding out before he could heal.

I felt a wave of pain come from Logan through the bond and that was enough to snap me out of my state of shock.

Evie instantly pushed forward. *"No one hurts our mate!"* she growled.

I didn't fight her and willingly let her take over. She lunged at my father and punched him so hard it looked like his head spun in a full circle. This momentarily stunned him, but he never let go of Logan and continued to choke him. Evie roared in my father's face, reached forward, and grabbed him by the throat.

She violently shook him three times, before he finally released Logan, who crawled rapidly towards Amber, sputtering for air.

Evie lifted my father in the air by his throat and squeezed him. Everyone heard the wind leave his body and the light cracking sound of his neck.

She got really close to his face with her fangs bared, dripping with saliva. "Who do you think you are, touching my mate? Give me one good reason why I shouldn't end you right here you fucking psychotic bastard!" Evie's voice was animalistic. I had never heard her like this.

"No one has ever hurt the other half of our soul before," she told me in between growls at my father.

My father at least had the decency to look frightened as he kicked his legs helplessly. Evie was relentless and continuously shook him every few seconds for good measure.

"Go ahead, Daddy dearest, tell me now why I shouldn't kill you? Logan is mine and you will never do anything to harm either of us or tear us apart. Do I make myself clear?" Evie growled at my father.

My father was still stubbornly clawing at my fist that Evie had wrapped tightly around his throat. He was putting in a valiant effort, but at that point, Evie was so pissed her strength was invincible. He would run out of air before she ran out of anger.

"I will ask you again, asshole, DID I MAKE MYSELF CLEAR?" Her voice lowered to the most dangerous tone I'd ever heard.

It clearly affected my father, because a wet spot appeared on the front of his pants and he struggled to nod his head in agreement.

"Fucking pussy!" Evie sneered in disgust.

The next moment, my father stopped clawing and kicking, his body just slumped forward.

"Oh my goddess, Evie, did we kill him? We can't kill him. That would make us Alpha! That has to go to Daniel." I was starting to panic.

"No Liv, we didn't kill him, look!"

It was at that moment I noticed my aunt Margot taking a step back from my father's now limp body that I still held onto tightly, she had a syringe in her hand.

"It's a sedative, Olivia. He'll wake up in a few hours. I'm sorry it took me so long to administer it; after the shock of him going feral wore off I had to run to my room and get the syringe." She bowed her head in embarrassment, as if she had failed me.

Evie slowly gave me back control of my body, and I dropped my father unceremoniously into a heap on the floor.

I ran over to Logan and pulled him into my arms, kissing him all over. "Are you okay? I am so sorry he hurt you. I will make sure he dies if he ever tries to touch you like that again." Angry tears were rolling down my face.

Logan reached out and wiped them away. "Please don't cry my love, I am okay, I promise! Norman was able to heal me. The doctor just looked me over and he said the damage wasn't that bad. You saved me, that's all that matters." He bent over and planted a sweet kiss on my lips.

Now that I knew my love was going to be fine, I turned my attention to Justin who was being looked after by the pack doctor.

"When did he get here?" I asked no one in particular.

Amber turned to me with a haunted expression on her face. "I linked him when Justin had been thrown, he came running right away."

"Thank you, Amber, for your quick thinking; you saved him. Justin, are you ok?"

He struggled to sit up, but once he did, he looked at me with a lopsided grin. "Never been better! The doc here wants me to go rest for about an hour to let my wolf finish healing me, after that, I'm as good as new!"

The pack doctor nodded in confirmation and I let out a huge sigh of relief. Logan and I helped Justin to his feet and brought him to his room.

"If you don't mind, my love, I will stay with Justin to watch over him. I also need a bit of quiet time to process what just happened," Logan said quietly.

"Of course, take all the time you need. I will deal with my father and then I will bring you both supper."

Justin smiled at me.

"That would be perfect! After supper, we will be hitting the road and heading back to Jade Moon to get our warriors for tomorrow as planned. I also want to bring baby Charlotte back to our pack. I think she would be safer hiding there with Melissa. If your father went that crazy today over a mate, I'm not sure I want to see what he will do when Daniel challenges him."

I agreed with Justin and let him know I would have Amber prepare a bag for Charlotte, for them to take when they leave later. I gave Logan one last little kiss and left them to rest.

I headed back down to the entry hall; my father was still crumpled on the floor where I had dropped his sorry ass. Margot was standing over him like a soldier. "Margot, you truly saved the day with your sedative. You ended that intense situation, before Evie did something unfathomable that would have bound me to a position I never wanted. I owe you one!" I leaned over and gave her a quick hug.

She returned the hug with a grateful smile on her face. "What are we going to do with this pile of shit?" she asked as she gave him a swift kick in the ribs.

I couldn't help but laugh at her actions. "How long have you been waiting to do that for?" I asked between laughs.

"Longer than you have been alive, my sweet niece." She grinned. I figured as much, so I nodded at her with my approval.

I suggested to the doctor that we move my father into the pack hospital to let him sleep off the sedative, and we could put him in restraints. He would wake up pissed as all Hell, but I didn't want him going on another rampage before Daniel came to challenge him.

The doctor agreed to my suggestion and, with the help of a few male omegas, they hauled his ass off to the hospital. The doctor promised to link me the moment he woke up; even though I was sure I'd hear him freaking out from there, when he was up.

Once the omegas took the trash out of sight, I turned to Margot. "Justin and Logan are heading back to Jade Moon with Charlotte after supper. Will you be going back with them?"

Margot thought it over for a moment and shook her head. "I'd like to stay here if possible? I'd like to go see my sister! She needs to know some truths before tomorrow. If Daniel shows up to challenge your father without your mother knowing he's alive, I fear it may kill her."

I hadn't thought about that with everything going on. I agreed with Margot and told her where she could find my mother. I needed to go call Daniel and Alpha Arnold, anyway, to let them know what had happened today, then I needed to bring the boys supper. I pointed Margot in the direction of my mother's room, and told her when she was done to come to my room; we'd discuss anything new that I might have found out from Daniel. We smiled at each other and parted ways, promising to meet up shortly.

"Good luck with your sister!" I shouted over my shoulder at Margot.

"She'll need all the luck she can get dealing with your mother," Evie snickered and I wholeheartedly agreed.

Chapter Twenty-Six

Margot

I waved at Olivia and went to the room she directed me to. I took a deep breath to steady my nerves, before I knocked on the door. I hadn't seen my sister in over twenty-five years.

I knew seeing me was going to be a huge shock to Angela, but not as great as seeing her dead son challenging her mate for the pack. I sent a prayer to the moon goddess that Angela would hear me out, and that I could open her eyes to what a monster Francis was.

I walked in and saw my sister standing by her window looking outside, lost in thought. "Angela?" I asked softly, but she was so lost in her own world that it scared her.

She jumped and spun around, her eyes growing wide and tears instantly springing into them, when she saw it was me. "Oh my goddess, Margot, is that you?"

"Yes, it's me, Angel!" I used her childhood nickname.

Angela let out a sob and ran over to me, throwing her arms around me in a huge hug. We stood like that for a long time, until Angela was finally able to speak.

"How? How is it possible you are here? Francis told me you abandoned the pack and died sometime after that."

Of course that prick would tell her I had abandoned the pack. I wasn't surprised he said that. I was surprised that my sister would believe him. I thought she knew me better than that. I guess love really does make us do weird things.

"He lied, Angel! He's lied about a lot of things and that's why I'm here. It's time you heard for yourself what your mate has done." She gave me a look of confusion and shook her head at me.

"Margot, what are you talking about? Francis is a good man, he wouldn't lie to me."

"He wouldn't? Then how do you explain my presence here right now?"

She paused momentarily. "He must have just gotten the wrong information from whoever told him you had died! He will be so happy to know you're alive and well." She tried to give me a big smile but it didn't reach her eyes.

I could tell she was trying to process everything, and she wasn't a hundred percent certain what she believed.

"Angela, you are such a smart woman, it kills me to know you are willingly being played by this asshole."

Anger flashed through her eyes. "Don't you dare disrespect my mate that way! You're the one who just randomly disappeared, you don't get to come back and call us names. How do I know that you're not the one that's lying, Margot?"

I let out a sharp barking laugh.

"I can assure you I'm not lying dear sister, you will soon find out for yourself what your mate has been lying about! I wanted to speak with you first, so it's not such a shock, but clearly you're happy with your head in the sand."

I moved towards the door in a bid to remove myself from the situation, because I was starting to get angry at how blind Angela was being. Anger would do no good in this situation. I needed to cool down and try to reason with her later on.

I was closing the door behind me when I stopped and looked at Angela, over my shoulder. "You should ask Francis what really happened to Corey."

The colour instantly drained from Angela's face and her jaw hit the floor. I didn't wait around for anything more to be said and closed the door, heading to Olivia's room as we had discussed. I would have to try again, later, to speak with Angela. I couldn't let it end like this for her.

Francis won once. Never again.

Olivia

Margot was off to speak with my mother, so I had a bit of time to prepare Amber for losing Charlotte later tonight, and to call Daniel. I linked Amber to meet me in my room. She told me she was already there waiting for me.

As I walked into my room, Amber burst into tears. "Liv, I have never been so scared in all my life! Your father was a raving lunatic. Poor Charlotte had been fussy all day; I think she was teething and she was just crying for a little while. He tried to grab her angrily from my arms but I whisked her away quickly, then I texted you to come home. I'm terrified to know what he would have done to her if he had gotten his hands on her."

I pulled Amber and Charlotte into a hug. "It's going to be ok, Amber. I will not let him harm one hair on her beautiful little head."

Amber sniffled and looked up at me with broken eyes."What are you going to do?"

"We are going to hide her, Cupcake! Justin and Logan will be going back to their pack after supper. They will take Charlotte with them and give her to Melissa to hide for the time being. Once Daniel takes over the pack, we will bring your little girl home, I promise!"

Amber nodded at me, but she looked utterly crushed by what had to be done.

"I understand it's for the best, I will go prepare a bag for the boys to bring with them," she muttered quietly, her head downcast.

"Perfect, you can bring the bag back here when you're done." I smiled, hoping to reassure her.

As Amber was leaving my room Margot was walking up to the door, they smiled at each other as they crossed paths. I bid Margot to come in. "Well, that was a fast conversation!"

Margot gave me a look that screamed...Don't go there! "She wasn't very receptive to what I had to say just now, I will have to try again later," she sighed in defeat.

"Margot, my mother has had her head in the sand for years, when it comes to my father's piss poor behaviour and treatment of everyone. I knew that it wasn't going to be a smooth ride for you." I gave her an apologetic look, she nodded at me.

"It's not your fault, Olivia. She was the same way before I got banished from the pack. I spent a lot of time trying to convince her she needed someone who would treat her better. She fell pregnant with Daniel not long after and any more efforts fell on deaf ears.

"Don't worry, Margot, we will get through to her, I promise. But for now, I need to call Daniel and Alpha Arnold."

Margot followed me to the couch near the window in my room, I grabbed my phone and dialed Daniel on speakerphone so we could both hear. Daniel picked up on the third ring.

"What happened, Olivia? Did you sort out the issue with our father?" Daniel asked hurriedly.

"Yeah you can say that...he's currently passed out and tied down in the pack hospital," I said, barking out a humourless laugh.

"What?!" he sputtered out in shock.

I had to laugh again at the shock in Daniel's voice. I went on to explain the whole situation to Daniel. When I was finished I had to ask if he was still on the phone, he had gone so quiet.

"So, what you're telling me is I'm going to have to challenge an unhinged madman tomorrow?" I could hear the loud gulp coming from the other end of the phone.

"Oh, come on now, Daniel. You already knew he was unhinged, he tried to kill you and you're his own flesh and blood!"

"Good point, sis. Still doesn't make me feel any braver!" He laughed nervously.

We then heard Alpha Arnold's muffled voice speaking in the background. "Suck it up, buttercup, this is your birthright! You're well trained and you've got plenty of backup, your father is a small man who had to have his Beta kill you." Evie perked up in my mind hearing Alpha Arnold's speech.

"I knew I liked that man! Francis isn't just a small man though, he's a pussy straight up!" I burst out laughing, which cut off Alpha Arnold on the other end.

I wiped tears from my eyes and told everyone what Evie had said. We all had a great laugh before we finalized our plan for tomorrow. As we bid each other goodbye, there was a knock on my door.

Margot went to open the door for me, while I hung up. She opened the door to my stunned mother. "Margot, what are you doing in here? Olivia, you know who this is?" She was sputtering and you could tell her brain was short-circuiting.

"Yes mother, I know who my Aunt Margot is." I put emphasis on aunt for extra effect.

"It was great to find out I had an aunt, also a brother as it turns out! Very kind of my family to tell me these things."

I didn't have time to say anything else before my mother passed out.

Margot was close enough, she was able to catch her before she hit the ground, dragging her over to my bed.

"Oops, I guess I should have kept the brother part to myself a little longer." I shrugged my shoulders and Margot just shook her head at me.

I ran to the bathroom for a cold washcloth, to bring my mother back to the land of the conscious. As I patted her face with the cool cloth, we heard a loud howl and a lot of angry cursing coming from across the pack house.

My mother jumped up in a panic.

"Well, I guess Daddy Dearest is awake," I chuckled and rolled my eyes.

A moment later, the doctor linked me that he was, in fact, awake and demanding to be untied. I told him under no circumstances was he to be let go. I advised the doctor and any staff to leave the hospital so they couldn't be Alpha commanded into untying him. I'd be down there shortly to have a chat with my Father.

"What have you done to your father?" My mother shrieked at me.

"Easy there, Mother, before you hurt yourself. I did nothing to that asshole."

My mother then did something I never guessed she would ever do and she took a swing at me. "Don't you ever call your father that name again."

I caught her fist easily and held it tightly, I looked her straight in the eyes and said that I'd stop calling him an asshole when he stopped acting like one.

"Your father is hard on you because he loves you, Olivia." She stubbornly defended him like she always did.

I told her that he had almost murdered a visiting Alpha, so this time he went a little too far and we had to sedate him.

If I thought my mother was pale before I'd have been wrong, she blanched even whiter than a sheet of paper.

"Come, Mother, let's go have a chat with my father!"

She got up as if she were in a trance and followed Margot and me out of my room towards the hospital.

Chapter Twenty-Seven

Chapter 27

Daniel

After hanging up with Olivia and my aunt Margot, I looked at Alpha Arnold with a worried expression. "Do you really think I can do this? Am I trained enough to go up against my father? Especially now that it seems he's losing his marbles and going feral!"

Arnold walked over to me and put his hand on my shoulder, squeezing tightly. "Daniel, you are like a son to me. I wouldn't send you into this situation if I didn't think you could beat him! I will be with you every step of the way to make sure you succeed and stay protected."

I reached out and pulled him into a hug, as tears sprang up in my eyes. I was so damn nervous about all of this; not just the challenge, but what would happen after. I would become the Alpha of Onyx Crescent.

I would have a whole pack to look out for; I couldn't even protect my mate and daughter. A lightning bolt of pain shot through my chest that made me wince.

How was I supposed to protect hundreds of other wolves?

"We will figure it out Daniel, we were born to be Alpha, we won't fail!" I felt Xander pouring strength and determination through our bond.

"Thank you, Xander. Knowing you believe in us makes me feel slightly better."

Alpha Arnold pulled me out of my conversation with Xander by patting my back. He suggested I should probably go back to my room and rest, extra sleep would help. I agreed with him, bidding him good night. I headed for my old room. I already knew I wouldn't be able to sleep for a while, my mind was just spiralling in every possible direction.

I even went so far as to think that if my father killed me, then I could be with Annabelle and Gabriella again! I was ashamed to admit that the thought brightened my mood.

"Knock it off Daniel, I know what you're thinking, remember?! Annabelle would be royally pissed off with you for thinking like that, she would never want you to die. Do you remember what Erin told me when we were in Selene's garden? Annabelle's last thoughts were a prayer to Selene to watch over you. Letting yourself die to be with her would be disrespectful to her sacrifice and memory." Xander finished his sentence with a low warning growl.

I knew he was right and I hung my head in shame for even letting myself think like that.

"I'm sorry, Xander. I just miss them both so damn much it hurts! Annabelle was always my greatest cheerleader, without her I'm feeling

lost. I promise you though that I won't sacrifice us, I will fight for her and Gabriella!"

I clenched my fists with a steel resolve rising within me, I would rid the world of the shit stain known as Francis Stevens. I would then live out the rest of my life remembering Annabelle and Gabriella, while protecting my pack members. Xander puffed out his chest proudly and nodded at me contentedly.

I had so much nervous energy, I decided I wanted to train before bed. I knew a workout wouldn't relieve all the anxiety, but it would make me feel less on edge, and hopefully exhaust me so I could get a good night's sleep.

"I know we're strong Xander, we just have to make sure we're faster than my father and we can't underestimate him."

"That isn't a problem Daniel, we're young and he's old. That makes us automatically faster," Xander boasted and chuckled to himself.

"Come on buddy don't think that way, he's the alpha for a reason. We have to watch our back, from what Olivia said the man is shady as Hell." I let loose and started pounding on the punching bag in front of me.

"I know I can handle him Daniel, so don't worry."

I wish I had Xander's faith, but sadly I was more of a realist than my wolf. At the end of the day this was happening, so I had to be prepared for anything.

After working on the boxing bag for over an hour, I decided to work on my speed and footwork, by the end I was completely spent. I went up to my room for a quick shower afterwards, I ended the night by throwing myself onto my bed and falling asleep fast just as I had hoped.

A little while later, I felt something cold nudge my shoulder and heard a whimper. I opened my eyes, looking into the face of Erin, Annabelle's wolf spirit. It took me several seconds to realize I wasn't in my room, I was back in Selene's garden with Erin staring at me intently. What was I doing here again?

Suddenly, I heard Selene's melodic voice. "Daniel, you've been through things that no one should have to, please accept this gift as an apology for the things your father has done to you." I couldn't see her but I could feel her presence all around me like a warm hug.

I stood up slowly and Erin bit my pant leg carefully, she started to drag me towards one of the ponds in the distance where there seemed to be a woman sitting with her feet in the water. The woman turned to look at me as we approached and my heart instantly stopped beating.

"Annabelle!?" I shouted and surged forward, breaking free of Erin's grip on my pants.

I picked her up off the ground swiftly but delicately. I feared she would break if I were not gentle enough. I gingerly ran my hand over her cheek and kissed her lips, Annabelle gave me one of her signature smiles.

"Well, hello there, my sweet Alpha. I am so happy I have gotten to see you one last time, to tell you how much I love you, and how proud I am of you."

"How is this even possible, Belle? Selene's garden is for our wolf spirits."

"Let's just say Selene pulled a few strings and may owe a favour or two moving forward." Annabelle giggled.

"Oh, I see, remind me to thank her before I leave!" I was having trouble coming to grips with the fact the moon goddess pulled strings for me to see my mate one last time. I was quickly brought out of my thoughts by Annabelle punching my shoulder full force.

"Ouch! What the hell was that for Belle?"

She gave me a pointed look with blazing eyes. "That was because of your thoughts earlier; wanting to let your father kill you tomorrow so we could be together again! You need to live so you can make changes to that pack moving forward, no one else should die senselessly as I did."

I promised her that I would never think like that again, and I would be fighting my father full force to win, for all the pack members he has ever mistreated, and avenge my family.

As we were speaking, a thought crossed my mind. "Belle, where is Gabriella? Did you not find each other on the other side? Is she okay?" I looked at her, hopeful that she'd pop out at any moment to give me a big hug.

But what Annabelle said next really floored me. "Daniel, she is not with me, Gabriella didn't die. I hid her before I was attacked by the guards." Her words hit me like a baseball bat between the eyes.

How was Gabriella still alive?

Alpha Arnold said they found the destroyed stroller. I couldn't wrap my head around this revelation. Did I not feel the familial bond snap when Gabriella died?

Seeing as Annabelle and I were chosen mates I never felt anything when she died, we didn't have a bond to snap. I tried hard to think back to that night and I was only in pain after finding out I lost Annabelle and Gabriella, but honestly, I couldn't remember feeling the snapping of the father-daughter bond any time before. I looked down at Annabelle in horror.

"Oh my goddess, Belle. That means our little girl is out there all by herself. What if she's hurt?"

Annabelle cupped my cheek and gave me a secretive smile. "I can't say much but Gabriella is safe. When the time is right you will find her again! I don't have much time left here with you, Daniel."

My heart fell at her words, I had just gotten here. I needed more time with my sweet Belle.

"Daniel, I need you to know that I believe in you and I know you will come out the victor against your father." I smiled bleakly at her.

"I know you're scared but you have no reason to be. Reach inside for that Alpha strength you were born with! I will always be proud of you." I perked up at this, she was proud of me?

"I will be watching over you and Gaby. Please live your new life and be happy. Think of our time together fondly, but give yourself the chance to love again. Promise me that?"

I nodded my response to her as she reached up and gave me one last beautiful kiss. We pulled apart as she slowly faded away with a smile on her face.

I should have felt crushed but I was left with a strong sense of peace. My baby was alive and I was going to take care of my father. My fears were suddenly lessened, and I felt like I just might have a chance at winning this. That was the best feeling I could have had, as everything went black around me.

Chapter Twenty-Eight

Chapter 28

***O**livia*

The walk across the pack house seemed endless as my mother was dragging her feet, barely able to stay upright. Margot, bless her soul, went up beside her sister, wrapped her arms around her hips, and helped her along, speeding up the process...

The closer we got, the louder and more obnoxious my father's rantings were becoming.

"Someone needs to shove something down his throat and shut him up." Evie shook her head from side to side, in pain from trying to silence the noise coming from the pack hospital.

We were almost at the room where my father was being held when I turned to Margot and whispered, "You stay hidden in the doorway, when the time is right, step forward so we can drive our point home."

She gave me a solemn nod, knowing exactly where I was heading with my request. We may not have known each other long or very well, but we were family, so I trusted that she had similar instincts.

My father had a lot of lies to fess up to and the only way my mother was going to believe us was to trap my father and get him to tell on himself.

I pushed the room door open with gusto, momentarily shocking my father into much-needed and appreciated silence.

"Oh, thank the goddess, Liv. Now if only he could stay silent like that it would be glorious", Evie snorted and I wholeheartedly agreed with her.

Unfortunately, we weren't that lucky. In a split second, the shock wore off and he started to curse us out loudly again, "ANGELA, look what our ungrateful little bitch of a daughter has done to me!!!! Get these ties off me immediately!" He spat at us viciously.

"Who's this pathetic pussy calling a bitch?" Evie was snarling in my mind and I ignored her for the moment. My mother was still in a catatonic state, staring blankly at my father.

"No can do daddy dearest!" I drawled sweetly as I walked towards him, leaving my mother half-leaning on the doorframe.

I knew Margot was behind her. If anything happened, she'd catch her again like she did earlier. The rage on my father's face as I approached him was laughable and caused me to smirk.

"Don't you dare laugh at me, you little bitch. I will make you pay for this dearly," he spat at me.

"Well, Daddy, it doesn't look like you're in much of a position to be making threats now, does it? I'm standing here freely and you're the one strapped to a bed." I patted his hand while giving him the most patronising look possible.

This had the desired effect I was looking for. I watched his eyes darken and it almost looked like foam was forming in the corners of his mouth. I've always lived to push my father's buttons, but I had to admit I was having more fun than usual.

"Let him have it, Liv. He's made our lives miserable for as long as we can remember, and all the lies he's told and hurtful things he's done to the people we love." Evie was getting agitated in my mind so I tried to calm her down a bit before continuing with my father.

While I was dealing with Evie, it seemed my mother had started to come out of her catatonic state, she was moving closer to my father's bedside, blinking rapidly.

"Olivia knows about Co...Corrrr...Co...Corrr..." She was trying desperately to say Corey's name but since she was under Alpha command she couldn't, she just ended up stuttering lamely, which enraged my father more.

"What are you mumbling about, you useless waste of space? Speak up and speak clearly! You know how much talking like that pisses me off," he growled at her.

This snapped me out of my conversation with Evie and I whipped around without missing a beat. "She's trying to tell you I know about Corey! Except, since you know, you Alpha commanded her against it, she can't say his name!"

I looked at him pointedly and that shut him up instantly. The man went from red as a tomato to white as a sheet in seconds. "What, wolf got your tongue, Daddy? Was I never supposed to find out about Corey?"

In all the years I've been alive, I had never known my father to be without words, but it seems I had rendered him speechless. He eventually began to sputter, "B-but...but...that's not possible...no, you couldn't know"

"Oh yes, Daddy. I know all about Corey, my sweet brother, whom you tried to have killed when he was just an innocent young boy, but who is still very much alive!"

My mother's head snapped towards me and her eyes narrowed as if she were seeing me for the first time, I nodded at her as if to say you need to believe this information.

My father instantly jumped to his own defense with a shrill, humourless laugh. "She's delusional, Angela. You're delusional, Olivia!" He looked quickly between the two of us. "Corey, was your brother, yes but he was killed by rogues and I Alpha commanded everyone not to speak about him because it was too painful to think about him. You know this Angela! You can't believe Olivia, he's not alive; she's insane and power hungry!"

He gave me a self-satisfied smirk as if he had won a prize, while my mother glared at me ready to agree with him before I cut her off. "Oh, really? So, you didn't command Beta Shane to finish Corey off after he was rendered unconscious by falling on a rock? And you didn't recognize him as one of the men from the other pack nearby? And you didn't have him locked up in our dungeon just two days ago?"

My mother swivelled her head between the two of us as I fired my questions at him. I could see by the look in his eyes that he was furious. The bomb was ticking and it was about to explode.

I could tell now that my mother was starting to put the pieces together for herself. I knew this final move would let her see exactly who her mate was without question. My father spoke in a deceivingly calm voice, "Olivia, where did you hear all this crazy bullshit from anyway?"

"She heard it from ME and her brother directly!" Margot said firmly as she stepped out of the shadows into the room.

"Oooh, here it comes, here it comes." Evie was giddy, I had to shush her to be able to concentrate on what was about to unfold.

My father's eyes went as big as dinner plates, and started swirling red and black with rage; if you looked hard enough you could even see steam coming out of his ears.

"Fire in the hole!" Evie yelled and I laughed with her in my head.

I didn't even get a chance to make it to a count of five before my father blew up just as I was hoping he would.

"What the fuck are you doing here, you no good bitch? I banished you!"

"Oh, I took care of that, Daddy! I invited her back and, since her tie had been severed from the pack, she could come back with no problem."

I smirked triumphantly in my father's direction, but he was too lost in rage to even notice.

"What's wrong Francis, you're not happy to see your dear sister in law?" Margot sneered at my father with a glint of amusement in her eyes.

"I've never considered you family, you useless waste of space." my father spat in our direction.

I noticed my mother flinch at his words and ball her fists.

"Oh come on now Francis I was the best part of being mated to my sister, I made life fun." Margot was laughing at how angry he was.

That was all it took for my father to put the nail in his own coffin, he bellowed at that point.

"I knew I should have had you killed at the same time as Corey. You were always no good, putting your nose in my business and you almost ruined everything," he growled and started thrashing around the bed.

I was so concentrated on my plan working out so well that I wasn't paying attention to my mother. That is why I didn't anticipate what she did next.

She launched herself at my father on the bed. jumped up, straddled him, and started rapid-fire punching him in the face.

"How could you order someone to kill my baby and banish my sister you arrogant lying asshole!! ALL THESE YEARS I believed my son was killed by rogues but it was really your doing! How dare you!!" She started to scream and sob as she punched the ever-loving shit out of my father.

"Liv, I'm impressed! I did not see that coming from your mother! Maybe we should stop her before she hurts herself or accidentally kills that bastard? I mean I want to see him dead but I think Daniel deserves that honour."

Evie was right. We needed to stop her. I shook off the shock and pulled on Evie's strength to mix with mine so we could make this extraction quick and easy.

"Okay Mother, that's enough for now. I'll let you have another go at him later," I told her as I hauled her off of my father's half-limp body.

I passed my squirming mother over to my aunt and linked the doctor to come back. Margot took my mother out of the room and said she'd take her upstairs and try to settle her down.

"I have some sleeping pills, I'll give her one of them." I nodded in confirmation to Margot, then turned my attention to the pack doctor who had just walked in.

"I want Alpha Francis to remain sedated overnight, he is to stay tied up and no one is to come near this room, am I clear, Doctor?" I ordered.

He agreed instantly with me and went to prepare the sedation drugs. I then linked Amber and Beta Shane to come see me in the room. They arrived pretty quickly.

"Where is Charlotte?" I asked a distraught-looking Amber.

"She's with Logan and Justin. She needed to get used to them, so I figured the practice would do them good," Amber replied.

"Makes sense!"

Beta Shane's eyes bulged out of his head when he saw the state my father was in. I raised my hands in surrender. "That wasn't my doing, that was my mother's."

"No, really? Way to go, Angela!" Amber fist-pumped the air much to her father's annoyance.

"Don't give your daughter that look, Beta, you know as well as everyone else what a trash Alpha my father is!" To give Shane credit when credit is due, he at least had the decency to look sheepish and apologised to Amber for his misplaced anger.

"Look, this isn't an ideal situation but I know you helped save my brother's life, Beta Shane. " I looked at him pointedly as his cheeks reddened. "Twice, in fact. That was very noble of you."

"You're a decent man who was sadly forced to follow a lunatic. My father will remain sedated overnight and I need you to guard him please Beta. You're the only one of all the men that I trust enough to actually listen to me."

Shane nodded at me firmly. "I won't let you down, Olivia," he promised sincerely.

"I know you won't, Beta. I believe in you." I squeezed his shoulder as I moved out of the way for the doctor to administer the sedative to my father.

"Doctor, tomorrow around mid-morning I will need you to give my father something that will wake him but keep him calm. Beta Shane will then escort him out into the pack yard. Please have an antidote on hand so that once my father is outside, we can remove the effects of the sedation." The doctor confirmed my request wouldn't be a problem and left us for the night.

Beta Shane turned to me with a questioning eyebrow raised.

"All will come to light tomorrow; all I need you to do is babysit this asshole for the night and drag him outside tomorrow." He nodded in understanding.

Amber and I bid her father good night and headed to Justin's room so we could see them on their way. I knocked on Justin's door and he opened it looking a million times better than earlier today. "I'm glad to see you're all healed!" I gave him a quick hug as we entered the room, I stopped dead in my tracks though as I looked further into the room and saw Logan rocking Charlotte in his arms.

"Oh, my OVARIES!" Evie cried dramatically, but she wasn't wrong.

I walked over and gave Charlotte a light kiss on top of her soft head of curly hair. "You take good care of my niece, you hear me!?!" I gave Logan a pointed, yet joking look.

He told me he would protect her with his life and I knew he wasn't kidding. Looking Logan over quickly I made sure any injuries he had were healed. A warm loving kiss was his reward as I told him to be safe and I'd see him around noon tomorrow.

We walked the boys and Charlotte to the car and helped them load everything up. Logan turned and gave me one last hug with a kiss on my forehead.

"Sleep well my love, I will see you tomorrow." He waved as they drove away.

I turned to Amber, who had giant tears rolling down her face. I took her into my arms and hugged her until the tears ran dry. "Come on, Cupcake, let's go get ready for bed. We've got a long and wild day tomorrow." We linked arms and walked back into the pack house, ready for a good night's rest.

Tomorrow was going to be life-changing, and we needed to be ready to face whatever was to come.

Amber looked at me with broken eyes, "do you really think she will be safe hiding in Justin's pack?" Her eyebrows knit together nervously.

I patted Amber on the back and reassured her Charlotte was going to be completely safe with Melissa. She turned and hugged me tight, she apologised for being a nervous wreck.

I chuckled lightly, "girl I would be a hot mess too if that was my child, you don't need to apologise. I'm here for you."

She gave me the shadow of a smile as we got to my room, I asked her if she wanted to stay with me for the night. Amber graciously accepted my offer; she didn't want to be alone in her room surrounded by Charlotte's things.

I didn't even make it out of the bathroom before Amber was passed out cold on my bed, I went and covered her. I gently kissed her head "sweet dreams Cupcake."

Chapter 29

Justin

The drive back to Jade Moon was quick. I wanted to get Charlotte settled with Melissa and get my men in order for tomorrow's challenge. I didn't know Daniel well, but he had a strong Alpha aura, and from what his Alpha said, he was well-trained, as well.

I wasn't so much worried about his skill as I was about what possible tricks Alpha Francis or his men might try and pull over on him. I would do everything in my power to ensure Daniel was safe and it was a fair fight.

I looked in the rear-view mirror and saw Charlotte lightly sleeping and couldn't help the smile that lit up my face. Logan chose that moment to look over at me. "Thinking about having your own pups?" he asked me with a grin on his face.

"Absolutely! I just need to get my father out of power, so I can properly claim your sister as my mate, then I'll fill her up with my pups."

Logan recoiled with a disgusted look on his face. "Dude, that's my sister, I don't want to think of what you're putting in her."

"Haha, you brought it up, my friend, so deal with the answer."

"Fair enough," he sighed as we pulled up on the side of the pack house to park. I didn't want anyone to see us unload Charlotte.

I turned to Logan when we parked. "What about you? Do you and Olivia want pups?"

Logan looked sheepish for a moment. "We haven't really spoken about that yet! I would love a couple of pups but ultimately it will be her decision."

I nodded at him as I got out of the car and gingerly removed Charlotte from her seat in the back. Logan grabbed her bag and we headed into the pack house cautiously. I had linked Melissa when we were coming up the driveway to meet me in her room.

Her door flew open before I had a chance to knock, she had the most beautiful smile on her face which quickly faded and was replaced by a slack jaw and shocked expression.

"Please tell me that is NOT your baby, Justin?" Anger and hurt were now present on her face.

Logan cut the tension by laughing. "Can we go inside where it's private and we'll explain." He half-shoved his sister back into her room.

Melissa went and sat on her bed crossing her arms and looking at me pointedly. "Explain!!"

"This is baby Charlotte. She belongs to Amber." I knew what she was thinking and before she could say it I explained how Amber came to have Charlotte after they left Jade Moon the other day.

Melissa jumped off her bed and ran over to me with a look of concern on her face. "Oh my goddess, the poor sweet child!"

I told her about what had happened today with Alpha Francis and why we took Charlotte with us. I did leave out the part where he wounded me. I didn't want her to worry, especially since she was already horrified that her brother had been attacked and injured.

"I will absolutely watch her and keep her safe while you go back to Onyx Crescent." She reached out and took Charlotte from my arms and held her tightly to her chest. "I've got you, little one. We're going to have fun while your uncles take care of that terrible Alpha."

Charlotte smiled up at Melissa and giggled, you saw her heart melt instantly and she looked at me with those beautiful eyes of hers.

"One day soon we will have our pups, I promise." I leaned over and gave her a loving kiss.

Logan gave Melissa the baby bag with everything she would need for a day or so. We bid her goodnight shortly after that, as I had to go speak with my men.

Daniel

I woke up feeling lighter than I thought I would. Spending that time in my dreams with Annabelle was just the boost I needed to give me the strength to get through today. I sent a heartfelt thank you to Selene for facilitating that meeting.

"You know we can't lose when we have the moon goddess herself rooting for us!" Xander was pacing in my mind.

"Right on, buddy. So then what's with the nervous energy right now?"

"I'm not sure, Daniel. I just feel like today is going to be wild in more ways than one." I could feel Xander's anxious energy rise through our bond.

"No matter what happens we just make sure we win so we can go find Gabriella!" Xander agreed that finding our pup would be top priority once my father is taken care of.

I got up and tried to prepare myself for battle. Once I was comfortably dressed, I headed down to Alpha Arnold's office where he was waiting for me with the few warriors that were accompanying us to Onyx Crescent.

Julie brought us a light breakfast with strong coffee which she insisted would keep us on our toes while we fought. She came over and gave me a huge hug, wished me well, and told me how proud she was of me.

Julie begged me to be careful, warning me that my father would not go down easily. I assured her that I would take every precaution during the fight. She then left us so that we could finish strategizing.

Around eleven, we started to wrap up and headed out towards the meeting spot we had agreed upon at Onyx Crescent. The closer we got, the more agitated Xander was becoming. I was about to ask him what was wrong when I stopped dead in my tracks, rooted to the spot in shock.

Olivia

I woke up energized and ready to get today rolling. My father needed to pay for his evil deeds and I couldn't wait to have my brother home so we could get to know each other and build that relationship that I so desperately wanted. I rolled over and nudged Amber to wake up. I felt bad because I knew she hadn't slept well. I felt her tossing and turning most of the night.

We decided that she would stay with me overnight. She was distraught about having to send Charlotte away and seeing all the baby things in her room the night before had sent her spiraling into a breakdown.

"Come on, Cupcake, it's a new day!"

"Five more minutes, please Liv?" As she put the blanket over her head.

"The quicker we deal with this shit show, the quicker we can go pick up Charlotte." I felt bad playing the Charlotte card but I knew that would work, and boy did it ever!

Amber threw the blanket off of her and jumped out of bed, she hit the floor running, making a mad dash for the bathroom. "I'll be ready in ten minutes, Liv. Let's go. Don't just sit there." I chuckled at her newfound perkiness.

"I kind of preferred her when she was mopey," Evie said dryly.

I got up and quickly got myself changed. As soon as Amber came out of the bathroom, I ran in to take care of my business. We went down to breakfast not long after.

    The dining room fell silent and many pairs of eyes stared at us as we entered the room, many held a look of relief mixed with curiosity. Then you had the ones that held a look of disgust and anger in them.

Most of those looks came from my father's best warriors, so I wasn't surprised, they would follow him right off of a cliff blindly.

As I sat down and was waiting for my breakfast to be served, I sent out a pack-wide mind-link advising all pack members that they needed to present themselves to the outdoor training ring at twelve-thirty today for a big announcement and that it was mandatory.

I heard back a lot of "Yes, Alpha." And a lot more dead silence, which was telling.

I repeated myself, this time putting Alpha command into the fact that this was non-negotiable.

This time I heard back many more "Yes, Alpha." Even if they were said begrudgingly, they at least agreed to be there. I knew this was going to be a huge hassle, but as long as they showed up, that's all that mattered.

I looked at Amber who was nervously chewing on her nails. I assumed it had to do with Charlotte. Amber confirmed this with a nod and a sad look, she was always so calm that it was starting to make me anxious seeing her so agitated.

We finished up breakfast rather quickly and took a quick detour to the hospital. I wanted to see for myself that everything was set for later today, before heading over to the meeting spot. Beta Shane greeted us at the door. He looked exhausted but still held a fierce determination to make sure my father stayed where he was.

"Did you sleep at all last night?" I asked him.

"No, I knew there would be trouble with some of our men. I didn't want to be caught sleeping on the job." I was a bit shocked that these idiots would try anything against Beta Shane, but I guess stupidity knows no bounds.

"Don't worry I took care of the few that showed up, they won't be a problem anymore," he said this with certainty as he cracked his neck, relieving the tension that had built up overnight. "The doctor came by twice this morning, Olivia. He's keeping your father knocked out until noon, that's when he will be coming back to ease the sedation so I can drag him outside like you asked. He has already given me the antidote that will give your father back full autonomy." He took a rolled-up cloth out of his pocket and showed us the needle.

I thanked him for his hard work and let him know that Amber and I were going out to patrol and if anything came up to link me immediately.

He nodded then asked us to be extra careful out there as my father's followers were quite angry and agitated.

"I have a bad feeling that some of the guards are plotting something Olivia, I don't like it." he looked nervously between me and Amber.

I assured him we would be safe and if anyone tried anything they would die on the spot.

I wasn't in the mood to play around today; if they wanted to fuck around they would find out really quickly. I wasn't the one to mess with.

We headed out of the pack house and towards the meeting spot. The closer we got, the more agitated Amber was getting.

"What's going on, Cupcake?"

"I don't know, Liv. I feel off and Lana is acting weird. Do you think something happened to Charlotte?" I saw tears glistening in her eyes, my heart went out to her, she really was attached to that little girl.

Before I had a chance to speak any words of comfort, Amber stopped dead in her tracks, her eyes widened to the size of dinner plates and she let out a strangled squeaking sound.

"Amber, what is..."

"Mate." I heard in stereo, one faint whisper from Amber and a loud thundering growl from DANIEL?!?!?!?!?!

Chapter Thirty

Chapter 30

Olivia

This couldn't be reality, my long-lost brother and my best friend were mates?

I was so excited I let out the biggest scream, which startled both Daniel and Amber. They were staring at each other intently, rooted to where they stood, neither of them made a move and I was worried about what that meant.

Amber was the first to speak. "How is this possible? We've met before, how did we not know then?"

Daniel looked at Alpha Arnold who cleared his throat. "I can answer that one. Daniel was given a potion as a child, to hide his real scent from this pack for his protection, the spell would only be broken when he turned thirty. Which he did yesterday, so he now has his real scent..."

Amber blinked rapidly, looking between Alpha Arnold and Daniel, I could see her trying to process this information.

Alpha Arnold continued. "...by coming into his real scent, it allowed your mate bond to come to the forefront, and your scent can now be recognized by Daniel's wolf."

I held my breath as Daniel walked up to Amber and extended his hand in greeting. I internally was urging Amber to accept him. I couldn't tell from the look on her face what she planned to do.

Daniel

When the scent of vanilla and coconut hit my nose, I was stunned. I instantly became rooted where I stood. Xander let out a mighty "*MATE!*", shocking me even more.

"*Xander, we just lost Annabelle. What are you doing?*"

"*I'm claiming what is ours, Daniel. I know you loved Annabelle; she was your best friend and perfect for you. She was a beautiful soul, I enjoyed her and Erin's company; but she is gone Daniel.*"

That was a punch in the gut, but Xander didn't care as he continued. "*This walking goddess is our fated mate. I will not lose her because you refuse to take action,*" Xander growled at me, which startled me.

I knew how much Xander wanted his true mate, and he had indulged me by letting me take Annabelle as my chosen mate.

"*I won't stop you from eventually claiming her, but it will take me some time to adjust, I don't want to disrespect Annabelle's memory.*"

"Don't forget your last meeting in Selene's garden, Annabelle did tell you she wanted you to move on and be happy, by not doing so you would be disrespecting her direct wishes," he said, his tone calmer this time.

It took me a moment to digest what he just said and he was right, Annabelle had told me to move on and be happy.

I chose to do what was right and go introduce myself. I walked up to my beautiful tiny mate and extended my hand to her. She looked up at me with shocked emerald green eyes. It took a moment for me to realize I was lost in her eyes and hadn't said anything yet.

"Hi, I'm Daniel Stevens, I'm happy to officially meet you, my little mate." I saw a faint red tint start to creep up her cheeks as she hesitantly reached her much smaller hand out to me.

"I'm Amber Small, future Beta of Onyx Crescent, it's nice to meet you, too." Our hands finally touched and sparks ran up my arm and coursed through my body, the feeling was so incredible I didn't want to ever let go.

Olivia chose this moment to interrupt with a cheery giggle. "I hate to interrupt you love birds, but we have a challenge to issue, and Amber, your father is bringing mine outside right now. We don't have a huge window of time."

I nodded to Olivia and turned back to Amber, kissing the top of her hand. "We have plenty of time after the challenge to get to know each other. Shall we?"

I gestured to her to walk back towards the pack, she smiled at me and slipped her hand out of mine, then went to walk with Olivia.

Amber

As we walked up to the group waiting for us, I was hit by the most decadent scent of chocolate and coffee.

This couldn't be happening right now, could it?

When I realised that the smell was coming from Olivia's brother Daniel, I was shocked to my core and stuck in place. I gurgled out some random noise until I was able to find my voice, and it barely came out...

"*Mate*," I whispered.

Daniel roared his response, which thrilled me and also terrified me all at once. I finally found my mate, and he was about to challenge my crazy asshole Alpha for his position. This wasn't ideal. What if he got seriously injured or, worse yet, died!? My heart squeezed at that thought.

"Don't worry, Amber. Mate is very strong. I can feel it!" Lana purred at me, I vowed right then and there that I would protect him if anything were to go sideways. *"That is the mark of a good mate, Amber, if you are willing to protect what is yours."* Lana proudly puffed out her chest at my vow. She was strong and would prove that by taking out anyone who dared to try and hurt her mate.

My shock wore off and I thought of something quite peculiar, which I shared with everyone. We had already met; how did we not know we were mates? Daniel's Alpha cleared that question up quickly, which I appreciated.

The next thing I knew, Daniel started moving towards me. My heart began beating wildly, Goddess, he was so tall and handsome.

"I'd like to climb him like a tree!" Lana grinned and panted in my mind.

I blocked her out as I looked up into his gorgeous hazel eyes, he reached out his hand and introduced himself. I returned the introduction and reached out to touch his large strong hand. The sparks instantly shot through me and made me feel very hot all of a sudden.

Olivia being Olivia, had to burst our bubble and let us know that time was ticking. Daniel kissed the top of my hand, which made my core clench. He said we had time to get better acquainted later, which I agreed with. I let go of his hand, instantly missing the warmth it provided and walked over to Olivia with a huge smile on my face. We started to walk back towards the pack house. My mind was going a mile a minute.

"Luna Cupcake has a nice ring to it!" I heard Olivia say as she burst out laughing. I stopped dead in my tracks while she continued ahead to speak with Daniel.

"Oh my goddess, Lana, she's right! Being mated to Daniel means I am going to be Luna..."

"I always knew we were meant for more, Amber. This is amazing!" Lana was excited but I was so worried.

Was I good enough to be Luna? What about Charlotte? Would Daniel accept a pup that wasn't his? My head started to spin and I began to get dizzy.

"Easy does it, I've got you." Alpha Arnold came up beside me and helped steady me. I thanked him for his assistance.

"I know this is overwhelming, Amber. I just wanted you to know it is going to be overwhelming for Daniel as well. He had a chosen mate that he recently lost, with a child. It was very tragic, so he's going to want to take things slow. I know you will be an amazing mate to Daniel, and I'm happy because he is like a son to me. I only want to see him happy." He patted me on the back and walked on, leaving me bewildered.

Daniel had a chosen mate and a child, who had died? That was so sad my heart broke for him. I knew at that moment I would need to proceed cautiously and make sure he was ready for whatever steps we would take together. I noticed then I had lagged behind and jogged to catch up.

Olivia

I walked over to Daniel and congratulated him for finding his mate. I told him I knew he had recently lost his chosen mate, but I hoped he would still accept Amber, because she was one of the most amazing women I knew.

I also warned him not to hurt her or I'd kick his ass again. This made him chuckle deeply. He assured me that he had no intention of rejecting Amber or hurting her. He would need a bit of time to adjust, but he would speak with Amber after the challenge was settled and lay all the cards on the table. He was worried she wouldn't accept him, for having had a chosen mate before her.

I assured him that my best friend wasn't like that and would love him no matter what. She had her own things she would need to share with him anyway.

I thought of Charlotte at that moment, that was going to be interesting to explain, but I knew they would be just fine as long as they communicated.

As we got closer to the pack house, I started hearing shouting and loud growls coming from the path between the pack house and the training ring, where we were heading.

I took off running ahead with Daniel coming up behind me. What we found in front of us really pissed me off. My father was being held by two of his men but was being blocked by two of what looked like Justin's men. Beta Shane was sparring back-to-back with Justin and Logan, against four other wolves, who followed my father blindly.

There didn't seem to be any injuries yet, but I had to put an end to this right now.

I let Evie push forward our Alpha aura and let our voices blend into a powerful tone. "That's enough, I command you all to stop right now."

The fighting and growling instantly stopped, and everyone just stared at me and Daniel, who had come up beside me.

"Release my father to Beta Shane immediately and stand down or face instant death." I let Evie snarl the last part and saw fear cross the faces of my father's men.

They grudgingly handed my father back to Beta Shane, who punched out one of the men holding my father up. I couldn't help but chuckle.

"Everyone is to go right now to the outdoor training ring; we have an announcement to make."

All the men started to move towards the ring, compelled by my Alpha command. My father's men looked angrily around them at Justin's men.

I walked up beside Justin and Logan, thanking them for helping Beta Shane. Justin told me they had just pulled up, when they saw Beta Shane get jumped by the loser he'd punched out. All Hell broke loose after that, so he and his men joined in.

He confirmed he was going to keep tabs on those men, who were clearly going to be trouble during the challenge. I thanked him again, gave Logan a chaste kiss on the cheek, and ran to the front of the group, so I could make it to the ring first.

Stepping into the middle of the training ring, I looked around and saw the entire pack showed up as I had ordered. My mother stood near the front clutching onto Margot, as if for dear life.

As Daniel walked up and stood next to me in the ring, my mother's face registered with shock, but then the tears came. Her baby was home. She started to move toward us, but Margot pulled her back and whispered something to her. She looked down at the ground and nodded in submission. I had to remember to thank Margot profusely later after all this was over.

"Let's get this show on the road, shall we?" I whispered to Daniel. He nodded to me and we watched Beta Shane walk into the ring with my father.

The ring fell silent, as most didn't understand why their Alpha was being led like a zombie into the ring. I was about to blow their minds. I took a deep breath and in a loud confident voice, I began to address the crowd.

"Onyx Crescent, I have asked you all to gather here today because recently something very important has come to light. This man standing beside me is my brother Daniel Stevens."

I could see everyone looking at each other with confusion, so I went on. "He was born Corey Stevens until our father, Alpha Francis, decided to have him murdered!" I waited for the shocked gasps to finish, before I continued.

"Alpha Francis lied about his death, and alpha commanded everyone to not speak about Corey. As you can see, Corey did not die but was taken in by a neighbouring pack and renamed Daniel. Daniel is the rightful heir to Onyx Crescent. He is our lost Alpha! He is here today to reclaim his birthright. Alpha Francis tried to murder an innocent child, his own child at that. Daniel had his life turned upside down and it's for that reason, today, he is issuing a challenge. He will fight against Alpha Francis Stevens, a fight to the death for the rights of Onyx Crescent."

Everyone started speaking at once, some excited, some panicked, and some angry, which I made a note of for later.

I gestured to Beta Shane that he could go ahead and administer the antidote to my father and bring him back to himself. The shot was given and Beta Shane backed away quickly, knowing full well my father was going to be enraged.

It took a moment for my father to stand tall with clear eyes; they began to scan the ring and landed on us.

At first shock and fear passed through his eyes, but that quickly turned to anger and disgust.

"If you think you two traitors will be getting my pack, you are sadly mistaken," he growled.

Daniel stepped forward and issued the challenge. "I Corey, now Daniel Stevens officially, challenge you, Alpha Francis Stevens. The winner will be the Alpha of Onyx Crescent." By our laws, my father had no choice but to comply with this.

Our father laughed wickedly. "See you in Hell, boy."

His wolf Sheldon took over, shifted quickly, and charged at Daniel.

Chapter Thirty-One

Chapter 31

Daniel

"See you in Hell, Boy." Was the last thing I heard before a large brown wolf came barreling across the ring at me.

I knew I wouldn't have time to shift into Xander before my father got to me. I stood my ground and waited to see what his next move would be.

He was clearly fighting angry because all he did was jump at me, he wasn't thinking about strategy. You could tell he just wanted to kill me and be done with it.

I easily dodged to my right and he flew past me snarling. I quickly gave Xander control and we shifted into my equally large sandy brown wolf.

We spun around and faced my father head-on.

The second time he came at us we didn't dodge. We let him launch himself at us, he landed on top of us and bit into our shoulder blade.

Xander let out a mighty roar from the pain. We instantly flipped over on top of him and did a barrel roll.

He let us go rather quickly. We scrambled to our feet and we circled each other, teeth bared.

We faked left and managed to grab onto his tail. Xander clamped down with all his might, earning a shriek from his wolf. We then spun ourselves in a circle and launched him a few feet away. He landed with a loud thud.

"I want to end this soon Xander, we're literally turning in circles here." Xander agreed and decided to end it.

He ran full force towards my father, fully expecting to grab my father by the throat, but he surprised us by doing a spin kick and sending us flying. We landed close to the edge of the ring, where some of his men were gathered.

They moved forward and took the liberty of kicking us several times in the ribs and face while we were momentarily stunned by being flung.

We heard Olivia roar. "Back away from the contestant or Alpha Francis will be instantly disqualified!" Justin's men appeared moments later to shove my father's men back.

"Back off you fools, if I lose because of you idiots you will be wishing for death by the time I'm done with you." My father was screaming angrily from the middle of the ring.

Xander had enough of the bullshit and got up quickly, we shook our head to clear the fog and ran back toward my father.

This time we attacked with no mercy, we bit, scratched, and managed to get several good hits. Our light sandy fur was splattered with red droplets of my father's blood.

"Now we're getting somewhere Xander, let's keep this up!"

We battled back and forth like that for a solid twenty minutes, exchanging blows. We were starting to get tired, but I could tell Francis was more exhausted than we were; he had more gaping wounds.

We weren't without injuries, but ours were more superficial and healed quicker. After one particularly nasty blow, my father limped off toward the side of the ring.

"Do you think he's giving up finally, Daniel?"

"I don't know Xander, but let's stay alert, you never know what he is planning."

One of his men approached him with water. Justin's men were on top of them rather quickly, so nothing sketchy could be done.

Xander let me shift back into my human form.

"Alpha Francis! You are tired and severely injured. Let's end this now, give up the pack, and you may live to see another day." I was feeling generous at this point. I wanted it to end.

My father shifted back as well and yelled at me loudly, "I would rather die and take you with me to Hell, than see this pack fall into your unworthy hands, you filthy mutt. You can count on me ending you today very soon, don't worry."

We both shifted back into our wolves and my father came charging back towards us. Xander held his ground and did not move, we stood solid like a brick wall.

Just as my father jumped up at us, Xander shifted our stance enough to grab him by the front paw and yanked really hard. Everyone heard the echo of the snap as his front leg broke.

His wolf whimpered, but we had no sympathy. In this situation, it was kill or be killed and I had no intention of dying today.

"We could never lose to this washed-up old Alpha, we've got this fight in the bag." Xander was boasting and prancing around the ring.

"Don't get cocky, Xander. This man is unhinged and he could easily kill us if he wanted."

My words seemed to fall on deaf ears as Xander continued to prance around the ring to applause from some of the pack members. I was not happy about this showboating, and was trying to force Xander to pay attention to no avail.

Before I knew what was happening, I heard Olivia shout out my name, but it was too late.

A moment later, I felt burning from our ribs to our hip. I stumbled slightly as I tried to turn around. When we were finally able to right ourselves, we turned and saw my father back in human form cradling a broken arm and brandishing a silver knife in his other hand. An evil smirk was plastered on his face and a wild look in his eyes.

"You see Xander, this is what I was trying to warn you about!" I yelled at him in exasperation, all he could do was whimper and try to heal us as quickly as possible.

We got really lucky though, with Xander moving around so much, my father missed his mark completely and didn't get the knife in very deep. It still hurt like a bitch because it was silver, which is usually deadly to a werewolf; but Xander wouldn't have a problem healing us since he was a strong Alpha wolf.

I moved towards the outer corner of the ring to get space from my father, who was stalking towards us with the knife, ready to stab us again.

"Running away so soon, son? Come back and play with your old man, we missed out on so many years together!" He cackled, maniacally.

I decided at that moment that I had to do something quickly to get that knife away from him. I knew the only way that was going to happen was if we were closer to him, this would be a huge risk, but this time Xander seemed to be laser-focused on the task at hand.

"Xander, when we are close enough I want you to fake lunge at him. When he lifts his arm to stab us, I want you to change course and bite his forearm, this should make him drop the knife."

I was really hoping my plan would work since I knew we would only have one shot at it.

We slowly and cautiously approached my father as he sneered at us.

"Glad to see you made the right choice, the ending is inevitable. You will die today, so let's get it over with so I can go punish your sister, and everyone else who went along with this crazy scheme."

"He really is delusional, isn't he?"

"Focus, Xander, we only have this one chance." Xander shut up and continued to move closer to my father.

"NOW!" I commanded, and he did a half jump. My father took the bait beautifully and lifted his arm to strike us down with the silver knife.

Xander bit my father's forearm, causing him to hiss and scream in pain. We gave one extra strong shake of our jaw to make sure we were effective, and the knife clattered to the ground.

We kicked it away with our back paw so it was out of reach. Xander then pinned my father to the ground, snarling in his face.

This was the end of the line for Alpha Francis and he knew it. I saw the fear in his eyes and could smell it coming off him in waves.

Not shockingly, he started to beg for his life.

"Now come on, son. You've proven you're stronger. Let me up and we'll go inside and discuss you becoming Alpha. You don't need to do this."

Xander only glared at him with pure hatred, there were so many things that needed to be said but I couldn't bring myself to say anything. Xander let out one mighty growl and went in for the kill. He was going to rip out his throat and that would be the end of that.

Xander's teeth were less than an inch from my father's jugular when we heard one person loudly clapping and laughing in a mocking tone.

"Ah, Francis, seems like you've gotten yourself into quite a predicament, haven't you?! I'm so happy I get to bear witness to the demise of the worst Alpha in history."

"DAD??" Was all I heard Justin yell, before my father headbutted us and sent us flying into a dazed heap on the ground.

Chapter 32

Justin

I was carefully keeping an eye on Alpha Francis's loyal men as we already had to step in twice so far. The second time, we somehow failed to see the silver knife being handed off. I was furious that this transpired, my men would be spoken with after the challenge was complete. This could never be allowed to happen again.

I was happy to see that Daniel finally had the upper hand and was about to finish his evil father off, when the sound of clapping and a familiar voice grabbed everyone's attention.

I was in complete and utter shock at who I saw standing there. It was impossible, wasn't it? What the hell was he doing here?

"DAD!" I shouted as I marched over to where he stood.

I didn't miss Daniel getting a headbutt from his father and being thrown on the ground. I groaned internally for him. I could only imagine how much that hurt.

"What are you doing here, Dad?" I demanded.

He whipped around and gave me the coldest stare-down I think he ever had in my entire life.

"Well, after finding out my own flesh and blood lied to me, I had to come see for myself the demise of my worst enemy."

"Lied? Who lied Dad?" I tried to play it off, but I was uneasy about who could have told my dad why we were truly here.

"Oh, come now son, did you honestly expect me to believe that you were bringing a dozen of my finest men to learn some new training maneuvers? We have the best-trained wolves in the territory, there was nothing this flea-ridden pack could have possibly taught my warriors," he finished with a snarl.

"So naturally, I pulled up the audio from the conference room and came to find out that you lied to me, son."

He held his chest dramatically as if I had wounded him, I was shell-shocked that he had secret recording devices in the conference room.

"I take it from your shocked expression that you didn't know the conference room had audio? Well, if that's the case this will really blow your mind, my boy...most of the pack house is wired! Do you think anything has happened in MY pack house without me knowing about it?"

The malicious glint in his eyes told me something worse was coming, my mind was reeling at where else he could have hidden recording devices. What else did he know? I was beginning to panic. I suddenly heard a familiar voice that made my heart stop and my blood run cold.

Beyond my dad, I saw two of his loyal men dragging Melissa along. She was arguing with them as she clutched poor sweet little Charlotte to her chest. I heard Amber gasp behind me and shriek out Charlotte's name.

My father began to cackle like a madman, which made my blood begin to boil.

"So, I was shocked and disgusted to learn that my only son was mated to a dirty, mangy omega, who is currently caring for the child of a worthless Beta's daughter. This whole scenario is quite intriguing, so you see my dear Justin, I just had to come down and be part of the festivities."

I gave Melissa a look of remorse for putting her in danger, she returned my gaze with one of terror, but also love for me above it all. This look gave me the strength I needed to confront my dad and try to negotiate her release.

"What will it take for you to let Melissa and the baby go?" I spoke in a clear and powerful voice.

"The baby, I will gladly let go of. I have no use for it. As for your little mate, she won't be let go, EVER. She will watch you die first, then I will kill her myself...or maybe I will have you kill her and then kill you myself!" He contemplated his options.

"What if I kill you first?" My eyes flashed black as my wolf tried to push forward.

"If you think you'll be able to kill me I wish you luck, boy! What if I have a fourth option for you?"

I didn't trust the man as far as I could throw him, but I wanted to keep him talking in the hope I could come up with a solution in that time frame.

"I think the fourth option would be in your best interest personally. I want you to challenge the new Alpha once he finishes off fuckup Francis over there! Once you win, I will then own Onyx Crescent and all the land between our two packs. I will allow you and your mate to live with one catch."

I indulged him by asking what that catch was, I wasn't holding out hope it would be anything good.

"The catch is you'd both live in the dungeon, in separate cells for as long as I feel generous enough to keep you alive and you, my dear boy, would do my bidding as I see fit."

I couldn't believe this piece of shit was my father, that entire fourth option made me want to throw up all over him. I agreed though to the fourth option simply to give us the time to regroup and eliminate my dad. Since I wouldn't start my challenge until Daniel finished his, I had time to plot.

Daniel, at that moment, was knocked out cold. I looked at Melissa and she nodded at me, understanding why I chose what I did.

Daniel

I wasn't sure how long I was out for but all I felt were the tingles coursing through my body, they felt so good it was almost like I was in a dream.

"This isn't a dream lover boy, this is a total nightmare!" Xander quipped as he came back to consciousness as well.

I heard Amber begging me to open my eyes and to be okay. I struggled for a moment, but my eyes eventually opened, they were instantly hit with a bright light shining in them. The light hurt so bad, I needed to shut my eyes again.

"Xander, we have a concussion, you need to heal us quickly, so we can kill my father and this new lunatic that arrived."

"On it!" I felt Xander's strength and healing flow through our body. He allowed me to shift back into my human form to give him more strength.

Amber was elated to have me conscious again. She wrapped her arms around me and held me tight. I felt a tear run down her cheek.

"Come now, don't cry, it will be okay!" I said as I reached up and wiped the tear away.

"I was so scared I had lost you, Daniel, we haven't even gotten a chance to know each other yet," she whispered.

"I know, but don't worry we will, I promise."

Our attention was suddenly pulled over to Justin and the other man who seemed to be his father, they were arguing furiously and a young woman was being held against her will.

Amber suddenly went ice cold and began to shake violently.

She gasped loudly and shrieked the name Charlotte. I assumed the young woman's name was Charlotte, but came to find out it was actually the baby's name, and the baby belonged to Amber?!

As if she knew what I was thinking, she told me quickly it was a long story and we would discuss it later.

I agreed and vowed that I would do what I could to help save Charlotte. Amber hugged me again and thanked me; she seemed to be coming out of her shocked state and began to help me up.

I had just finished standing when my father's voice boomed over the training grounds.

"How dare you, Renato, come into my territory uninvited! And who do you think you are announcing another challenge against me? I will not be the one dying today at anyone's hands. If anything, it will be you who dies!" He then ordered his men to attack, and that's when all Hell broke loose.

Olivia

I couldn't believe this was happening. Daniel almost had the challenge finished until the king of assholes himself, Renato, decided to crash the party.

What a shit show this turned out to be and if this whole thing wasn't messed up enough, Alpha Renato had Melissa and Charlotte as prisoners. I knew Amber was panicking and I prayed to the goddess that we could get Charlotte out of there safely.

I looked over at Logan who was seething in anger, and just as equally terrified for his sister. I wished I could have been next to him, so I could hold him, but I didn't dare move now. I had to be able to attack if need be, and I had a better position where I currently was.

My father spoke out against Alpha Renato and ordered his men to attack. At that moment, all Hell broke loose and I shifted to Evie immediately. People were running and screaming everywhere.

I linked the entire pack and ordered those who were trained and capable to stay and fight, the rest needed to seek cover right away. I looked around the training field and dozens of men supporting Alpha Renato had appeared. He came packing and we were horribly outnumbered.

Justin's loyal men shifted and came to stand on our side with the paltry few men Alpha Arnold was able to bring with him, then there were the men loyal to my father and that was it.

Sadly, even those who could fight that didn't like my father ran for cover, and I couldn't even be mad!

"I wouldn't risk my life either for that egotistical Alphahole," Evie scoffed.

I linked Amber as I surged towards the fighting.

"I will distract them as much as I can, while you grab Charlotte and make a run for it." Amber agreed and shifted to Lana.

Moving in tandem, we stalked towards where Melissa was standing. Evie and I bit the leg of one of the men holding Melissa. He screamed out and we pounced on him, ripping his throat out.

We had no time for mercy.

The other guy threw Melissa to the side and came at us with a glint of madness in his eyes. Meanwhile, Amber took Melissa, who was still clutching Charlotte to her chest and ran off towards the pack house.

I internally breathed a sigh of relief, before turning back to the other guy.

"Play stupid games, win stupid prizes," Evie said as we pounced on him and tore his throat out, the same as his friend before. *"Did this guy actually think he had a chance against me? In human form, no less?"* She shook her head in distaste.

I suddenly felt a surge of pain course through me and knew it was from Logan. We turned in time to see him get thrown into a tree. Evie yelped and ran full force into the wolf who hurt our mate.

We speared the wolf so hard he went rolling, ass over head, stopping near Logan. We stalked over and slashed his throat, leaving him to bleed out as we went to check on Logan.

I shifted back and asked him if he was okay.

Logan looked up at me with his beautiful blue eyes and smiled., "You're my hero, Olivia, I'm fine, just a little sore. Nothing Norman can't heal."

I was relieved he was fine. I gave him a quick peck on the lips and went back into the fray.

I set my sights on taking out as many of Alpha Renato's men as possible to give us an even playing field. Evie and I were a well-oiled killing machine and made fast work of most of them.

The numbers were significantly reduced and it was beginning to look like we had good odds.

Justin was fighting his father and Daniel had gone back to taking care of our father, who was still trying to fight him in human form, since now he had his men to protect him.

Daniel was doing well, until I saw our father creeping up on him while he was fighting one of the men. Our father was going to stab Daniel in the heart with the large silver knife.

I screamed his name but it was too late. Our father jabbed his arm out, I closed my eyes out of fear and that's when I heard Amber's blood-curdling scream from behind me.

Chapter Thirty-Three

Chapter 33

Olivia

My eyes were closed tightly, I couldn't watch as my only brother who I had just found, faced his end at the hands of our unhinged father.

Amber's blood-curdling scream cut through me like lightning. I whipped around, tearing my eyes open. The sight before me made my blood run cold and my heart stopped.

There stood Daniel in wolf form, frozen in place with a look of horror in his eyes. Lying on the ground crumpled at his feet, with the silver knife lodged in his chest to the hilt, was Beta Shane.

I didn't even have time to think of my next move when Evie pushed forward and we charged at my father, knocking him back several feet and laying him flat on the ground.

We pressed our large paw into his throat, cutting off his airways. Daniel joined me as we snarled in our father's face. He knew he had met his end and he wasn't leaving that ring.

He begged and pleaded with us to spare him, but neither of us had any mercy to give today.

Alpha Francis Stevens would cease to exist in mere moments, no one would ever give him a second thought again.

Daniel and I looked at each other, even though we couldn't link, we both knew what the other was thinking. Without wasting any more time on that pathetic excuse of a human, we let our wolves tear our father apart, working together in unison.

His shrill screams of agony and terror echoed around the ring and pack lands as body parts flew in every direction.

No one paid him any attention or came to his rescue.

Eventually, the screams ended abruptly as his life was no longer; blood soaked into the dirt and our wolves' fur, but we didn't notice. Daniel and I shifted instantly and ran back over to where Beta Shane was lying on the ground with Amber cradling his head on her lap while she sobbed.

I threw my arms around Amber's shoulders to comfort her as Daniel knelt beside Beta Shane and took his hand in his own.

"It's over now, he's gone! He will no longer burden our lives. Thank you for stepping in and protecting me from him, for the third time in my life." Daniel's words caught in his throat as a giant lump formed and tears welled up in his eyes.

Beta Shane smiled up at Daniel, and even though he was struggling to breathe he managed to speak a few last words.

"I had to do it, son, I failed to protect you as a young boy. This was my final gift to you, in the hopes you could forgive me for not being strong enough to protect you all those years ago."

"There is nothing to forgive, sir. You did the best with what you had at the time and you saved my life. I am forever grateful and thankful you were there that day."

A violent cough wracked Shane's body as he turned to look up at Amber, the smile he gave her broke my heart.

"I'm proud of you, my little princess. Always remember that." Amber leaned in to tell him how much she loved him and thanked him for saving her mate.

A look of shock and delight spread across his face as he looked between both Amber and Daniel.

Shane's breathing was becoming increasingly more laboured, I recognized that the end was fast approaching.

Suddenly I heard a familiar shriek, as my mother came flying at Shane from across the ring; Margot was not far behind her.

My mother threw herself on her knees by his side weeping. "You can't leave me like this Shane! You're my best friend, what am I supposed to do without you?"

Shane weakly smiled at her and spoke barely above a whisper. "I've always loved you, Angel and I'll be watching over you from above. Take care of our babies, they are mates."

My mother's stunned face looked up at Amber and Daniel for confirmation. They both nodded at her in unison.

"Be happy and watch out for one another." Those were his final words as he let out his last breath with a peaceful smile on his face.

My mother and Amber both fell on his chest sobbing and begging him to come back. Daniel leaned over and gently closed his eyes for the last time. Hot tears were rolling down my face as I watched my best friend and my mother grieve for their father and best friend.

My mother kept wailing about how much she loved him and that he needed to come back. This broke me, and I needed to turn away from that scene. I sensed Daniel wrap his arms around my shoulders from behind and gave me a hug, which I greatly appreciated at that moment.

Justin

I had been battling my father for over half an hour and it felt like there was no end in sight. Olivia had helped me greatly, by thinning out the number of extra men, so I could concentrate solely on eliminating my father.

I was focused on our fight, but also aware of what was going on in the ring.

From what I was piecing together, Beta Shane had stepped in and saved Daniel by taking the brunt of Alpha Francis's surprise attack. I silently commended him for his bravery.

I was then surprised to see Olivia and Daniel team up to take on their father. I wasn't expecting to see them tearing him apart in unison. I was sure he would be brought to The Elders and put on trial for his crimes. However, I was glad they were able to lay their terrible past to rest, and move on to a brighter future now without delay.

I noticed my father's movements starting to get sloppy and correctly assumed he was tired. A few more minutes and this whole ordeal would be over.

However, that thought went out the window, when he kicked sand into our eyes. While my wolf was temporarily blinded, he jumped on my back and bit into my neck hard; causing blood to gush out and for me to let out a wild howl of pain.

Next thing I knew, he kicked me to the side and pounced on me again, this time biting the other side of my neck, tearing out a significant chunk of flesh. The blood was gushing out of the wound staining the ground red, my father puffed out his chest and walked a few yards away to boast to himself. I was losing blood rapidly and could not hold my wolf form.

I shifted back into my human form, curling into a ball to protect myself.

I heard a loud gasp and then suddenly I felt the tingles. "No Melissa, you need to go back to the pack house, he's going to kill you. I won't survive if he kills you, I love you and need you to be with me."

"I can't leave you, Justin, you're bleeding so heavily, our mate bond will help your wolf heal faster."

I knew she was right, but the risk to her was high and I didn't like it, yet here she was not leaving my side, holding her rolled-up sweater against my neck to stop the bleeding as best she could. I had my eyes closed trying to concentrate on the healing, when I felt the sweater and Melissa's weight get ripped off of me.

I opened my eyes in time to see Melissa hitting the ground a few feet away with a loud thud and a whimper. I struggled to sit up as I wasn't fully healed yet, but I had to try and get to her.

My father had shifted back into his human form as well and was cackling like a deranged maniac. "This is sheer perfection, I can kill two birds with one stone. Two love birds, that is." He flashed an evil sick grin between Melissa and I.

A chill ran down my spine at the implication.

"Now, boy, did you actually think I was going to let you ruin my pack by mating with this unworthy, dirty, filthy mutt? Haha! No, no, no my dear son, instead you are going to watch me kill her and then

I am going to take great pleasure in ripping you apart, the same way that loser Francis just was." He continued to laugh psychotically.

I struggled to stand and failed miserably, too weak to hold myself up. I couldn't believe I wasn't able to protect Melissa and was starting to freak out, when out of nowhere a large brown wolf flew past me and jumped on my father.

It took me a moment to recognize Logan's wolf, Norman, was the one currently assaulting my father. He wasn't playing around, he ripped one leg clean off my father's body, causing him to scream like the little bitch he was.

Then, without hesitation, he tore out his throat and we all watched as the asshole's lifeless body hit the ground.

A wave of relief and freedom passed over me as I crawled over to Melissa. Logan was faster and had already made it to her side, checking on her. She wasn't injured. Thank the goddess, she was only slightly stunned.

She turned and folded herself carefully into my arms and we just held each other, rocking on the ground for what seemed like an hour. Finally, I felt that I was fully healed and pulled both Melissa and myself to our feet.

We walked over to Logan who was holding a crying Olivia in his arms.

"Logan, you are a hero, you saved both mine and Melissa's life. Thank you from the bottom of my heart." I reached out and squeezed his shoulder with affection.

"Justin, you're my best friend and my brother-in-law. I need you as much as my sister. I did what I had to do and I have no regrets. I would do it all over again if I could, really. That son of a bitch deserved so much worse for everything he's done to us, but I wanted it to be over as quickly as possible."

I nodded in agreement, as he turned around to shield Olivia's naked body from me. I saw her snuggle into Logan with a content sigh as she wiped away some stray tears.

I turned and pulled Melissa back to me. "Thank you for being so brave and coming to my rescue, my sweet Luna." I kissed her on the top of her head and held her close.

We were now officially free from two evil assholes who had caused a lot of harm over the years. I was very excited about starting this new chapter and seeing where the future was going to take us.

Daniel

I had done it, I won the fight against my father.

"Thanks largely in part to Olivia and Beta Shane, without them we were toast!" Xander sighed with exhaustion. The stress leading up to this moment and the fight really wiped out all his energy.

"You're absolutely right, buddy. They saved our lives today." I was still shocked and moved by Beta Shane's sacrifice.

He lived for all those years with the guilt of what happened when I was a kid. He gave up his own life now for me to live on, and take over this pack to make it a better place. It touched me deeply that someone I barely knew could care so much about me.

"Mate cares about us too and she just lost her father, don't forget!" Xander was right, he saved me. But in the process, she lost her father.

The guilt hit me hard and fast. I looked over at Amber who was still sitting next to his body with her arms wrapped around herself. A few stray tears still flowed freely down her face.

"Go to her Daniel, and comfort her. I feel your hesitation. Do not feel guilty about her father's choices; he gave you both the gift of a life together." Xander was right again.

I quickly walked over to her, gently bent down, and scooped her up into my arms. She gasped in surprise and looked me in the eyes with shock. I gave her a gentle smile and that's when the dam burst.

She wrapped her arms around my neck, buried her head into my shoulder, and just sobbed harder than I had ever heard anyone cry before. I held her tight as her body shook violently, the tingles shot through both of us as I rubbed her back in comfort.

Soon enough, the crying and shaking stopped. She looked up at me with broken bashful eyes and apologized for breaking down like that.

"You never need to apologize to me for your emotions, Amber, I am going to be here for you no matter what, we are going to get through this together. I promise."

I leaned over and kissed her forehead gently, I knew my heart wasn't fully ready to belong to Amber yet, I still had some letting go to do but I knew soon enough this woman was going to own my heart and my soul.

I gently put her on the ground and steadied her as she wobbled, ever so slightly. That's when she noticed I was naked. Amber turned the cutest shade of crimson red and looked away quickly.

She told me to wait a moment and went to go get a pair of shorts for me behind a nearby bush. I put them on and thanked her, then took her hand and we walked towards my sister and her mate.

As we approached Olivia and Logan, I looked over to see my aunt Margot walking over with my mother, well, the woman who was once my mother. She looked at me shyly and approached cautiously. Olivia saw this and decided she'd make it all a little easier for everyone.

"Mom, this is your son, Daniel; Daniel, this is your mom, Luna Angela!" She gave me a little wink and I had to chuckle at how cheeky she was.

I reached out my hand to shake hers, her tiny hand touched mine and it was shaking like a leaf. "Ma...ma...may...may I hug you?" The request was barely audible, but I managed to catch it. I took a moment to think it through but ultimately decided she was as much a victim in all of this as I was, so I gently pulled her in for a hug.

Once she was in my arms she began to cry hysterically. "My baby, my baby's home! I missed you so much, I swear I didn't know what that asshole did to you! If I knew you were still alive I would have searched until the end of the earth for you, but I foolishly believed that son of a bitch. Is there any chance you have room in your heart to forgive me?" She pleaded between sobs.

I held her for a few more moments while she cried herself out. I told her that there was nothing to forgive, that she was a victim just like me, he had lied to her and kept the truth hidden. Worse yet, he had forbidden her to even mourn her dead child or talk about him. She was as innocent as I was and I told her as much.

When I finally let her go, she seemed lighter somehow, as if my forgiveness had removed twenty-six years of heartbreak and guilt. Now that all the waterworks were taken care of, I had something extremely important to take care of. I needed to go find my pup, she was out there somewhere.

I turned to Olivia and Amber and asked that we head back to the pack house. I needed to address the pack as their new Alpha and make sure no traitors remained amongst them. I also desperately needed a shower to get rid of the remnants of my father that still clung to me.

I had a lot of work to do, but I knew it would be worth it, so my sweet little pup could come home to her new safe pack.

We started to walk back as I daydreamed about Gabriella.

Chapter 34

Olivia

Daniel asked to go back to the pack house to address the pack as their new Alpha, as we walked back I took in our surroundings. There were dead bodies littered everywhere that would need to be removed as soon as possible.

Luckily, we suffered very little loss of life on our side. Only one of Justin's soldiers fell against his own pack mate, the few men Alpha Arnold brought all survived, thankfully.

A few of my father's loyal men fell, the rest would soon be imprisoned or sentenced to death for the role they played in interfering with the challenge. The other warriors were all Alpha Renato's men and the asshole himself. Justin would advise how he wanted those bodies handled.

Once we cleaned house on our side, Daniel would have to set up more training, because we were left with very few loyal warriors after this fiasco. I would gladly take over the training and I'm sure Amber would be happy to help. Although, maybe not, since she was now our Luna and had little Charlotte to take care of.

We would have to cross that bridge at a later time. For now, the most important thing was to get Daniel sworn in as Alpha.

As we approached the pack house, I linked the entire pack, commanding them to come out of hiding and present themselves outside at the front of the pack house.

Daniel, Amber, Logan, and I all climbed up a few stairs so we could look out on the crowd that was slowly building. We waited a solid half hour, before the final straggler finally appeared at the back of the group looking sheepish to have been dead last.

I looked at Daniel and nodded that he could now commence. I was so proud of my big brother, and even happier that I could say I had a big brother now.

Daniel

We stood on the steps of the pack house for what felt like an eternity as pack members slowly and cautiously filtered into the area.

"Should I push forward and roar? Assert our dominance from the get-go?" Xander chuckled.

"*No buddy, these people were treated like shit by my father; I'm nothing like him. We will lead with kindness, strength, and dignity.*"

"Fine, we'll do it your way, but can I at least snap a traitor's neck or two in front of them all?" I saw him giving me puppy eyes and couldn't help but laugh.

"We'll see Xander!" He curled into a ball to pout as Olivia nodded at me, letting me know that I could now speak to the pack.

I would deal with my sulky blood-thirsty wolf after I spoke to the pack. I wasn't going to lie; I was nervous as hell. I had never led anything, even though I was born for the role, I was never given any type of training. This transition could be rough.

I looked out over the crowd of some hopeful, some scared and some angry faces. I told Xander to remember those faces, he'd be having fun with them later. That perked him right up, I smiled as best I could at everyone, took a deep breath, and began to speak in the loudest, strongest voice I could muster.

"Onyx Crescent, I am Daniel Stevens, I challenged your Alpha, my estranged father, for the title of Alpha and I have prevailed."

I paused momentarily to take a breath, and as I was about to continue one of the angry faces in the crowd who was undoubtedly a follower of my father yelled.

"How do we know you really killed him and it wasn't someone else?!" Murmurs began to spread through the crowd, and I knew this could go sideways very quickly so I decided to end it.

"There were many witnesses to his demise, but if you want proof here!" I grabbed a good-sized piece of his flesh I had stuck to me and flung it at the man in the crowd, it landed on his cheek and the colour drained from his face. I had never seen someone move so fast, he ripped it off his face, flinging it to the ground in disgust, and then threw up.

"You don't seem to have a very strong stomach, do you? Feel free to take that piece to the pack hospital and have them test it as proof it belonged to my father!" The man just angrily glared at me as he wiped his mouth with his sleeve. "Anyone else have a comment for me?"

"I will NEVER follow you," the same man once again interrupted,

"Not a problem, friend. I don't want you following me either with that attitude. What would you like to do?" I waited for the man to answer, but he only glared at me more fiercely.

"If you swear to pledge your loyalty to me, I will show you how a real pack should be run." He spat on the ground and yelled that I could go fuck myself.

"Very well, it seems like you have made your decision." I motioned to Justin, who sent one of his men to grab the guy and escort him off to go calm down in the cells. I would go speak with him later and see where he stood.

Once he was gone, I continued, "I am not my father. I will not harm you or treat the pack members like they are nothing. We all belong here, and we all have great worth, but I do require respect as your Alpha. I will respect you all from this moment forward, but I expect the same in return. I can't promise you this transition will be easy. However, I promise you as your Alpha, I will be respectful to all situations, to be fair, and to protect you all. My Luna, Amber, and I will make this pack better than it has ever been."

I looked over at Amber and smiled. She looked shocked that I had mentioned her to the crowd. I reached out my hand and pulled her to me, giving her a kiss on the forehead.

The pack was talking now like crazy; people seemed a lot lighter at hearing that I wasn't the same as the dick they had before.

Olivia cut in at that moment, and announced to the pack she was going to swear me in as Alpha. She was given the pack's ceremonial knife by an omega, who was standing at the side of the steps.

Olivia walked over and said, "Daniel Stevens, do you swear to give your life to protect this pack and all its members, from harm?"

I looked her in the eyes and smiled. "Yes, I swear to put my life above all else, to protect this pack and all its people until my last breath."

She then sliced both our palms and pushed them together. Once our blood mingled, a giant gust of wind swept through the pack yard and swirled around us like a tornado. I felt the connection to everyone clicking into place and people welcoming me home through the mind-link.

Olivia smiled up at me. "It's done! Welcome home, my big brother Alpha."

We both laughed at this before I stumbled back a bit. I was starting to get dizzy from all the voices in my head. I wasn't used to it. Olivia understood what was happening and told me how to create a block for the masses. That really helped, and I thanked her for her assistance.

Olivia turned to the pack and announced loudly, "Our Lost Alpha has returned. Let us all give him a howl!"

All at once, the entire pack let out one hell of an impressive howl, which warmed my heart.

I let everyone settle back down before I finished off by asking the pack to give me at least a week, to go through my father's things and get everything in working order. I would pick our ranked members, and we would do a proper ceremony for everything when all was settled.

I dismissed everyone then and turned to walk into the pack house, really needing that shower. I noticed an omega handing Amber what appeared to be her baby, and walked over to her.

"Was Baby Charlotte harmed?" I asked gently as Amber looked up at me happily.

"No, she was completely unharmed. Thank the goddess, I know I owe you an explanation. Where would you like me to start?"

"Well, first I'd love to see this pup of yours. May I meet her?"

I knew I was covered in blood, but I felt compelled to hold this little bundle, and it was the blanket that would take the brunt of the dirt.

She handed the baby over to me, and my heart stopped when I saw her sweet face.

The world began to spin and I fell forward onto my knees clutching the baby with a loud sob escaping my throat. Amber shrieked my name and threw herself on the ground to catch the baby and me. Olivia and Logan ran over to see what was happening, but I didn't care if I was causing a scene.

My baby, my sweet Gabriella, was alive, safe, and with my mate this entire time. I wouldn't need to send out a search party, she was right here waiting.

"Just like Annabelle told you she would be when you had your last dream date with her," Xander reminded me in wonder.

I was sobbing hysterically, happy tears flowing down my face as I rocked my baby. Amber was sitting next to me with a look of shock and panic, not knowing what to do.

I heard Alpha Arnold come over and he started to talk to me. I didn't understand a word he said, all I could do was look up at him and point to Gabriella. He gasped and gave a shout of joy, throwing his arms around me to celebrate with me.

"Can someone please let us in on what the hell is going on?" Olivia asked, with utter confusion in her voice.

I was finally able to calm myself down enough to take a deep breath and speak. "This isn't baby Charlotte, this is my missing daughter, Gabriella. We thought she was dead, and I can't believe she's been here, safe the whole time with my mate."

I looked over at Amber, who looked like I had just knocked her in the gut with a giant wooden beam. It hit me at that moment that we both had a lot to discuss. I kissed Gabriella and handed her to Olivia, who took her without question.

I grabbed Amber's hands and helped her up. "Let's go inside, clean up, and have a little chat, shall we?"

She nodded vigorously and followed me without question into the pack house. I had no idea how this conversation was going to go, but I prayed to Selene that it would end with Amber still as my mate.

CHAPTER THIRTY-FIVE

Chapter 35

Amber

    I followed Daniel into the pack house in a daze. My mind was swirling like a tornado. I found my mate, he was my best friend's long-lost brother and our new Alpha, which made me a Luna.

I had just lost my father, the only living relative that I had left. I had found a baby who I was head over heels for, and she turned out to be my mate's child; who he had with a chosen mate prior to meeting me.

All of this information was just too much. I felt like I couldn't breathe, it got really hot all of a sudden and the room began to spin. I started to wobble as I walked, Daniel felt me lose my footing, and turned around with a look of concern on his gorgeous face.

"Amber, are you okay? Talk to me." Before I could say anything, everything went black around me.

The last thing I remember is Daniel screaming my name and his arms wrapping around me before I could hit the floor. I felt the sparks running over my knuckles slowly and softly, I then smelt that wonderful chocolate coffee smell.

Finally, I forced myself to open my eyes, blinking at the harsh light in the room. "Oh, let me turn that down for you." Daniel jumped off the bed, hurried to the dimmer switch, and lowered the lights to a manageable level.

He came back over and helped me sit up a bit, then, he shocked me by folding me into a giant hug. I was stunned but couldn't help but nestle into his arms. Lana enjoyed the hug as well, she was purring in my head like crazy. We stayed like that for several minutes. I was enjoying being held by him, when Daniel broke the silence.

"You scared me to death before, I thought I had lost you." I gently pushed back and looked up to see tears shining in his eyes. Seeing tears in Daniels' eyes shocked me to my core. How was he that worried about me?

"Amber, don't forget he lost a mate recently and we don't know his story yet," Lana reproached me.

"Thank you, Lana, I completely forgot about that!"

Losing someone you love was traumatic, especially since I knew how his other mate died, so I couldn't blame him for being paranoid. I gave Daniel a small smile and reached up to cup his cheek.

"There was nothing to worry about. I'm perfectly fine and not going anywhere. I can promise you I'm strong and healthy, I think I just got overwhelmed by everything that's happened today." I looked down to hide my embarrassment as my cheeks heated up.

I felt his fingers hook under my chin and lift my face so we could look into each other's eyes. "Don't be embarrassed, Amber. Today was a wildly emotional day, and I'm pretty much at the end of my rope, as well. Don't you remember I was hysterically crying on the front steps only a few hours ago?" He chuckled and shook his head, his cheeks turning the cutest shade of pink.

I couldn't help but smile and giggle with him. "That's a little different Daniel, you had just found out your daughter was alive! Oh my goddess, where is Gabriella?" I panicked and looked around the room frantically, now that I realised she wasn't with us.

"Don't worry. Olivia and Logan are on aunty and uncle babysitting duty tonight. After I took you upstairs, Olivia came and sat with you while I showered quickly. She said they would watch Gabriella for us so we could talk." I nodded and calmed down, settling back into the pillows on my bed.

"So, where should we start?" I asked, shyly.

Daniel smiled down at me and said he'd do all the talking first since the bigger part of the story was his. I agreed and settled in to listen. A slight nervous twinge started to creep up my spine which I didn't like. Goddess I hope I could live with whatever he was about to tell me.

Daniel

I looked down at Amber and smiled, I took her small hands in mine and held them firmly for support as I took a breath and began to tell her my story.

I explained how, growing up in the Blood Viper pack, we never had hope of finding our mates, unless they somehow found their way to our pack. Otherwise, because we were so small and unknown, we either stayed single or took a chosen mate; if we fell in love with someone.

I told her how Annabelle and I had fallen hard for each other and that Gabriella came from that union. I then went on to tell her about going to Onyx Crescent, being captured, and then rescued by her father.

I saw a small sob catch in her throat and I squeezed her hands for comfort. I continued on to how I found out Annabelle had been murdered, and thought that Gabriella had been too. She looked pained as I told her that part.

"Daniel, I knew about Annabelle's death, I didn't know who she was to you or that Gabriella was yours." This confession shocked me slightly.

"How did you know?" I was curious.

"Olivia and I were driving home from Jade Moon and I just had an intense feeling we needed to pull over. My wolf, Lana, led us to Gabriella; we found our guard's dead body and the remains of Annabelle later and pieced it together. We also heard later on from two other guards who were there that they had killed her. I am so sorry." I watched as a tear rolled down her cheek which I wiped away. I leaned over and gave her a chaste kiss on the cheek.

"There is nothing for you to be sorry about, Amber. You saved my little girl and kept her safe. I am eternally indebted to you for that." Amber looked at me with a small smile and blushed.

I continued on with my story about how I met Annabelle in my dreams, and she had told me that Gabriella was still alive out there, waiting for me. I also alluded to the fact that Annabelle had told me to love again, but I wasn't quite ready to tell her those words, and run the risk of her rejecting me.

I also apologized to Amber for never looking for her, and I told her I hoped that she could forgive me for having a child with another. My heart gave a little squeeze of trepidation as I asked her that. She looked up at me with an expression I couldn't quite read which made me panic.

"Way to go, Romeo. Now, she's going to reject us." Xander sounded so depressed as he readied himself for the inevitable.

Amber sat up straight, locking eyes with me, and she took a deep breath. Closing my eyes; I knew what was coming. I gulped as I braced myself for the words and the pain I knew was about to hit me.

"I, Amber Small, accept you, Daniel Stevens, as my mate."

"What??" Both Xander and I exclaimed at the same time. My eyes flew open in shock and my jaw hit the bed.

"Holy Shit, Casanova, you did it. Not sure how, but she accepted us." Xander was doing a happy wolf dance in my head. I didn't know what to say back to her. *"How about we accept her back and not leave her hanging like an idiot? She may still change her mind if you aren't careful."* Xander was right.

I regained my composure quickly, and said back to her, "I, Daniel Stevens, accept you, Amber Small, as my mate."

I felt the bond snap into place. Amber gave a cute little squeak and threw herself into my arms. I wrapped her in a tight hug and breathed in her intoxicating scent.

"I know your heart isn't ready yet, Daniel. I will never push you but I want you to know I am here for you. No matter what, we will figure it out together. Your past is valid, even if you had gone out to look for me you were under the witches' potion to hide your true scent; we never would have found out. I am happy that Annabelle was there to love you and gave you Gabriella, who is a true gift. We will honour Annabelle, and I will love Gabriella as my own."

I couldn't believe she was saying those words to me. I felt like I was in a dream. I couldn't believe I had gotten this lucky twice in one lifetime. I didn't want to get her hopes up, so I kept it to myself, but I knew it wasn't going to be too long before I made peace with my past, and my heart was ready to love again.

That night we ended up falling asleep on top of the bed in each other's arms completely dressed. I dreamed of Annabelle standing with Amber's father smiling at both of us. She mouthed to me 'Be Happy' and then they were gone.

No matter what was to come, I knew I would be able to face it with Amber by my side.

Afterword

I would like to thank you all for joining me on this journey. The Lost Alpha wouldn't have been possible if I didn't have the support of all my readers from Dreame who encouraged me to continue no matter how hard it got. I took a leap of faith getting back to my passion of writing after years of time constraints. I was blown away by the warm reception my readers gave me. Your excitement for my book has touched my heart more than you will ever know. My family were my rock through it all, bless them for putting up with my late-night writing sessions and constant chatter about Daniel and Olivia.

I also have an amazing group of Friends who have supported me and encouraged me this entire time.

Amanda, Sarah, Alex, Kathryn, Ginger, Bex, Christin, Aura, Leah, Jenny, Jackie, Jennifer, Lois, Angie, Den, Shantella, Nikki, Aurora, Steph, Emm, Claire, Ianna, Julie, Courtney, Maxine, Eve and Avalina.

You are all unique, strong, funny, creative, kind and loving women. You ladies mean the world to me! XxxX

Manufactured by Amazon.ca
Acheson, AB